The yellowbacks... classics of popular fiction

The yellowjackets or yellowbacks were a great series of bestselling adventure and crime thrillers that had its origins in the mid to late 19th century following on from the 'penny dreadfuls'. They virtually began the mass market revolution of the early 20th century with a clear standard format and imprint/series livery (what would today be called branding). Hodder & Stoughton published the yellowjackets in two main series with series run dates of: 1923-1939 and later 1949-1957.

As the tagline ('where thrillers really began') on the back cover implies, the imprint and series focused on thrillers that were the bestsellers of their time. This current reissue or retro revival if you will, brings back many of these masterpieces, now classics in their own way and extends it further by including key titles from that period that were either great crime or thriller or even general commercial fiction (including sub-genres of noir, horror, gothic, romance, westerns, etc.) influences of their time. There are some perennial favourites and many rarities either lost or not easily available being revived in the current series. Writers and characters ranged from adventure heroes like Bulldog Drummond, Allan Quatermain, Richard Hannay or the Saint through thriller grandmasters Edgar Wallace and E. Phillips Oppenheim, crime and mystery maestros like Patricia Wentworth, G.K. Chesterton, Agatha Christie and the Detection club, to western and swashbucklers like Zane Grey, Max Brand, Captain Blood and even romance or general fiction classics like Hermina Black, Denise Robins, Marie Corelli or Stella Morton. These were books that had storytelling at their heart and always entertained.

The yellowbacks had both hardback (with varying design elements) and paperback (which built the series look) versions with the latter still carrying the imprint 'yellowjacket'. The current reissues pay tribute to both and use an amalgam of elements from both editions while retaining the complete yellow (or 'mustard-plaster') livery with the author's name in blue beveled type with a 'simulated emboss' effect and a white outer 'outline', and the book title in black. These reissues retain the distinctive size of the original mass market paperback and follow the three main category variations—the thrillers (crime, westerns, mystery, adventure) had blue lettering for the author's name, while Romance and softer general fiction had red; and other categories like humour had green.

For more details and a full list of titles visit https://www.hachetteindia.com/home/yellowbacks

THE SECRET TOMB

THE SECRET TOMB

Maurice Marie Émile Leblanc was a French novelist and writer of short stories, known primarily as the creator of the gentleman burglar, adventurer and detective Arsène Lupin, often described as a French counterpart to Arthur Conan Doyle's Sherlock Holmes and E.W. Hornung's Raffles.

Refusing the career that his father had set up for him at a card factory, Leblanc instead went to Paris in 1888, to pursue writing as a journalist. But he soon turned novelist and storyteller. His first novel, *Une femme (A Woman),* published in 1893 was a success and was followed by other works, such as *Des couples (The Couples), Voici des ailes (Here are Wings)* and a play *La pitié,* released in 1902, which was a flop. In 1905, Pierre Lafitte, the director of the monthly *Je sais tout,* commissioned a short story from Leblanc, with the brief that he was to combine the appeal of A.J Raffles by Ernest William Hornung and Sherlock Holmes. The result was 'L'Arrestationd'Arsène Lupin' ('The Arrest of Arsène Lupin') which was a huge success. Two years later, *Arsène Lupin, Gentleman Burglar* was released, and the rest was history – with one of the most successful series being born.

THE SECRET TOMB

Maurice Leblanc

Frontispiece By
George W. Gage

HODDER AND STOUGHTON
YELLOW JACKET
hachette

The Secret Tomb
First published in 1923 in French as 'Dorothée, Danseuse de Corde'.

1

The texts in these editions in most cases have been reprinted as is, with minimal editorial changes and by and large no bowdlerizing for political correctness; though in some editions, a few words and phrases considered archaic, or those considered offensive now, along with archaic punctuation may have been modified in places to make the text more accessible to today's readers. The narratives, language, beliefs, social mores and/or cultural depictions, in these volumes are a reflection of their times and must be viewed as such. They may also contain certain cultural, racial and gender prejudices and stereotypes that may be outdated or clearly wrong then and wrong today; but their removal would be tantamount to claiming these prejudices never existed. The Publisher does not endorse or support those depictions or stereotypes; and these books have been made available for a discerning audience that will read it for entertainment value and a chronicle/record of popular fiction of past times.

Cover design by Priya Singh adapted from the original classic yellowjacket by Hodder & Stoughton.

Cover illustration by Ishan Trivedi.

Series note: Some of the books in the series (unless otherwise credited) may have cover or inside illustrations from the original yellowbacks or early editions, and while full restoration has been attempted, some images may be grainy or faded due to the condition of the original material. The end notes or bonus material or blurb details may have been sourced from the public domain or free use publications such as Wikipedia and attribution is hereby made also allowing similar free use reproduction from here. Sources requiring further specific attribution may write in and further detailing and/or corrections shall be made in subsequent printings/editions.

Reprint specifications may be subject to change including but not limited to finishes, paper, colour sections.

ISBN: 978-93-5731-229-5

Hachette Book Publishing India Pvt. Ltd.
4th & 5th Floors, Corporate Centre,
Plot No. 94, Sector 44, Gurugram - 122 003, India

Typeset in Electra LT STD 10/12.5 pt by Manipal Technologies Limited, Manipal

Printed and bound in India by Manipal Technologies Limited, Manipal

FSC www.fsc.org MIX Paper from responsible sources FSC™ C043100

CONTENTS

"Leave me alone!... I forbid you to touch me!"

I

THE CHÂTEAU DE ROBOREY

Under a sky heavy with stars and faintly brighter for a low-hanging sickle moon, the gipsy caravan slept on the turf by the roadside, its shutters closed, its shafts stretched out like arms. In the shadow of the ditch nearby a stertorous horse was snoring.

Far away, above the black crest of the hills, a bright streak of sky announced the coming of the dawn. A church clock struck four. Here and there a bird awoke and began to sing. The air was soft and warm.

Abruptly, from the interior of the caravan, a woman's voice cried:

"Saint-Quentin! Saint-Quentin!"

A head was thrust out of the little window which looked out over the box under the projecting roof.

"A nice thing this! I thought as much! The rascal has decamped in the night. The little beast! Nice discipline this is!"

Other voices joined in the grumbling. Two or three minutes passed, then the door in the back of the caravan opened and a shadowy figure descended the five steps of the ladder while two tousled heads appeared at the side window.

"Dorothy! Where are you going?"

"To look for Saint-Quentin!" replied the shadowy figure.

"But he came back with you from your walk last night; and I saw him settle down on the box."

"You can see that he isn't there any longer, Castor."

"Where is he?"

"Patience! I'm going to bring him back to you by the ears."

But two small boys in their shirts came tumbling down the steps of the caravan and implored her:

"No, no, mummy Dorothy! Don't you go away by yourself in the night-time. It's dangerous..."

"What are you making a fuss about, Pollux? Dangerous? It's no business of yours!"

She smacked them and kicked them gently, and brought them quickly back to the caravan into which they climbed. There, sitting on the stool, she took their two heads, pressed them against her face, and kissed them tenderly.

"No ill feeling, children. Danger? I'll find Saint-Quentin in half an hour from now."

"A nice business!... Saint-Quentin!... A beggar who isn't sixteen!"

"While Castor and Pollux are twenty—taken together!" retorted Dorothy.

"But what does he want to go traipsing about like this at night for? And it isn't the first time either... Where is it he makes these expeditions to?"

"To snare rabbits," she said. "There's nothing wrong in it, you see. But come, there's been talk enough about it. Go to by-by again, boys. And above all, Castor and Pollux, don't fight. D'you hear? And no noise. The Captain's asleep; and he doesn't like to be disturbed, the Captain doesn't."

She took herself off, jumped over the ditch, crossed a meadow, in which her feet splashed up the water in the puddles, and gained a path which wound through a copse of young trees which only reached her shoulders. Twice already, the evening before, strolling with her comrade Saint-Quentin, she had followed this half-formed path, so that she went briskly forward without hesitating. She crossed two roads, came to a stream, the white pebbly bottom of which gleamed under the quiet water, stepped into it, and walked up it against the current, as if she wished to hide her tracks, and when the first light of day began to invest objects with clear shapes, darted forth afresh through the woods, light, graceful, not very tall, her legs bare below a very short skirt from which streamed behind her a flutter of many-colored ribbons.

She ran, with effortless ease, surefooted, with never a chance of spraining an ankle, over the dead leaves, among the flowers of early spring, lilies of the valley, violet anemones, or white narcissi.

Her black hair, not very long, was divided into two heavy masses which flapped like two wings. Her smiling face, parted lips, dilated nostrils, her half-closed eyes proclaimed all her delight in her swift course through the fresh air of the morning. Her neck, long and flexible, rose from a blouse of gray linen, closed by a kerchief of orange silk. She looked to be fifteen or sixteen years old.

The wood came to an end. A valley lay before her, sunk between two walls of rock and turning off abruptly. Dorothy stopped short. She had reached her goal.

Facing her, on a pedestal of granite, cleanly cut down, and not more than a hundred feet in diameter, rose the main building of a château, which though it lacked grandeur of style itself, yet drew from its position and the impressive nature of its construction an air of being a seigniorial residence. To the right and left the valley, narrowed to two ravines, appeared to envelop it like an old-time moat. But in front of Dorothy the full breadth of the valley formed a slightly undulating glacis, strewn with boulders and traversed by hedges of briar, which ended at the foot of the almost vertical cliff of the granite pedestal.

"A quarter to five striking," murmured the young girl. "Saint-Quentin won't be long."

She crouched down behind the enormous trunk of an uprooted tree and watched with unwinking eyes the line of demarcation between the château itself and its rocky base.

A narrow shelf of rock lengthened this line, running below the windows of the ground floor; and there was a spot in this exiguous cornice at which there came to an end a slanting fissure in the face of the cliff, very narrow, something of the nature of a crevice in the face of a wall.

The evening before, during their walk, Saint-Quentin had said, his finger pointing at the fissure:

"Those people believe themselves to be perfectly secure; and yet nothing could be easier than to haul one's self up along that crack to one of the windows... Look; there's one which is actually half-open... the window of some pantry."

Dorothy had no doubt whatever that the idea of climbing the granite pedestal had gripped Saint-Quentin and that that very night he had stolen away to attempt it. What had become of him after the attempt? Had there not been someone in the room he had entered? Knowing nothing of the place he was exploring nor of the dwellers in it, had he not let himself be taken? Or was he merely waiting for the break of day?

She was greatly troubled. For all that she could see no sign of a path along the ravine, some countryman might come along at the very moment at which Saint-Quentin took the risk of making his descent, a far more difficult business than climbing up.

Of a sudden she quivered. One might have said that in thinking of this mischance she had brought it on them. She heard the sound of heavy footfalls coming along the ravine and making for its main entrance. She buried herself among the roots of the tree and they hid her. A man came in sight. He was wearing a long blouse; his face was encircled and hidden by a gray muffler; old, furred gloves covered his hands; he carried a gun on his arm, a mattock over his shoulder.

She thought that he must be a sportsman, or rather a poacher, for he walked with an uneasy air, looking carefully about him, like one who feared to be seen, and who was carefully changing his usual bearing. But he came to a standstill near the wall fifty or sixty yards from the spot at which Saint-Quentin had made the ascent, and studied the ground, turning over some flat stones and bending down over them.

At last he made up his mind and seizing one of these slabs by its narrower end, he raised it and set it up on end in such a manner that it was balanced after the fashion of a cromlech. So doing he uncovered a hole which had been hollowed out in the center of the deep imprint left by the slab. Then he took his mattock and set about enlarging it, removing the earth very quietly, evidently taking great care to make no noise.

A few minutes more slipped away. Then the inevitable event which Dorothy had at once desired and feared took place. The window of the château, through which Saint-Quentin had climbed the night before, opened; and there appeared a long body clad in a long black coat, its head covered with a high hat, which, even at that distance, were plainly shiny, dirty, and patched.

Squeezed flat against the wall, Saint-Quentin lowered himself from the window and succeeded in setting his two feet on the rocky shelf. On the instant Dorothy, who was at the back of the man in the blouse, was on the point of rising and making a warning signal to her comrade. The movement was useless. The man had perceived what looked to be a black devil clinging to the face of the cliff, and dropping his mattock, he slipped into the hole.

For his part, Saint-Quentin, absorbed in his job of getting down, was paying no attention to what was going on below him, and could only have seen it by turning round, which was practically impossible. Uncoiling a rope, which he had, without doubt, picked up in the mansion, he ran it round a pillar of the balcony of the window in such a fashion that the two ends hung down the face of the cliff an equal distance. With the help of this double rope the descent presented no difficulty.

Without losing a second, Dorothy, uneasy at being no longer able to see the man in a blouse, sprang from her hiding-place and raced to the hole. As she got a view of it, she smothered a cry. At the bottom of the hole, as at the bottom of a trench, the man, resting the barrel of his gun on the rampart of earth he had thrown up, was about to take deliberate aim at the unconscious climber.

Call out? Warn Saint-Quentin? That was to precipitate the event, to make her presence known and find herself engaged in an unequal struggle with an armed adversary. But do something she must. Up there Saint-Quentin was availing himself of the fissure in the face of the cliff, for all the world as if he were descending the shaft of a chimney. The whole of him stuck out, a black and lean silhouette. His high hat had been crushed down, concertina fashion, right on to his ears.

The man set the butt of his gun against his shoulder and took aim. Dorothy leapt forward and flung herself at the stone which stood up behind him and with the impetus of her spring and all her weight behind her outstretched hands, shoved it. It was badly balanced, gave at the shock, and toppled over, closing the excavation like a trap-door of stone, crushing the gun, and imprisoning the man in the blouse. The young girl got just a glimpse of his head as it bent and his shoulders as they were thrust down into the hole.

She thought that the attack was only postponed, that the enemy would lose no time in getting out of his grave, and dashed at full speed to the bottom of the fissure at which she arrived at the same time as Saint-Quentin.

"Quick... quick!" she cried. "We must bolt!"

In a flurry, he dragged down the rope by one of the ends, mumbling as he did so:

"What's up? What d'you want? How did you know I was here?"

She gripped his arm and tugged at it.

"Bolt, idiot!... They've seen you!... They were going to take a shot at you!... Quick! They'll be after us!"

"What's that? Be after us? Who?"

"A queer-looking beggar disguised as a peasant. He's in a hole over yonder. He was going to shoot you like a partridge when I tumbled the slab on to the top of him."

"But—"

"Do as I tell you, idiot! And bring the rope with you. You mustn't leave any traces!"

She turned and bolted; he followed her. They reached the end of the valley before the slab was raised, and without exchanging a word took cover in the wood.

Twenty minutes later they entered the stream and did not leave it till they could emerge on to a bank of pebbles on which their feet could leave no print.

Saint-Quentin was off again like an arrow; but Dorothy stopped short, suddenly shaken by a spasm of laughter which bent her double.

"What is it?" he said. "What's the matter with you?"

She could not answer. She was convulsed, her hands pressed against her ribs, her face scarlet, her teeth, small, regular, whitely-gleaming teeth, bared. At last she managed to stutter:

"You—you—your high—high hat!... That b-b-black coat!... Your b-b-bare feet!... It's t-t-too funny!... Where did you sneak that disguise from?... Goodness! What a sight you are!"

Her laughter rang out, young and fresh, on the silence in which the leaves were fluttering. Facing her, Saint-Quentin, an awkward stripling who had outgrown his strength, with his face too pale, his hair too fair, his ears sticking out, but with admirable, very kindly black eyes, gazed, smiling, at the young girl, delighted by this diversion which seemed to be turning aside from him the outburst of wrath he was expecting.

Of a sudden, indeed, she fell upon him, attacking him with thumps and reproaches, but in a half-hearted fashion, with little bursts of laughter, which robbed the chastisement of its sting.

"Wretch and rogue! You've been stealing again, have you? You're no longer satisfied with your salary as acrobat, aren't you, my fine fellow? You must still prig money or jewels to keep yourself in high hats, must you? What have you got, looter? Eh? Tell me!"

By dint of striking and laughing she had soothed her righteous indignation. She set out again and Saint-Quentin, thoroughly abashed, stammered:

"Tell you? What's the good of telling you? You've guessed everything, as usual... As a matter of fact I did get in through that window, last evening... It was a pantry at the end of a corridor which led to the ground-floor rooms... Not a soul about... The family was at dinner... A servant's staircase led me up into another passage, which ran round the house, with the doors of all the rooms opening into it. I went through them all. Nothing—that is to say, pictures and other things too big to carry away. Then I hid myself in a closet, from which I could see into a little sitting-room next to the prettiest bedroom. They danced till late; then came upstairs... fashionable people... I saw them through a peep-hole in the door... the ladies décolletées, the gentlemen in evening dress... At last one of the ladies went into the boudoir. She put her jewels into a jewel-box and the jewel-box into a small safe, saying out loud as she opened it the three letters of the combination of the lock, R.O.B... So that, when she went to bed, all I had to do was to make use of them... After that... I waited for daylight... I wasn't going to chance stumbling about in the dark."

"Let's see what you've got," she commanded.

He opened his hand and disclosed on the palm of it two earrings, set with sapphires. She took them and looked at them. Her face changed; her eyes sparkled; she murmured in quite a different voice:

"How lovely they are, sapphires!... The sky is sometimes like that—at night... that dark blue, full of light..."

At the moment they were crossing a piece of land on which stood a large scarecrow, simply clad in a pair of trousers. On one of the cross-sticks which served it for arms hung a jacket. It was the jacket of Saint-Quentin. He had hung it there the evening before, and in order to render himself unrecognizable, had borrowed the scarecrow's long coat and high hat. He took off that long coat, buttoned it over the plaster bosom of the scarecrow, and replaced the hat. Then he slipped on his jacket and rejoined Dorothy.

She was still looking at the sapphires with an air of admiration.

He bent over them and said: "Keep them, Dorothy. You know quite well that I'm not really a thief and that I only got them for you... that you might have the pleasure of looking at them and touching them... It often goes to my heart to see you running about in that beggarly get-up!... To think of you dancing on the tight-rope! You who ought to live in luxury!... Ah, to think of all I'd do for you, if you'd let me!"

She raised her head, looked into his eyes, and said: "Would you really do anything for me?"

"Anything, Dorothy."

"Well, then, be honest, Saint-Quentin."

They set out again; and the young girl continued:

"Be honest, Saint-Quentin. That's all I ask of you. You and the other boys of the caravan, I've adopted you because, like me, you're war-orphans, and for the last two years we have wandered together along the high roads, happy rather than miserable, getting our fun, and on the whole, eating when we're hungry. But we must come to an understanding. I only like what is clean and straight and as clear as a ray of sunlight. Are you like me? This is the third time you've stolen to give me pleasure. Is this the last time? If it is, I pardon it. If it isn't, it's 'goodbye.'"

She spoke very seriously, emphasizing each phrase by a toss of the head which made the two wings of her hair flap.

Overwhelmed, Saint-Quentin said imploringly:

"Don't you want to have anything more to do with me?"

"Yes. But swear you won't do it again."

"I swear I won't."

"Then we won't say anything more about it. I feel that you mean what you say. Take back these jewels. You can hide them in the big basket under the caravan. Next week you will send them back by post. It's the Château de Chagny, isn't it?"

"Yes, and I saw the lady's name on one of her band-boxes. She's the Comtesse de Chagny."

They went on hand in hand. Twice they hid themselves to avoid meeting peasants, and at last, after several detours, they reached the neighborhood of the caravan.

"Listen," said Saint-Quentin, pausing to listen himself. "Yes. That's what it is—Castor and Pollux fighting as usual, the rascals!"

He dashed towards the sound.

"Saint-Quentin!" cried the young girl. "I forbid you to hit them!"

"You hit them often enough!"

"Yes. But they like me to hit them."

At the approach of Saint-Quentin, the two boys, who were fighting a duel with wooden swords, turned from one another to face the common enemy, howling:

"Dorothy! Mummy Dorothy! Stop Saint-Quentin! He's a beast! Help!"

There followed a distribution of cuffs, bursts of laughter, and hugs.

"Dorothy, it's my turn to be hugged!"

"Dorothy, it's my turn to be smacked!"

But the young girl said in a scolding voice:

"And the Captain? I'm sure you've gone and woke him up!"

"The Captain? He's sleeping like a sapper," declared Pollux. "Just listen to his snoring!"

By the side of the road the two urchins had lit a fire of wood. The pot, suspended from an iron tripod, was boiling. The four of them ate a steaming thick soup, bread and cheese, and drank a cup of coffee.

Dorothy did not budge from her stool. Her three companions would not have permitted it. It was rather which of the three should rise to serve her, all of them attentive to her wants, eager, jealous of one another, even aggressive towards one another. The battles of Castor and Pollux were always started by the fact that she had shown favor to one or the other. The two urchins, stout and chubby, dressed alike in pants, a shirt, and jacket, when one least expected it and for all that they were as fond of one another as brothers, fell upon one another with ferocious violence, because the young girl had spoken too kindly to one, or delighted the other with a too affectionate look.

As for Saint-Quentin, he cordially detested them. When Dorothy fondled them, he could have cheerfully wrung their necks. Never would she hug him. He had to content himself with good comradeship, trusting and affectionate, which only showed itself in a friendly hand-shake or a pleasant smile. The stripling delighted in them as the only reward which a poor devil like him could possibly deserve. Saint-Quentin was one of those who love with selfless devotion.

"The arithmetic lesson now," was Dorothy's order. "And you, Saint-Quentin, go to sleep for an hour on the box."

Castor brought his arithmetic. Pollux displayed his copy-book. The arithmetic lesson was followed by a lecture delivered by Dorothy on the Merovingian kings, then by a lecture on astronomy.

The two children listened with almost impassioned attention; and Saint-Quentin on the box took good care not to go to sleep. In teaching, Dorothy gave full play to her lively fancy in a fashion which diverted her pupils and never allowed them to grow weary. She had an air of learning herself whatever she chanced to be teaching. And her discourse, delivered in a very gentle voice, revealed a considerable knowledge and understanding and the suppleness of a practical intelligence.

At ten o'clock the young girl gave the order to harness the horse. The journey to the next town was a long one; and they had to arrive in time to secure the best place in front of the town-hall.

"And the Captain? He hasn't had breakfast!" cried Castor.

"All the better," said she. "The Captain always eats too much. It will give his stomach a rest. Besides if anyone wakes him he's always in a frightful temper. Let him sleep on."

They set out. The caravan moved along at the gentle pace of One-eyed Magpie, a lean old mare, but still strong and willing. They called her "One-eyed Magpie" because she had a piebald coat and had lost an eye. Heavy, perched on two high wheels, rocking, jingling like old iron, loaded with boxes, pots and pans, steps, barrels, and ropes, the caravan had recently been repainted. On both sides it bore the pompous inscription, "Dorothy's Circus, Manager's Carriage," which led one to believe that a file of wagons and vehicles was following at some distance with the staff, the properties, the baggage, and the wild beasts.

Saint-Quentin, whip in hand, walked at the head of the caravan. Dorothy, with the two small boys at her side, gathered flowers from the banks, sang choruses of marching songs with them, or told them stories. But at the end of half an hour, in the middle of some crossroads, she gave the order: "Halt!"

"What is it?" asked Saint-Quentin, seeing that she was reading the directions on a sign-post.

"Look," she said.

"There's no need to look. It's straight on. I looked it up on our map."

"Look," she repeated. "Chagny. A mile and a half."

"Quite so. It's the village of our château of yesterday. Only to get to it we made a short cut through the woods."

"Chagny. A mile and a half. Château de Roborey."

She appeared to be troubled and in a low voice she murmured again:

"Roborey—Roborey."

"Doubtless that's the proper name of the château," hazarded Saint-Quentin. "What difference can it make to you?"

"None—none."

"But you look as if it made no end of a difference."

"No. It's just a coincidence."

"In what way?"

"With regard to the name of Roborey—"

"Well?"

"Well, it's a word which was impressed on my memory... a word which was uttered in circumstances—"

"What circumstances, Dorothy?"

She explained slowly with a thoughtful air:

"Think a minute, Saint-Quentin. I told you that my father died of his wounds, at the beginning of the war, in a hospital near Chartres. I had been summoned; but I did not arrive in time... But two wounded men, who occupied the beds next to his in the ward, told me that during his last hours he never stopped repeating the same word again and again: 'Roborey... Roborey.' It came like a litany, unceasingly, and as if it weighed on his mind. Even when he was dying he still uttered the word: 'Roborey... Roborey.'"

"Yes," said Saint-Quentin. "I remember... You did tell me about it."

"Ever since then I have been asking myself what it meant and by what memory my poor father was obsessed at the time of his death. It was, apparently, more than an obsession... it was a terror... a dread. Why? I have never been able to find the explanation of it. So now you understand, Saint-Quentin, on seeing this name... written there, staring me in the face... on learning that there was a château of that name..."

Saint-Quentin was frightened:

"You never mean to go there, do you?"

"Why not?"

"It's madness, Dorothy!"

The young girl was silent, considering. But Saint-Quentin felt sure that she had not abandoned this unprecedented design. He was seeking for arguments to dissuade her when Castor and Pollux came running up:

"Three caravans are coming along!"

They issued on the instant, one after the other in single file, from a sunken lane, which opened on to the crossroads, and took the road to Roborey. They were an Aunt Sally, a Rifle-Range, and a Tortoise Merry-go-round. As he passed in front of Dorothy and Saint-Quentin, one of the men of the Rifle-Range called to them:

"Are you coming along too?"

"Where to?" said Dorothy.

"To the château. There's a village fête in the grounds. Shall I keep a pitch for you?"

"Right. And thanks very much," replied the young girl.

The caravans went on their way.

"What's the matter, Saint-Quentin?" said Dorothy.

He was looking paler than usual.

"What's the matter with you?" she repeated. "Your lips are twitching and you are turning green!"

He stammered:

"The p-p-police!"

From the same sunken lane two horsemen came into the crossroads, they rode on in front of the little party.

"You see," said Dorothy, smiling, "they're not taking any notice of us."

"No; but they're going to the château."

"Of course they are. There's a fête there; and two policemen have to be present."

"Always supposing that they haven't discovered the disappearance of the earrings and telephoned to the nearest police-station," he groaned.

"It isn't likely. The lady will only discover it tonight, when she dresses for dinner."

"All the same, don't let's go there," implored the unhappy stripling. "It's simply walking into the trap... Besides, there's that man... the man in the hole."

"Oh, he dug his own grave," she said and laughed.

"Suppose he's there... Suppose he recognizes me?"

"You were disguised. All they could do would be to arrest the scarecrow in the tall hat!"

"And suppose they've already laid an information against me? If they searched us they'd find the earrings."

"Drop them in some bushes in the park when we get there. I'll tell the people of the château their fortunes; and thanks to me, the lady will recover her earrings. Our fortunes are made."

"But if by any chance—"

"Rubbish! It would amuse me to go and see what is going on at the château which is named Roborey. So I'm going."

"Yes; but I'm afraid... afraid for you as well."

"Then stay away."

He shrugged his shoulders.

"We'll chance it!" he said, and cracked his whip.

II

DOROTHY'S CIRCUS

The château, situated at no great distance from Domfront, in the most rugged district of the picturesque department of the Orne, only received the name of Roborey in the course of the eighteenth century. Earlier it took its name of the Château de Chagny from the village which was grouped round it. The village green is in fact only a prolongation of the courtyard of the château. When the iron gates are open the two form an esplanade, constructed over the ancient moat, from which one descends on the right and left by steep slopes. The inner courtyard, circular and enclosed by two battlemented walls which run to the buildings of the château, is adorned by a fine old fountain of dolphins and sirens and a sun-dial set up on a rockery in the worst taste.

Dorothy's Circus passed through the village, preceded by its band, that is to say that Castor and Pollux did their best to wreck their lungs in the effort to extract the largest possible number of false notes from two trumpets. Saint-Quentin had arrayed himself in a black satin doublet and carried over his shoulder the trident which so awes wild beasts, and a placard which announced that the performance would take place at three o'clock.

Dorothy, standing upright on the roof of the caravan, directed One-eyed Magpie with four reins, wearing the majestic air of one driving a royal coach.

Already a dozen vehicles stood on the esplanade; and round them the showmen were busily setting up their canvas tents and swings and wooden horses, etc. Dorothy's Circus made no such preparations. Its directress went to the mayor's office to have her license viséd, while Saint-Quentin unharnessed One-eyed Magpie, and the two musicians changed their profession and set about cooking the dinner.

The Captain slept on.

Towards noon the crowd began to flock in from all the neighboring villages. After the meal Saint-Quentin, Castor, and Pollux took a siesta beside the caravan. Dorothy again went off. She went down into the ravine, examined the slab over the excavation, went up out of it again, moved among the groups of peasants and strolled about the gardens, round the château, and everywhere else that one was allowed to go.

"Well, how's your search getting on?" said Saint-Quentin when she returned to the caravan.

She appeared thoughtful, and slowly she explained:

"The château, which has been empty for a long while, belongs to the family of Chagny-Roborey, of which the last representative, Count Octave, a man about forty, married, twelve years ago, a very rich woman. After the war the Count and Countess restored and modernized the château. Yesterday evening they had a house-warming to which they invited a large party of guests who went away at the end of the evening. Today they're having a kind of popular house-warming for the villagers."

"And as regards this name of Roborey, have you learned anything?"

"Nothing. I'm still quite ignorant why my father uttered it."

"So that we can get away directly after the performance," said Saint-Quentin who was very eager to depart.

"I don't know... We'll see... I've found out some rather queer things."

"Have they anything to do with your father?"

"No," she said with some hesitation. "Nothing to do with him. Nevertheless I should like to look more closely into the matter. When there is darkness anywhere, there's no knowing what it may hide... I should like..."

She remained silent for a long time. At last she went on in a serious tone, looking straight into Saint-Quentin's face:

"Listen: you have confidence in me, haven't you? You know that I'm quite sensible at bottom... and very prudent. You know that I have a certain amount of intuition... and good eyes that see a little more than most people see... Well, I've got a strong feeling that I ought to remain here."

"Because of the name of Roborey?"

"Because of that, and for other reasons, which will compel me perhaps, according to circumstances, to undertake unexpected enterprises... dangerous ones. At that moment, Saint-Quentin, you must follow me—boldly."

"Go on, Dorothy. Tell me what it is exactly."

"Nothing... Nothing definite at present... One word, however. The man who was aiming at you this morning, the man in the blouse, is here."

"Never! He's here, do you say? You've seen him? With the policemen?"

She smiled.

"Not yet. But that may happen. Where have you put those earrings?"

"At the bottom of the basket, in a little cardboard box with a rubber ring round it."

"Good. As soon as the performance is over, stick them in that clump of rhododendrons between the gates and the coach-house."

"Have they found out that they've disappeared?"

"Not yet," said Dorothy. "From the things you told me I believe that the little safe is in the boudoir of the Countess. I heard some of the maids talking; and nothing was said about any robbery. They'd have been full of it." She added: "Look! there are some of the people from the château in front of the shooting-gallery. Is it that pretty fair lady with the grand air?"

"Yes. I recognize her."

"An extremely kind-hearted woman, according to what the maids said, and generous, always ready to listen to the unfortunate. The people about her are very fond of her... much fonder of her than they are of her husband, who, it appears, is not at all easy to get on with."

"Which of them is he? There are three men there."

"The biggest... the man in the gray suit... with his stomach sticking out with importance. Look; he has taken a rifle. The two on either side of the Countess are distant relations. The tall one with the grizzled beard which runs up to his tortoise-shell spectacles, has been at the château a month. The other more sallow one, in a velveteen shooting-coat and gaiters, arrived yesterday."

"But they look as if they knew you, both of them."

"Yes. We've already spoken to one another. The bearded nobleman was even quite attentive."

Saint-Quentin made an indignant movement. She checked him at once.

"Keep calm, Saint-Quentin. And let's go closer to them. The battle begins."

The crowd was thronging round the back of the tent to watch the exploits of the owner of the château, whose skill was well known. The dozen bullets which he fired made a ring round the center of the target; and there was a burst of applause.

"No, no!" he protested modestly. "It's bad. Not a single bull's-eye."

"Want of practice," said a voice near him.

Dorothy had slipped into the front ranks of the throng; and she had said it in the quiet tone of a connoisseur. The spectators laughed. The bearded gentleman presented her to the Count and Countess.

"Mademoiselle Dorothy, the directress of the circus."

"Is it as circus directress that mademoiselle judges a target or as an expert?" said the Count jocosely.

"As an expert."

"Ah, mademoiselle also shoots?"

"Now and then."

"Jaguars?"

"No. Pipe-bowls."

"And mademoiselle does not miss her aim?"

"Never."

"Provided, of course, that she has a first-class weapon?"

"Oh, no. A good shot can use any kind of weapon that comes to hand... even an old-fashioned contraption like this."

She gripped the butt of an old pistol, provided herself with six cartridges, and aimed at the cardboard target cut out by the Count.

The first shot was a bull's-eye. The second cut the black circle. The third was a bull's-eye.

The Count was amazed.

"It's marvelous... She doesn't even take the trouble to aim. What do you say to that, d'Estreicher?"

The bearded nobleman, as Dorothy called him, cried enthusiastically:

"Unheard of! Marvelous! You could make a fortune, Mademoiselle!"

Without answering, with the three remaining bullets she broke two pipe-bowls and shattered an empty egg-shell that was dancing on the top of a jet of water.

And thereupon, pushing aside her admirers, and addressing the astonished crowd, she made the announcement:

"Ladies and gentlemen, I have the honor to inform you that the performance of Dorothy's Circus is about to take place. After exhibitions of marksmanship, choregraphic displays, then feats of strength and skill and tumbling, on foot, on horseback, on the earth and in the air. Fireworks, regattas, motor races, bull-fights, train hold-ups, all will be on view there. It is about to begin, ladies and gentlemen."

From that moment Dorothy was all movement, liveliness, and gayety. Saint-Quentin had marked off a sufficiently large circle, in front of the door of the caravan, with a rope supported by stakes. Round this arena, in which chairs were reserved for the people of the château, the spectators were closely packed together on benches and flights of steps and on anything they could lay their hands on.

And Dorothy danced. First of all on a rope, stretched between two posts. She bounced like a shuttlecock which the battledore catches and drives yet higher; or again she lay down and balanced herself on the rope as on a hammock, walked backwards and forwards, turned and saluted right and left; then leapt to the earth and began to dance.

An extraordinary mixture of all the dances, in which nothing seemed studied or purposed, in which all the movements and attitudes appeared unconscious and to spring from a series of inspirations of the moment. By turns she was the London dancing-girl, the Spanish dancer with her castanets, the Russian who bounds and twirls, or, in the arms of Saint-Quentin, a barbaric creature dancing a languorous tango.

And every time all that she needed was just a movement, the slightest movement, which changed the hang of her shawl, or the way her hair was arranged, to become from head to foot a Spanish, or Russian, or English, or Argentine girl. And all the while she was an incomparable vision of grace and charm, of harmonious and healthy youth, of pleasure and modesty, of extreme but measured joy.

Castor and Pollux, bent over an old drum, beat with their fingers a muffled, rhythmical accompaniment. Speechless and motionless the spectators gazed and admired, spellbound by such a wealth of fantasy and the multitude of images which passed before their eyes. At the very moment when they were regarding her as a guttersnipe turning cartwheels, she suddenly appeared to them in the guise of a lady with a long train, flirting her fan and dancing the minuet. Was she a child or a woman? Was she under fifteen or over twenty?

She cut short the clamor of applause which burst forth when she came to a sudden stop, by springing on to the roof of the caravan, and crying, with an imperious gesture:

"Silence! The Captain is waking up!"

There was, behind the box, a long narrow basket, in the shape of a closed sentry-box. Raising it by one end, she half opened the cover and cried:

"Now, Captain Montfaucon, you've had a good sleep, haven't you? Come now, Captain, we're a bit behind-hand with our exercises. Make up for it, Captain!"

She opened the top of the basket wide and disclosed in a kind of cradle, very comfortable, a little boy of seven or eight, with golden curls and red cheeks, who yawned prodigiously. Only half awake, he stretched out his hands to Dorothy who clasped him to her bosom and kissed him very tenderly.

"Baron Saint-Quentin," she called out. "Catch hold of the Captain. Is his bread and jam ready? Captain Montfaucon will continue the performance by going through his drill."

Captain Montfaucon was the comedian of the troupe. Dressed in an old American uniform, his tunic dragged along the ground, and his corkscrew trousers had their bottoms rolled up as high as his knees. This made a costume so hampering that he could not walk ten steps without falling full length. Captain

Montfaucon provided the comedy by this unbroken series of falls and the impressive air with which he picked himself up again. When, furnished with a whip, his other hand useless by reason of the slice of bread and jam it held, his cheeks smeared with jam, he put the unbridled One-eyed Magpie through his performance, there was one continuous roar of laughter.

"Mark time!" he ordered. "Right-about-turn!... Attention, One-eye' Magpie!"—he could never be induced to say "One-eyed"—"And now the goose-step. Good, One-eye' Magpie... Perfect!"

One-eyed Magpie, promoted to the rank of circus horse, trotted round in a circle without taking the slightest notice of the captain's orders, who, for his part, stumbling, falling, picking himself up, recovering his slice of bread and jam, did not bother for a moment about whether he was obeyed or not. It was so funny, the phlegm of the little man, and the undeviating course of the beast, that Dorothy herself was forced to laugh with a laughter that re-doubled the gayety of the spectators. They saw that the young girl, in spite of the fact that the performance was undoubtedly repeated every day, always took the same delight in it.

"Excellent, Captain," she cried to encourage him. "Splendid! And now, captain, we'll act 'The Gipsy's Kidnaping,' a drama in a brace of shakes. Baron Saint-Quentin, you'll be the scoundrelly kidnaper."

Uttering frightful howls, the scoundrelly kidnaper seized her and set her on One-eyed Magpie, bound her on her, and jumped up behind her. Under the double burden the mare staggered slowly off, while Baron Saint-Quentin yelled:

"Gallop! Hell for leather!"

The Captain quietly put a cap on a toy gun and aimed at the scoundrelly kidnaper.

The cap cracked; Saint-Quentin fell off; and in a transport of gratitude the rescued gypsy covered her deliverer with kisses.

There were other scenes in which Castor and Pollux took part. All were carried through with the same brisk liveliness. All were caricatures, really humorous, of what diverts or charms us, and revealed a lively imagination, powers of observation of the first order, a keen sense of the picturesque and the ridiculous.

"Captain Montfaucon, take a bag and make a collection. Castor and Pollux, a roll of the drum to imitate the sound of falling water. Baron Saint-Quentin, beware of pickpockets!"

The Captain dragged through the crowd an enormous bag in which were engulfed pennies and dirty notes; and from the top of the caravan Dorothy delivered her farewell address:

"Very many thanks, agriculturists and towns-people! It is with regret that we leave this generous locality. But before we depart we take this opportunity of informing you that Mademoiselle Dorothy (she saluted) is not only the directress of a circus and a first-class performer. Mademoiselle Dorothy (she saluted) will also demonstrate her extraordinary excellence in the sphere of clairvoyance and psychic powers. The lines of the hand, the cards, coffee grounds, handwriting, and astrology have no secrets for her. She dissipates the darkness. She solves enigmas. With her magic ring she makes invisible springs burst forth, and above all, she discovers in the most unfathomable places, under the stones of old castles, and in the depths of forgotten dungeons, fantastic treasures whose existence no one suspected. A word to the wise is enough. I have the honor to thank you."

She descended quickly. The three boys were packing up the properties.

Saint-Quentin came to her.

"We hook it, don't we, straight away? Those policemen have kept an eye on me the whole time."

She replied:

"Then you didn't hear the end of my speech?"

"What about it?"

"What about it? Why, the consultations are going to begin—the superlucid clairvoyant Dorothy. Look, here come some clients... the bearded nobleman and the gentleman in velveteen... I like the gentleman in velveteen. He is very polite; and there's no side about his fawn-colored gaiters—the complete gentleman-farmer."

The bearded nobleman was beside himself. He loaded the young girl with extravagant compliments, looking at her the while in an uncommonly equivocal fashion. He introduced himself as "Maxime d'Estreicher," introduced his companion as "Raoul Davernoie," and finally, on behalf of the Countess Octave, invited her to come to tea in the château.

"Alone?" she asked.

"Certainly not," protested Raoul Davernoie with a courteous bow. "Our cousin is anxious to congratulate all your comrades. Will you come, mademoiselle?"

Dorothy accepted. Just a moment to change her frock, and she would come to the château.

"No, no; no toilet!" cried d'Estreicher. "Come as you are... You look perfectly charming in that slightly scanty costume. How pretty you are like that!"

Dorothy flushed and said dryly:

"No compliments, please."

"It isn't a compliment, mademoiselle," he said a trifle ironically. "It's the natural homage one pays to beauty."

He went off, taking Raoul Davernoie with him.

"Saint-Quentin," murmured Dorothy, looking after them. "Keep an eye on that gentleman."

"Why?"

"He's the man in the blouse who nearly brought you down this morning."

Saint-Quentin staggered as if he had received the charge of shot.

"Are you sure?"

"Very nearly. He has the same way of walking, dragging his right leg a little."

He muttered:

"He has recognized me!"

"I think so. When he saw you jumping about during the performance it recalled to his mind the black devil performing acrobatic feats against the face of the cliff. And it was only a step from you to me who shoved the slab over on to his head. I read it all in his eyes and his attitude towards me this afternoon—just in his manner of speaking to me. There was a touch of mockery in it."

Saint-Quentin lost his temper:

"And we aren't hurrying off at once! You dare stay?"

"I dare."

"But that man?"

"He doesn't know that I penetrated his disguise... And as long as he doesn't know—"

"You mean that your intention is?"

"Perfectly simple—to tell them their fortunes, amuse them, and puzzle them."

"But what's your object?"

"I want to make them talk in their turn."

"What about?"

"What I want to know."

"What do you want to know?"

"That's what I don't know. It's for them to teach me."

"And suppose they discover the robbery? Suppose they cross-examine us?"

"Saint-Quentin, take the Captain's wooden gun, mount guard in front of the caravan, and when the policemen approach, shoot them down."

When she had made herself tidy, she took Saint-Quentin with her to the château and on the way made him repeat all the details of his nocturnal expedition. Behind them came

Castor and Pollux, then the Captain, who dragged after him by a string a little toy cart loaded with tiny packages.

They entertained them in the large drawing-room of the château. The Countess, who indeed was, as Dorothy had said, an agreeable and amiable woman, and of a seductive prettiness, stuffed the children with dainties, and was wholly charming to the young girl. For her part, Dorothy seemed quite as much at her ease with her hosts as she had been on the top of the caravan. She had merely hidden her short skirt and bodice under a large black shawl, drawn in at the waist by a belt. The ease of her manner, her cultivated intonation, her correct speech, to which now and then a slang word gave a certain spiciness, her quickness, and the intelligent expression of her brilliant eyes amazed the Countess and charmed the three men.

"Mademoiselle," d'Estreicher exclaimed, "if you can foretell the future, I can assure you that I too can clearly foresee it, and that certain fortune awaits you. Ah, if you would put yourself in my hands and let me direct your career in Paris! I am in touch with all the worlds and I can guarantee your success."

She tossed her head:

"I don't need anyone."

"Mademoiselle," said he, "confess that you do not find me congenial."

"Neither congenial nor uncongenial. I don't really know you."

"If you really knew me, you'd have confidence in me."

"I don't think so," she said.

"Why?"

She took his hand, turned it over, bent over the open palm, and as she examined it said slowly:

"Dissipation... Greedy for money... Conscienceless..."

"But I protest, mademoiselle! Conscienceless? I? I who am full of scruples."

"Your hand says the opposite, monsieur."

"Does it also say that I have no luck?"

"None at all."

"What? Shan't I ever be rich?"

"I fear not."

"Confound it... And what about my death? Is it a long way off?"

"Not very."

"A painful death?"

"A matter of seconds."

"An accident, then?"

"Yes."

"What kind of accident?"

She pointed with her finger:

"Look here—at the base of the forefinger."

"What is there?"

"The gallows."

There was an outburst of laughter. D'Estreicher was enchanted. Count Octave clapped his hands.

"Bravo, mademoiselle, the gallows for this old libertine; it must be that you have the gift of second sight. So I shall not hesitate..."

He consulted his wife with a look of inquiry and continued:

"So I shall not hesitate to tell you..."

"To tell me," finished Dorothy mischievously, "the reasons for which you invited me to tea."

The Count protested:

"Not at all, mademoiselle. We invited you to tea solely for the pleasure of becoming acquainted with you."

"And perhaps a little from the desire to appeal to my skill as a sorceress."

The Countess Octave interposed:

"Ah, well, yes, mademoiselle. Your final announcement excited our curiosity. Moreover, I will confess that we haven't much belief in things of this kind and that it is rather out of curiosity that we should like to ask you certain questions."

"If you have no faith in my poor skill, madame, we'll let that pass, and all the same I'll manage to gratify your curiosity."

"By what means?"

"Merely by reflecting on your words."

"What?" said the Countess. "No magnetic passes? No hypnotic sleep?"

"No, madame—at least not for the present. Later on we'll see."

Only keeping Saint-Quentin with her, she told the children to go and play in the garden. Then she sat down and said:

"I'm listening, madame."

"Just like that? Perfectly simply?"

"Perfectly simply."

"Well, then, mademoiselle—"

The Countess spoke in a tone the carelessness of which was not perhaps absolutely sincere.

"Well, then, mademoiselle, you spoke of forgotten dungeons and ancient stones and hidden treasures. Now, the Château de Roborey is several centuries old. It has undoubtedly been the scene of adventures and dramas; and it would amuse us to know whether any of its inhabitants have by any chance left in some out-of-way corner one of these fabulous treasures of which you spoke."

Dorothy kept silent for some little time. Then she said:

"I always answer with all the greater precision if full confidence is placed in me. If there are any reservations, if the question is not put as it ought to be..."

"What reservations? I assure you, mademoiselle—"

The young girl broke in firmly:

"You asked me the question, madame, as if you were giving way to a sudden curiosity, which did not rest, so to speak, on any real base. Now you know as well as I do that excavations have been made in the château."

"That's very possible," said Count Octave. "But if they were, it must have been dozens of years ago, in the time of my father or grandfather."

"There are recent excavations," Dorothy asserted.

"But we have only been living in the château a month!"

"It isn't a matter of a month, but of some days... of some hours..."

The Countess declared with animation:

"I assure you, mademoiselle, that we have not made researches of any kind."

"Then the researches must have been made by someone else."

"By whom? And under what conditions? And in what spot?"

There was another silence. Then Dorothy went on:

"You will excuse me, madame, if I have been going into matters which do not seem to be any business of mine. It's one of my faults. Saint-Quentin often says to me: 'Your craze for trespassing and ferreting about everywhere will lead people to say unpleasant things about you.' But it happened that, on arriving here, since we had to wait for the hour of the performance, I took a walk. I wandered right and left, looking at things, and in the end I made a certain number of observations which, as it seemed to me, are of some importance. Thus..."

The Count and Countess drew nearer in their eagerness to hear her. She went on:

"Thus, while I was admiring the beautiful old fountain in the court of honor, I was able to make sure that, all round it, holes have been dug under the marble basin which catches the water. Was the exploration profitable? I do not know. In any case, the earth has been put back into its place carefully, but not so well that one cannot see that the surface of the soil is raised."

The Count and his guests looked at one another in astonishment.

One of them objected:

"Perhaps they've been repairing the basin... or been putting in a waste pipe?"

"No," said the Countess in a tone of decision. "No one has touched that fountain. And, doubtless, mademoiselle, you discovered other traces of the same kind of work."

"Yes," said Dorothy. "Someone has been doing the same thing a little distance away—under the rockery, the pedestal on which the sun-dial stands. They have been boring across that rockery. An iron rod has been broken. It's there still."

"But why?" cried the excited Countess. "Why these two spots rather than others? What are they searching for? What do they want? Have you any indication?"

They had not long to wait for her answer; and Dorothy delivered it slowly, as if to make it quite clear that here was the essential point of her inquiry:

"The motive of these investigations is engraved on the marble of the fountain. You can see it from here? Sirens surround a column surmounted by a capital. Isn't it so? Well, on one of the faces of the capital are some letters—almost effaced letters."

"But we've never noticed them!" cried the Countess.

"They are there," declared the young girl. "They are worn and hard to distinguish from the cracks in the marble. However, there is one word—a whole word—that one can reconstruct and read easily when once it has appeared to you."

"What word?"

"The word FORTUNA."

The three syllables came long-drawn-out in a silence of stupefaction. The Count repeated them in a hushed voice, staring at Dorothy, who went on:

"Yes; the word FORTUNA. And this word you find again also on the column of the sun-dial. Even yet more obliterated, to such a degree that one rather divines that it is there rather than actually reads it. But it certainly is there. Each letter is in its place. You cannot doubt it."

The Count had not waited for her to finish speaking. Already he was out of the house; and through the open windows they saw him hurry to the fountain. He cast but one glance at it, passed in front of the sun-dial, and came quickly back.

"Everything that mademoiselle says is the exact truth. They have dug at both spots... and the word FORTUNA, which I saw at once, and which I had never seen before, gives the reason for their digging... They have searched... and perhaps they have found."

"No," the young girl asserted calmly.

"Why do you say no? What do you know about it?"

She hesitated. Her eyes met the eyes of d'Estreicher. He knew now, doubtless, that he was unmasked, and he began to understand what the young girl was driving at. But would she dare to go to extremities and join battle? And then what were the reasons for this unforeseen struggle?

With an air of challenge he repeated the Countess's question:

"Yes; why do you say that they have found nothing?"

Boldly Dorothy accepted the challenge.

"Because the digging has gone on. There is in the ravine, under the walls of the château, among the stones which have fallen from the cliff, an ancient slab, which certainly comes from some demolished structure. The word FORTUNA is to be deciphered on the base of it also. Let someone move that slab and they will discover a perfectly fresh excavation, and the tracks of feet muddled up by the hand."

III

EXTRA-LUCID

This last blow re-doubled the uneasiness of Count and Countess; and they took counsel in a low voice for a moment with their cousins d'Estreicher and Raoul Davernoie.

Saint-Quentin on hearing Dorothy reveal the events in the ravine and the hiding-place of the man in the blouse had fallen back among the cushions of the great easy chair on which he was sitting. She was going mad! To set them on the trail of the man in the blouse was to set them on their own trail, his and Dorothy's. What madness!

She, however, in the midst of all this excitement and anxiety remained wholly calm. She appeared to be following a quite definite course with her goal clearly in view, while the others, without her guidance, stumbled in a panic.

"Mademoiselle," said the Countess, "your revelations have upset us considerably. They show how extraordinarily acute you are; and I cannot thank you enough for having given us this warning."

"You have treated me so kindly, madame," she replied, "that I am only too delighted to have been of use to you."

"Of immense use to us," agreed the Countess. "And I beg you to make the service complete."

"How?"

"By telling us what you know."

"I don't know any more."

"But perhaps you could learn more?"

"In what way?"

The Countess smiled:

"By means of that skill in divination of which you were telling us a little while ago."

"And in which you do not believe, madame."

"But in which I'm quite ready to believe now."

Dorothy bowed.

"I'm quite willing... But these are experiments which are not always successful."

"Let's try."

"Right. We'll try. But I must ask you not to expect too much."

She took a handkerchief from Saint-Quentin's pocket and bandaged her eyes with it.

"Astral vision, on condition of being blind," she said. "The less I see the more I see."

And she added gravely:

"Put your questions, madame. I will answer them to the best of my ability."

"Remaining in a state of wakefulness all the time?"

"Yes."

She rested her two elbows on the table and buried her face in her hands. The Countess at once said:

"Who has been digging? Who has been making excavations under the fountain and under the sun-dial?"

A minute passed slowly. They had the impression she was concentrating and withdrawing from all contact with the world around her. At last she said in measured tones which bore no resemblance to the accents of a pythoness or a somnambulist.

"I see nothing on the esplanade. In that quarter the excavations must already be several days old, and all traces are obliterated. But in the ravine—"

"In the ravine?" said the Countess.

"The slab is standing on end and a man is digging a hole with a mattock."

"A man? What man? Describe him."

"He is wearing a very long blouse."

"But his face?..."

"His face is encircled by a muffler which passes under a cap with turned-down brim... You cannot even see his eyes. When he has finished digging he lets the slab fall back into its place and carries away the mattock."

"Nothing else?"

"No. He has found nothing."

"Are you sure of that?"

"Absolutely sure."

"And which way does he go?"

"He goes back up the ravine... He comes to the iron gates of the château."

"But they're locked."

"He has the key. He enters... It is early in the morning... No one is up... He directs his steps to the orangerie... There's a small room there."

"Yes. The gardener keeps his implements in it."

"The man sets the mattock in a corner, takes off his blouse and hangs it on a nail in the wall."

"But he can't be the gardener!" exclaimed the Countess. "His face? Can you see his face?"

"No... no... It remains covered up."

"But his clothes?"

"His clothes?... I can't make them out... He goes out... He disappears."

The young girl broke off as if her attention were fixed on someone whose outline was blurred and lost in the shadow like a phantom.

"I do not see him any longer," she said. "I can see nothing any longer... Do I?... Ah yes, the steps of the château... The door is shut quietly... And then... then the staircase... A long corridor dimly lighted by small windows... However I can distinguish some prints... galloping horses... sportsmen in red coats... Ah! The man!... The man is there, on his knees, before a door... He turns the handle of the door... It opens."

"It must be one of the servants," said the Countess in a hollow voice. "And it must be a room on the first floor, since there are prints on the passage walls. What is the room like?"

"The shutters are closed. The man has lit a pocket-lamp and is hunting about... There's a calendar on the chimney-piece... It's today, Wednesday... And an Empire clock with gilded columns..."

"The clock in my boudoir," murmured the Countess.

"The hands point to a quarter of six... The light of the lamp is directed to the other side of the room, on to a walnut cupboard with two doors. The man opens the two doors and reveals a safe."

They were listening to Dorothy in a troubled silence, their faces twitching with emotion. How could anyone have failed to believe the whole of the vision the young girl was describing, seeing that she had never been over the château, never crossed the threshold of this boudoir, and that nevertheless she was describing things which must have been unknown to her.

Dumfounded, the Countess exclaimed:

"The safe was unlocked!... I'm certain of it... I shut it after putting my jewels away... I can still hear the sound of the door banging!"

"Shut—yes. But the key there."

"What does that matter? I have muddled up the letters of the combination."

"Not so. The key turns."

"Impossible!"

"The key turns. I see the three letters."

"The three letters! You see them!"

"Clearly—an R, an O, and a B, that is to say the first three letters of the word Roborey. The safe is open. There's a jewel-case inside it. The man's hand gropes in it... and takes..."

"What? What? What has he taken?"

"Two earrings."

"Two sapphires, aren't they? Two sapphires?"

"Yes, madame, two sapphires."

Thoroughly upset and moving jerkily, the Countess went quickly out of the room, followed by her husband, and Raoul Davernoie. And Dorothy heard the Count say:

"If this is true, you'll admit, Davernoie, that this instance of divination would be uncommonly strange."

"Uncommonly strange indeed," replied d'Estreicher who had gone as far as the door with them.

He shut the door on them and came back to the middle of the drawing-room with the manifest intention of speaking to the young girl.

Dorothy had removed the handkerchief from her eyes and was rubbing them like a person who has come out of the dark. The bearded nobleman and she looked at one another for a few moments. Then, after some hesitation, he took a couple of steps back towards the door. But once more he changed his mind and turning towards Dorothy, stroked his beard at length, and at last broke into a quiet, delighted chuckle.

Dorothy, who was never behind-hand when it came to laughing, did as the bearded nobleman had done.

"You laugh?" said he.

"I laugh because you laugh. But I am ignorant of the reason of your gayety. May I learn it?"

"Certainly, mademoiselle. I laugh because I find all that very amusing."

"What is very amusing?"

D'Estreicher came a few steps further into the room and replied:

"What is very amusing is to mix up into one and the same person the individual who was making an excavation under the slab of stone and this other individual who broke into the château last night and stole the jewels."

"That is to say?" asked the young girl.

"That is to say, to be yet more precise, the idea of throwing beforehand the burden of robbery committed by M. Saint-Quentin—"

"Onto the back of M. d'Estreicher," said Dorothy, ending his sentence for him.

The bearded nobleman made a wry face, but did not protest. He bowed and said:

"That's it, exactly. We may just as well play with our cards on the table, mayn't we? We're neither of us people who have eyes for the purpose of not seeing. And if I saw a black silhouette slip out of a window last night. You, for your part, have seen—"

"A gentleman who received a stone slab on his head."

"Exactly. And I repeat, it's very ingenious of you to try to make them out to be one and the same person. Very ingenious... and very dangerous."

"In what way is it dangerous?"

"In the sense that every attack provokes a counter-attack."

"I haven't made any attack. But I wished to make it quite clear that I was ready to go to any lengths."

"Even to the length of attributing the theft of this pair of earrings to me?"

"Perhaps."

"Oh! Then I'd better lose no time proving that they're in your hands."

"Be quick about it."

Once more he stopped short on the threshold of the door and said:

"Then we're enemies?"

"We're enemies."

"Why? You're quite unacquainted with me."

"I don't need to be acquainted with you to know who you are."

"What? Who I am? I'm the Chevalier Maxime d'Estreicher."

"Possibly. But you're also the gentleman who, secretly and without his cousins' knowledge, seeks... that which he has no right to seek. With what object if not to steal it?"

"And that's your business?"

"Yes."

"On what grounds?"

"It won't be long before you learn."

He made a movement—of anger or contempt? He controlled himself and mumbled:

"All the worse for you and all the worse for Saint-Quentin. Goodbye for the present."

Without another word he bowed and went out.

It was an odd fact, but in this kind of brutal and violent duel, Dorothy had kept so cool that hardly had the door closed before, following her instincts of a street Arab, she indulged in a high kick and pirouetted half across the room. Then, satisfied with herself and the way things were going, she opened a glass-case, took from it a bottle of smelling-salts, and went to Saint-Quentin who was lying back in his easy chair.

"Smell it, old chap."

He sniffed it, began to sneeze, and stuttered:

"We're lost!"

"You're a fine fellow, Saint-Quentin! Why do you think we're lost?"

"He's off to denounce us."

"Undoubtedly he's off to buck up the inquiries about us. But as for denouncing us, for telling what he saw this morning, he daren't do it. If he does, I tell in my turn what I saw."

"All the same, Dorothy, there was no point in telling them of the disappearance of the jewels."

"They were bound to discover it sooner or later. The fact of having been the first to speak of it diverts suspicion."

"Or turns it on to us, Dorothy."

"In that case I accuse the bearded nobleman."

"You need proofs."

"I shall find them."

"How you do detest him!"

"No: but I wish to destroy him. He's a dangerous man, Saint-Quentin. I have an intuition of it; and you know that I hardly ever deceive myself. He has all the vices. He is betraying his cousins, the Count and Countess. He is capable of anything. I wish to rid them of him by any means."

Saint-Quentin strove to reassure himself:

"You're amazing. You make combinations and calculations; you act; you foresee. One feels that you direct your course in accordance with a plan."

"In accordance with nothing at all, my lad. I go forward at a venture, and decide as Fortune bids."

"However..."

"I have a definite aim, that's all. Four people confront me, who, there's no doubt about it, are linked together by a common secret. Now the word 'Roborey,' uttered by my father when he was dying, gives me the right to try to find out whether he himself did not form part of this group, and if, in consequence, his daughter is not qualified to take his place. Up to now the four people hold together and keep me at a distance. I have vainly attempted the impossible to obtain their confidence in the first place and after it their confessions, so far without any result. But I shall succeed."

She stamped her foot, with an abruptness in which was suddenly manifest all the energy and decision which animated this smiling and delicate creature, and she said again:

"I shall succeed, Saint-Quentin. I swear it. I am not at the end of my revelations. There is another which will persuade them perhaps to be more open with me."

"What is it, Dorothy?"

"I know what I'm doing, my lad."

She was silent. She gazed through the open window near which Castor and Pollux were fighting. The noise of hurrying footsteps re-ëchoed about the château. People were calling out to one another. A servant ran across the court at full speed and shut the gates, leaving a small part of the crowd and three or four caravans, of which one was Dorothy's Circus, in the courtyard.

"The p-p-policemen! The p-p-policemen!" stammered Saint-Quintin. "There they are! They're examining the Rifle-Range!"

"And d'Estreicher is with them," observed the young girl.

"Oh, Dorothy, what have you done?"

"It's all the same to me," she said, wholly unmoved. "These people have a secret which perhaps belongs to me as much as to them. I wish to know it. Excitement, sensations, all that works in my favor."

"Nevertheless..."

"Pipe, Saint-Quentin. Today decides my future. Instead of trembling, rejoice... a fox-trot, old chap!"

She threw an arm round his waist, and propping him up like a tailor's dummy with wobbly legs, she forced him to turn; climbing in at the window, Castor and Pollux, followed by Captain Montfaucon, started to dance round the couple, chanting the air of the Capucine, first in the drawing-room, then across the large hall. But a fresh failure of Saint-Quentin's legs dashed the spirits of the dancers.

Dorothy lost her temper.

"What's the matter with you now?" she cried, trying to raise him and keep him upright.

He stuttered:

"I'm afraid... I'm afraid."

"But why on earth are you afraid? I've never seen you in such a funk. What are you afraid of?"

"The jewels..."

"Idiot! But you've thrown them into the clump!"

"No."

"You haven't?"

"No."

"But where are they then?"

"I don't know. I looked for them in the basket as you told me to. They weren't there any longer. The little cardboard box had disappeared."

During his explanation Dorothy grew graver and graver. The danger suddenly grew clear to her.

"Why didn't you tell me about it? I should not have acted as I did."

"I didn't dare to. I didn't want to worry you."

"Ah, Saint-Quentin, you were wrong, my lad."

She uttered no other reproach, but added:

"What's your explanation?"

"I suppose I made a mistake and didn't put the earrings in the basket... but somewhere else... in some other part of the caravan... I've looked everywhere without finding them... But those policemen—they'll find them."

The young girl was overwhelmed. The earrings discovered in her possession, the theft duly verified meant arrest and jail.

"Leave me to my fate," groaned Saint-Quentin. "I'm nothing but an imbecile... A criminal... Don't try to save me... Throw all the blame on me, since it is the truth."

At that moment a police-inspector in uniform appeared on the threshold of the hall, under the guidance of one of the servants.

"Not a word," murmured Dorothy. "I forbid you to utter a single word."

The inspector came forward:

"Mademoiselle Dorothy?"

"I'm Mademoiselle Dorothy, inspector. What is it you want?"

"Follow me. It will be necessary..."

He was interrupted by the entrance of the Countess who hurried in, accompanied by her husband and Raoul Davernoie.

"No, no, inspector!" she exclaimed. "I absolutely oppose anything which might appear to show a lack of trust in mademoiselle. There is some misunderstanding."

Raoul Davernoie also protested. But Count Octave observed:

"Bear in mind, dear, that this is merely a formality, a general measure which the inspector is bound to take. A robbery has been committed, it is only right that the inquiry should include everybody— "

"But it was mademoiselle who informed of the robbery," interrupted the Countess. "It is she who for the last hour has been warning us of all that is being plotted against us!"

"But why not let her be questioned like everybody else? As d'Estreicher said just now, it's possible that your earrings were not stolen from your safe. You may have put them in your ears without thinking today, and then lost them out-of-doors... where someone has picked them up."

The inspector, an honest fellow who seemed very much annoyed by this difference of opinion between the Count and Countess, did not know what to do. Dorothy helped him out of the awkward situation.

"I quite agree with you, Count. My part in the business may very well appear suspicious to you; and you have the right to ask how I know the word that opens the safe, and if my talents as a diviner are enough to explain my clairvoyance. There isn't any reason then for making an exception in my favor."

She bent low before the Countess and gently kissed her hand.

"You mustn't be present at the inquiry, madame. It's not a pleasant business. For me, it's one of the risks we strolling entertainers run; but you would find it painful. Only, I beg you, for reasons which you will presently understand, to come back to us after they have questioned me."

"I promise you I will."

"I'm at your service, inspector."

She went off with her four companions and the inspector of police. Saint-Quentin had the air of a condemned criminal being led to the gallows. Captain Montfaucon, his hands in his pockets, the string round his wrist, dragged along his baggage-wagon and whistled an American tune, like a gallant fellow who knows that all these little affairs always end well.

At the end of the courtyard, the last of the country folk were departing through the open gates, beside which the gamekeeper was posted. The showmen were grouped about their tents and in the orangery where the second policeman was examining their licenses.

On reaching her caravan, Dorothy perceived d'Estreicher talking to two servants.

"You then are the director of the inquiry, monsieur?" she said gayly.

"I am indeed, mademoiselle—in your interest," he said in the same tone.

"Then I have no doubt about the result of it," she said; and turning to the inspector, she added: "I have no keys to give you. Dorothy's Circus has no locks. Everything is open to the world. Empty hands and empty pockets."

The inspector seemed to have no great relish for the job. The two servants did their best and d'Estreicher made no bones about advising them.

"Excuse me, mademoiselle," he said to the young girl, taking her on one side. "I'm of the opinion that no effort should be spared to make your complicity quite out of the question."

"It's a serious business," she said ironically.

"In what way?"

"Well, recall our conversation. There's a criminal: if it isn't me, it's you."

D'Estreicher must have considered the young girl a formidable adversary, and he must have been frightened by her threats, for while he remained quite agreeable, gallant even, jesting with her, he was indefatigable in his investigation. At his bidding the servants lifted down the baskets and boxes, and displayed her wretched wardrobe, in the strongest contrast to the brilliantly colored handkerchiefs and shawls with which the young girl loved to adorn herself.

They found nothing.

They searched the walls and platform of the caravan, the mattresses, the harness of One-eyed Magpie, the sack of oats, and the food. Nothing.

They searched the four boys. A maid felt Dorothy's clothes. The search was fruitless. The earrings were not to be found.

"And that?" said d'Estreicher, pointing to the huge basket loaded with pots and pans which hung under the vehicle.

With a furtive kick on the ankle Dorothy straightened Saint-Quentin who was tottering.

"Let's bolt!" he stuttered.

"Don't be a fool. The earrings are no longer there."

"I may have made a mistake."

"You're an idiot. One doesn't make a mistake in a case like that."

"Then where is the cardboard box?"

"Have you got your eyes stuffed up?"

"You can see it, can you?"

"Of course I can see it—as plainly as the nose in the middle of your face."

"In the caravan?"

"No."

"Where?"

"On the ground ten yards away from you, between the legs of the bearded one."

She glanced at the wagon of Captain Montfaucon which the child had abandoned to play with a doll, and the little packages from which, miniature bags and trunks and parcels, lay on the ground beside d'Estreicher's heels.

One of these packages was nothing else than the cardboard box which contained the earrings. Captain Montfaucon had that afternoon added it to what he called his haulage material.

In confiding her unexpected discovery to Saint-Quentin, Dorothy, who did not suspect the keenness of the subtlety and power of observation of the man she was fighting, committed an irreparable imprudence. It was not on the young girl that d'Estreicher was keeping watch from behind the screen of his spectacles, but on her comrade Saint-Quentin whose distress and feebleness he had been quick to notice. Dorothy herself remained impassive. But would not Saint-Quentin end by giving some indication?

That was what happened. When he recognized the little box with the red gutta-percha ring round it, Saint-Quentin heaved a great sigh in his sudden relief. He told himself that it would never occur to anyone to untie these child's toys which lay on the ground for anyone to pick up. Several times, without the slightest suspicion, d'Estreicher had brushed them aside with his feet and stumbled over the wagon, winning from the Captain this sharp reprimand:

"Now then, sir! What would *you* say, if you had a car and I knocked it over?"

Saint-Quentin raised his head with a cheerful air. D'Estreicher followed the direction of his gaze and instinctively understood. The earrings were there, under the protection of Fortune and with the unwitting complicity of the captain. But in which of the packages? The cardboard box seemed to him to be the most likely. Without a word he bent quickly down and seized it. He drew himself up, opened it with a furtive movement, and perceived, among some small white pebbles and shells, the two sapphires.

He looked at Dorothy. She was very pale.

IV

THE CROSS-EXAMINATION

"Let's bolt!" again said Saint-Quentin, who had sunk down on to a trunk and would have been incapable of making a single step.

"A splendid idea!" said Dorothy in a low voice. "Harness One-eyed Magpie; let's all five of us hide ourselves in the caravan and hell for leather for the Belgian frontier!"

She gazed steadfastly at her enemy. She felt that she was beaten. With one word he could hand her over to justice, throw her into prison, and render vain all her threats. Of what value are the accusations of a thief?

Box in hand, he balanced himself on one foot then on the other with ironical satisfaction. He had the appearance of waiting for her to weaken and become a suppliant. How he misjudged her! On the contrary she maintained an attitude of defiance and challenge as if she had had the audacity to say to him:

"If you speak, you're lost."

He shrugged his shoulders and turning to the inspector who had seen nothing of this by-play, he said:

"We may congratulate ourselves on having got it over, and entirely to mademoiselle's advantage. Goodness, what a disagreeable job!"

"You had no business to set about it at all," said the Countess, coming up with the Count and Raoul Davernoie.

"Oh yes, I had, dear cousin. Your husband and I had our doubts. It was just as well to clear them up."

"And you've found nothing?" said the Count.

"Nothing... less than nothing—at the most an odd trifle with which Mr. Montfaucon was playing, and which Mademoiselle Dorothy had been kind enough to give me. You do, don't you, Mademoiselle?"

"Yes," said Dorothy simply.

He displayed the cardboard box, round which he had again drawn the rubber ring, and handing it to the Countess:

"Take care of that till tomorrow morning, will you, dear lady?"

"Why should I take care of it and not you?"

"It wouldn't be the same thing," said he. "To place it in your hands is as it were to affix a seal to it. Tomorrow, at lunch, we'll open it together."

"Do you make a point of it?"

"Yes. It's an idea... of sorts."

"Very good," said the Countess. "I accept the charge if mademoiselle authorizes me to do so."

"I ask it, madame," replied Dorothy, grasping the fact that the danger was postponed till the morrow. "The box contains nothing of importance, only white pebbles and shells. But since it amuses monsieur, and he wants a check on it, give him this small satisfaction."

There remained, however, a formality which the inspector considered essential in inquiries of this kind. The examination of identification papers, delivery of documents, compliance with the regulations, were matters which he took very seriously indeed. On the other hand, if Dorothy surmised the existence of a secret between the Count and Countess and their cousins, it is certain that her hosts were not less puzzled by the strange personality which for an hour or two had dominated and disturbed them. Who was she? Where did she come from? What was her real name? What was the explanation of the fact that this distinguished and intelligent creature, with her supple cleverness and distinguished manners, was wandering about the country with four street-boys?

She took from a locker in the caravan a passport-case which she carried under her arm; and when they all went into the orangery which was now empty, she took from this case a sheet of paper black with signatures and stamps and handed it to the inspector.

"Is this all you've got?" he said almost immediately.

"Isn't it sufficient? The secretary at the mayor's office this morning was satisfied with it."

"They're satisfied with anything in mayors' offices," he said scornfully. "And what about these names?... Nobody's named Castor and Pollux?... And this one... Baron de Saint-Quentin, acrobat!"

Dorothy smiled:

"Nevertheless it is his name and his profession."

"Baron de Saint-Quentin?"

"Certainly he was the son of a plumber who lived at Saint-Quentin and was called Baron."

"But then he must have the paternal authorization."

"Impossible."

"Why?"

"Because his father died during the occupation."

"And his mother?"

"She's dead too. No relations. The English adopted the boy. Towards the end of the war he was assistant-cook in a hospital at Bar-le-Duc, where I was a nurse. I adopted him."

The inspector uttered a grunt of approval and continued his examination.

"And Castor and Pollux."

"I don't know where they come from. In 1918, during the German push towards Châlons, they were caught in the storm and picked up on a road by some French soldiers who gave them their nicknames. The shock was so great that they've lost all memory of the years before those days. Are they brothers? Were they acquaintances? Where are their families? Nobody knows. I adopted them."

"Oh!" said the inspector, somewhat taken aback. Then he went on: "There remains now Sire Montfaucon, captain in the American army, decorated with the Croix de guerre."

"Present," said a voice.

Montfaucon drew himself stiffly upright in a soldierly attitude, his heels touching, and his little finger on the seam of his enormous trousers.

Dorothy caught him on to her knee and gave him a smacking kiss.

"A brat, about whom also nobody knows anything. When he was four he was living with a dozen American soldiers who had made for him, by way of cradle, a fur bag. The day of the great American attack, one of the twelve carried him on his back; and it happened that of all those who advanced, it was this soldier who went furthest, and that they found his body next day near Montfaucon hill. Beside him, in the fur bag, the child was asleep, slightly wounded. On the battlefield, the colonel decorated him with the Croix de guerre, and gave him the name and rank of Captain Montfaucon of the American army. Later it fell to me to nurse him at the hospital to which he was brought in. Three months after that the colonel wished to carry him off to America. Montfaucon refused. He did not wish to leave me. I adopted him."

Dorothy told the child's story in a low voice full of tenderness. The eyes of the Countess shone with tears and she murmured:

"You acted admirably—admirably, mademoiselle. Only that gave you four orphans to provide for. With what resources?"

Dorothy laughed and said:

"We were rich."

"Rich?"

"Yes, thanks to Montfaucon. Before he went his colonel left two thousand francs for him. We bought a caravan and an old horse. Dorothy's Circus was formed."

"A difficult profession to which you have to serve an apprenticeship."

"We served our apprenticeship under an old English soldier, formerly a clown, who taught us all the tricks of the trade and all the wheezes. And then I had it all in my blood. The tight-rope, dancing, I was broken in to them years ago. Then we set out across France. It's rather a hard life, but it keeps one in the best of health, one is never dull, and taken all round Dorothy's Circus is a success."

"But does it comply with the official regulations?" asked the inspector whose respect for red tape enabled him to control the sympathy he was feeling for her. "For after all this document is only valuable from the point of view of references. What I should like to see is your own certificate of identity."

"I have that certificate, inspector."

"Made out by whom?"

"By the Prefecture of Châlons, which is the chief city of the department in which I was born."

"Show it to me."

The young girl plainly hesitated. She looked at Count Octave then at the Countess. She had begged them to come just in order that they might be witnesses of her examination and hear the answers she proposed to give, and now, at the last moment, she was rather sorry that she had done so.

"Would you prefer us to withdraw?" said the Countess.

"No, no," she replied quickly. "On the contrary I insist on your knowing."

"And us too?" said Raoul Davernoie.

"Yes," she said smiling. "There is a fact which it is my duty to divulge to you. Oh, nothing of great importance. But... all the same."

She took from her case a dirty card with broken corners.

"Here it is," she said.

The inspector examined the card carefully and said in the tone of one who is not to be humbugged:

"But that isn't your name. It's a *nom de guerre* of course—like those of your young comrades?"

"Not at all, inspector."

"Come, come, you're not going to get me to believe..."

"Here is my birth certificate in support of it, inspector, stamped with the stamp of the commune of Argonne."

"What? You belong to the village of Argonne!" cried the Count de Chagny.

"I did, Monsieur le Comte. But this unknown village, which gave its name to the whole district of the Argonne, no longer exists. The war has suppressed it."

"Yes... yes... I know," said the Count. "We had a friend there—a relation. Didn't we, d'Estreicher?"

"Doubtless it was Jean d'Argonne?" she asked.

"It was. Jean d'Argonne died at the hospital at Clermont from the effects of a wound... Lieutenant the Prince of Argonne. You knew him."

"I knew him."

"Where? When? Under what conditions?"

"Goodness! Under the ordinary conditions in which one knows a person with whom one is closely connected."

"What? There were ties between you and Jean d'Argonne... the ties of relationship?"

"The closest ties. He was my father."

"Your father! Jean d'Argonne! What are you talking about? It's impossible! See why... Jean's daughter was called Yolande."

"Yolande, Isabel, Dorothy."

The Count snatched the card which the inspector was turning over and over again, and read aloud in a tone of amazement:

"Yolande Isabel Dorothy, Princess of Argonne!"

She finished the sentence for him, laughing:

"Countess Marescot, Baroness de la Hêtraie, de Beaugreval, and other places."

The Count seized the birth certificate with no less eagerness, and more and more astounded, read it slowly syllable by syllable:

"Yolande Isabel Dorothy, Princess of Argonne, born at Argonne, on the 14th of October, 1900, legitimate daughter of Jean de Marescot, Prince of Argonne, and of Jessie Varenne."

Further doubt was impossible. The civil status to which the young girl laid claim was established by proofs, which they were the less inclined to challenge since the unexpected fact explained exactly everything which appeared inexplicable in the manners and even in the appearance of Dorothy.

The Countess gave her feelings full play:

"Yolande? You are the little Yolande about whom Jean d'Argonne used to talk to us with such fondness."

"He was very fond of me," said the young girl. "Circumstances did not allow us to live always together as I should have liked. But I was as fond of him as if I had seen him every day."

"Yes," said the Countess. "One could not help being fond of him. I only saw him twice in my life, in Paris, at the beginning of the war. But what delightful recollections of him I retain! A man teeming with gayety and lightheartedness! Just like you, Dorothy. Besides, I find him again in you... the eyes... and above all the smile."

Dorothy displayed two photographs which she took from among her papers.

"His portrait, madame. Do you recognize it?"

"I should think so! And the other, this lady?"

"My mother who died many years ago. He adored her."

"Yes, yes, I know. She was formerly on the stage, wasn't she? I remember. We will talk it all over, if you will, and about your own life, the misfortunes which have driven you to live like this. But first of all, how came you here? And why?"

Dorothy told them how she had chanced to see the word Roborey, which her father had repeated when he was dying. Then the Count interrupted her narration.

He was a perfectly commonplace man who always did his best to invest matters with the greatest possible solemnity, in order that he might play the chief part in them, which his rank and fortune assigned to him. As a matter of form he consulted his two comrades, then, without waiting to hear their answers, he dismissed the inspector with the lack of ceremony of a grand seignior. In the same fashion he turned out Saint-Quentin and the three boys, carefully closed the two doors, bade the two women sit down, and walked up and down in front of them with his hands behind his back and an air of profound thoughtfulness.

Dorothy was quite content. She had won a victory, compelled her hosts to speak the words she wanted. The Countess held her tightly to her. Raoul appeared to be a friend. All was going well. There was, indeed, standing a little apart from them, hostile and formidable, the bearded nobleman, whose hard eyes never left her. But sure of herself, accepting the combat, full of careless daring, she refused to bend before the menace of the terrible danger which, however, might at any moment crush her.

"Mademoiselle," said the Count de Chagny with an air of great importance. "It has seemed to us, to my cousins and me, since you are the daughter of Jean d'Argonne, whose loss we so deeply deplore—it has seemed to us, I say, that we ought in our turn, to enlighten you concerning events of which he was cognizant and of which he would have informed you had he not been prevented by death... of which he actually desired, as we know, that you should be informed."

He paused, delighted with his preamble. On occasions like this he loved to indulge in a pomposity of diction employing only the most select vocabulary, striving to observe the rules of grammar, and fearless of subjunctives. He went on:

"Mademoiselle, my father, François de Chagny, my grandfather, Dominique de Chagny, and my great-grandfather, Gaspard de Chagny, lived their lives in the sure conviction that great wealth would be... how shall I put it?... would be offered to them, by reason of certain unknown conditions of which each of them was confident in advance that he would be the beneficiary. And each of them took the greater joy in the fact and indulged in a hope all the more agreeable because the Revolution had ruined the house of the Counts de Chagny from the roof-tree to the basement. On what was this conviction based? Neither François, nor Dominique, nor Gaspard de Chagny ever knew. It came from vague legends which described exactly neither the nature of the riches nor the epoch at which they would appear, but all of which had this in common that they evoked the name of Roborey. And these legends could not have gone very far back since this château, which was formerly called the Château de Chagny, only received the name of Chagny-Roborey in the reign of Louis XVI. Is it this designation which brought about the excavations that were made from time to time? It is extremely probable. At all events it is a fact that at the very moment the war broke out I had formed the resolution of restoring this Château de Roborey, which had become merely a shooting-box and definitely settling down in it, for all that, and I am not ashamed to say it, my recent marriage with Madame de Chagny had enabled me to wait for these so-called riches without excessive impatience."

The Count smiled a subtle smile in making this discreet allusion to the manner in which he had regilded his heraldic shield, and continued:

"It is needless to tell you, I hope, that during the war the Count de Chagny did his duty as a good Frenchman. In 1915, as lieutenant of light-infantry, I was in Paris on leave when a series of coincidences, brought about by the war, brought me into touch with three persons with whom I had not previously been acquainted, and whose ties of kinship with the Chagny-Roborey I learnt by accident. The first was the father of Raoul Davernoie, Commandant Georges Davernoie, the second Maxime d'Estreicher, the last Jean d'Argonne. All four of us were distant cousins, all four on leave or recovering from wounds. And so it came about that in the course of our interviews, that we learnt, to our great surprise, that the same legend had been handed down in each of our four families. Like their fathers and their grandfathers Georges Davernoie, d'Estreicher, and Jean d'Argonne were awaiting the fabulous fortune which was promised them and which was to settle the debts which this conviction had led them on to contract. Moreover, the same ignorance prevailed among the four cousins. No proof, no indication—"

After a fresh pause intended to lead up to an impressive effect, the Count continued: "But yes, one indication, however: Jean d'Argonne remembered a gold medal the importance of which his father had formerly impressed on him. His father died a few days later from an accident in the hunting-field without having told him anything more. But Jean d'Argonne declared that this medal bore on it an inscription, and that one of these words, he did not recall it at once, was this word Roborey, on which all our hopes are undoubtedly concentrated. He informed us then of his intention of ransacking the twenty trunks or so, which he had been able in August, 1914, to bring away from his country seat before its imminent pillage, and to store in a shed at Bar-le-Duc. But before he went, since we were all men of honor, exposed to the risks of war, we all four took a solemn oath that all our discoveries relative to the famous treasure, should be common property. Henceforth and forever, the treasure, should Providence decide to grant it to us, belonged to all the four; and Jean d'Argonne, whose leave expired, left us."

"It was at the end of 1915, wasn't it?" asked Dorothy. "We passed a week together, the happiest week of my life. I was never to see him again."

"It was indeed towards the end of 1915," the Count agreed. "A month later Jean d'Argonne, wounded in the North, was sent into hospital at Chartres, from which he wrote to us a long letter... never finished."

The Countess de Chagny made a sudden movement. She appeared to disapprove of what her husband had said.

"Yes, yes, I will lay that letter before you," said the Count firmly.

"Perhaps you're right," murmured the Countess. "Nevertheless—"

"What are you afraid of, madame?" said Dorothy.

"I am afraid of our causing you pain to no purpose, Dorothy. The end of it will reveal to you very painful things."

"But it is our duty to communicate it to her," said the Count in a peremptory tone. And he drew from his pocket-book a letter stamped with the Red Cross and unfolded it. Dorothy felt her heart flutter with a sudden oppression. She recognized her father's handwriting. The Countess squeezed her hand. She saw that Raoul Davernoie was regarding her with an air of compassion; and with an anxious face, trying less to understand the sentences she heard than to guess the end of this letter, she listened to it.

"My dear Octave,

"I will first of all set your mind at rest about my wound. It is a mere nothing, no complications to be afraid of. At the most a little fever at night, which bothers the major; but all that will pass. We will say no more about it, but come straight to my journey to Bar-le-Duc.

"Octave, I may tell you without any beating about the bush that it has not been useless, and that after a patient search I ended by ferreting out from among a pile of boots and that conglomeration of useless objects which one brings away with one when one bolts, the precious medal. At the end of my convalescence when I come to Paris I will show it to you. But in the meantime, while keeping secret the indications engraved on the face of the medal, I may tell you that on the reverse are engraved these three Latin words: '*In Robore Fortuna.*' Three words which may be thus translated: 'Fortune is in the firm heart,' but which, in view of the presence of this word 'Robore' and in spite of the difference in the spelling, doubtless point to the Château de Roborey as the place in which the fortune, of which our family legends tell will consequently be hidden.

"Have we not here, my dear Octave, a step forward on our path towards the truth? We shall do better still. And perhaps we shall be helped in the matter, in the most unexpected fashion, by an extremely nice young person, with whom I have just passed several days which have charmed me—I mean my dear little Yolande.

"You know, my dear friend, that I have very often regretted not having been the father I should like to have been. My love for Yolande's mother, my grief at her death, my life of wandering during the years which followed it, all kept me far away from the modest farm which you call my country seat, and which, I am sure, is no longer anything but a heap of ruins.

"During that time, Yolande was living in the care of the people who farmed my land, bringing herself up, getting her education from the village priest, or the schoolmaster, and above all from Nature, loving the animals, cultivating her flowers, light-hearted and uncommonly thoughtful.

"Several times, during my visits to Argonne, her common sense and intelligence astonished me. On this occasion I found her, in the field-hospital of Bar-le-Duc, in which she has, on her own initiative, established herself as an assistant-nurse, a young girl. Barely fifteen, you cannot imagine the ascendancy she exercises over everyone about her. She decides matters like a grown person and she makes those decisions according to her own judgment. She has an accurate insight into reality, not merely into appearances but into that which lies below appearances.

"'You do see clearly,' I said to her. 'You have the eyes of a cat which moves, quite at its ease, through the darkness.'

"My dear Octave, when the war is finished, I shall bring Yolande to you; and I assure you that, along with our friends, we shall succeed in our enterprise—"

The Count stopped. Dorothy smiled sadly, deeply touched by the tenderness and admiration which this letter so clearly displayed. She asked:

"That isn't all, is it?"

"The letter itself ends there," said the Count. "Dated the 16th of January, it was not posted till the 20th. I did not receive it, for various reasons, till three weeks later. And I learnt later that on the 15th of January Jean d'Argonne had a more violent attack of fever, of that fever which baffled the surgeon-major and which indicated a sudden infection of the wound of which your father died... or at least—"

"Or at least?" asked the young girl.

"Or at least which was officially stated to be the cause of his death," said the Count in a lower voice.

"What's that you say? What's that you say?" cried Dorothy. "My father did not die of his wound?"

"It is not certain," the Count suggested.

"But then what did he die of? What do you suggest? What do you suppose?"

V

"WE WILL HELP YOU"

The Count was silent.

Dorothy murmured fearfully, full of the dread with which the utterance of certain words inspired one:

"Is it possible? Can they have murdered... Can they have murdered my father?"

"Everything leads one to believe it."

"And how?"

"Poison."

The blow had fallen. The young girl burst into tears. The Count bent over her and said:

"Read it. For my part, I am of the opinion that your father scribbled these last pages between two attacks of fever. When he was dead, the hospital authorities finding a letter and an envelope all ready for the post, sent it all on to me without examining it. Look at the end... It is the writing of a very sick man... The pencil moves at random directed by an effort of will which was every moment growing weaker."

Dorothy dried her tears. She wished to know and judge for herself, and she read in a low voice:

"What a dream!... But was it really a dream?... What I saw last night, did I see it in a nightmare? Or did I actually see it?... The rest of the wounded men... my neighbors... not one of them was awakened. Yet the man... the men made a noise... There were two of them. They were talking in a low voice... in the garden... under a window... which was certainly open on account of the heat... And then the window was pushed... To do that one of the two must have climbed on to the shoulders of the other. What did he want? He tried to pass his arm through... But the window caught against the table by the side of the bed... And then he must have slipped off his jacket... In spite of that his sleeve must have caught in the window and only his arm... his bare arm, came through... preceded by a hand which groped in my direction... in the direction of the drawer... Then I understood... The medal was in the drawer... Ah, how I wanted to cry out! But my throat was cramped... Then another thing terrified me. The hand held a small bottle... There was on the table a glass of water, for me to drink with a dose of my medicine... The hand poured several drops from the bottle into the glass. Horror!... Poison beyond a doubt!... But I will not drink my medicine—no, no!... And I write this, this morning, to make sure of being able to recall it... I write that the hand afterwards opened the drawer... And while it was seizing the medal... I saw... I saw on the naked arm... above the elbow... words written—"

Dorothy had to bend lower so shaky and illegible did the writing become; and it was with great difficulty that she was able, syllable by syllable, to decipher it:

"Three words written... tattooed... as sailors do... three words... Good God!... these three words! The words on the medal!... *In robore fortuna!*"

That was all. The unfinished sheet showed nothing more but undecipherable characters, which Dorothy did not even try to make out.

For a long while she sat with bowed head, the tears falling from her half-closed eyes. They perceived that the circumstances in which, in all likelihood, her father had died, had brought back all her grief.

The Count, however, continued:

"The fever must have returned... the delirium... and not knowing what he was doing, he must have drunk the poison. Or, at any rate, it is a plausible hypothesis... for what else could it have been that this hand poured into the glass? But I confess that we have not arrived at any certainty in the matter. D'Estreicher and Raoul's father, at once apprized by me of what had happened, accompanied me to Chartres. Unfortunately, the staff, the surgeon-major and the two nurses had been changed, so that I was brought up short against the official document which ascribed the death to infectious complications. Moreover, ought we to have made further researches? My two cousins were not of that opinion, neither was I? A crime?... How to prove it? By means of these lines in which a sick man describe a nightmare which has ridden him? Impossible. Isn't that your opinion, mademoiselle?"

Dorothy did not answer; and it put the Count rather out of countenance. He seemed to defend himself—not without a touch of temper:

"But we could not, Mademoiselle! Owing to the war, we ran against endless difficulties. It was impossible! We had to cling to the one fact which we had actually learned and not venture beyond this actual fact which I will state in these terms: In addition to us four, to us three rather, since Jean d'Argonne, alas! was no more, there was a fourth person attacking the problem which we had set ourselves to solve; and that person, moreover, had a considerable advantage over us. A rival, an enemy had arisen, capable of the most infamous actions to attain his end. What enemy?

"Events did not allow us to busy ourselves with this affair, and what is more, prevented us from finding you as we should have wished. Two letters that I wrote to you at Bar-le-Duc remained unanswered. Months passed. Georges Davernoie was killed at Verdun, d'Estreicher wounded in Artois, and I myself despatched on a mission to Salonica from which I did not return till after the Armistice. In the following year the work here was begun. The house-warming took place yesterday, and only today does chance bring you here.

"You can understand, Mademoiselle, how amazed we were when we learned, step by step, first that excavations were being made without our knowing anything about it, that the places in which they had been made were explained by the word Fortuna, which bore out exactly the inscription which your father had read twice, on the gold medal and on the arm which stole the gold medal from him. Our confidence in your extraordinary clearsightedness became such that Madame de Chagny and Raoul Davernoie wished you to be informed of the complete history of the affair; and I must admit that the Countess de Chagny displayed remarkable intuition and judgment since the confidence we felt in you was really placed in that Yolande d'Argonne whom her father recommended to us. It is then but natural, mademoiselle, that we should invite you to collaborate with us in our attempt. You take the place of Jean d'Argonne, as Raoul Davernoie has taken the place of Georges Davernoie. Our partnership is unbroken."

A shadow rested on the satisfaction that the Count de Chagny was feeling in his eloquence and magnanimous proposal. Dorothy maintained an obstinate silence. Her eyes gazed vacantly before her. She did not stir. Was she thinking that the Count had not taken much trouble to discover the daughter of his kinsman Jean d'Argonne and to rescue her from the life she was leading? Was she still feeling some resentment on account of the humiliation she had suffered in being accused of stealing the earrings?

The Countess de Chagny questioned her gently:

"What's the matter, Dorothy? This letter has filled you with gloom. It's the death of your father, isn't it?"

"Yes," said Dorothy after a pause in a dull voice. "It's a terrible business."

"You also believe that they murdered him?"

"Certainly. If not, the medal would have been found. Besides, the last sheets of the letter are explicit."

"And it's your feeling that we ought to have striven to bring the murderer to book?"

"I don't know... I don't know," said the young girl slowly.

"But if you think so, we can take the matter up again. You may be sure that we will lend you our assistance."

"No," she said. "I will act alone. It will be best. I will discover the guilty man; and he shall be punished. I promise my father he shall. I swear it."

She uttered these words with measured gravity, raising her hand a little.

"We will help you, Dorothy," declared the Countess. "For I hope that you won't leave us... Here you are at home."

Dorothy shook her head. "You are too kind, madame."

"It isn't kindness: it's affection. You won my heart at first sight, and I beg you to be my friend."

"I am, madame—wholly your friend. But—"

"What? You refuse?" exclaimed the Count de Chagny in a tone of vexation. "We offer the daughter of Jean d'Argonne, our cousin, a life befitting her name and birth and you prefer to go back to that wretched existence!"

"It is not wretched, I assure you, monsieur. My four children and I are used to it. Their health demands it."

The Countess insisted: "But we can't allow it—really! You're going to stay with us at least some days; and from this evening you will dine and sleep at the château."

"I beg you to excuse me, madame. I'm rather tired... I want to be alone."

In truth she appeared of a sudden to be worn out with fatigue. One would never have supposed that a smile could animate that drawn, dejected face.

The Countess de Chagny insisted no longer.

"Ah well, postpone your decision till tomorrow. Send your four children to dinner this evening. It will give us great pleasure to question them... Between now and tomorrow you can think it over, and if you persist, I'll let you go your way. You'll agree to that, won't you?"

Dorothy rose and went towards the door. The Count and Countess went with her. But on the threshold she paused for a moment. In spite of her grief, the mysterious adventure which had during the last hour or two been revealed to her continued to exercise her mind, without, so to speak, her being aware of it; and throwing the first ray of light into the darkness, she asserted:

"I really believe that all the legends that have been handed down in our families are based on a reality. There must be somewhere about here buried, or hidden, treasure; and that treasure one of these days will become the property of him, or of those who shall be the possessors of the talisman—that is to say, of the gold medal which was stolen from my father. That's why I should like to know whether any of you, besides my father, has ever heard of a gold medal being mentioned in these legends."

It was Raoul Davernoie who answered:

"That's a point on which I can give you some information, mademoiselle. A fortnight ago I saw in the hands of my grandfather, with whom I live at Hillocks Manor in Vendée, a large gold coin. He was studying it; and he put it back in its case at once with the evident intention of hiding it from me."

"And he didn't tell you anything about it?"

"Not a word. However, on the eve of my departure he said to me: 'When you come back I've an important revelation to make to you. I ought to have made it long ago.'"

"You believe that he was referring to the matter in hand?"

"I do. And for that reason on my arrival at Roborey I informed my cousins, de Chagny and d'Estreicher, who promised to pay me a visit at the end of July when I will inform them of what I have learned."

"That's all?"

"All, mademoiselle; and it appears to me to confirm your hypothesis. We have here a talisman of which there are doubtless several copies."

"Yes... yes... there's no doubt about it," murmured the young girl. "And the death of my father is explained by the fact that he was the possessor of this talisman."

"But," objected Raoul Davernoie, "was it not enough to steal it from him? Why this useless crime?"

"Because, remember, the gold medal gives certain indications. In getting rid of my father they reduced the number of those who, in perhaps the near future, will be called upon to share these riches. Who knows whether other crimes have not been committed?"

"Other crimes? In that case my grandfather is in danger."

"He is," she said simply.

The Count became uneasy and, pretending to laugh, he said:

"Then we also are in danger, mademoiselle, since there are signs of recent excavation about Roborey."

"You also, Count."

"We ought then to be on our guard."

"I advise you to."

The Count de Chagny turned pale and said in a shaky voice:

"How? What measures should we take?"

"I will tell you tomorrow," said Dorothy. "You shall know tomorrow what you have to fear and what measures you ought to take to defend yourselves."

"You promise that?"

"I promise it."

D'Estreicher, who had followed with close attention every phase of the conversation, without taking part in it, stepped forward:

"We make all the more point of this meeting tomorrow, mademoiselle, because we still have to solve together a little additional problem, the problem of the cardboard box. You haven't forgotten it?"

"I forget nothing, monsieur," she said. "Tomorrow, at the hour fixed, that little matter and other matters, the theft of the sapphire earrings among other things, shall be made clear."

She went out of the orangery.

The night was falling. The gates had been re-opened; and the showmen, having dismantled their shows, were departing. Dorothy found Saint-Quentin waiting for her in great anxiety and the three children lighting a fire. When the dinner-bell rang, she sent them to the château and remained alone to make her meal of the thick soup and some fruit. In the evening, while waiting for them, she strolled through the night towards the parapet which looked down on to the ravine and rested her elbows on it.

The moon was not visible, but the veil of light clouds, which floated across the heavens, were imbued with its light. For a long while she was conscious of the deep silence, and, bare-headed, she presented her burning brow to the fresh evening airs which ruffled her hair.

"Dorothy..."

Her name had been spoken in a low voice by someone who had drawn near her without her hearing him. But the sound of his voice, low as it was, made her tremble. Even before recognizing the outline of d'Estreicher she divined his presence.

Had the parapet been lower and the ravine less profound she might have essayed flight, such dread did this man inspire in her. However, she braced herself to keep calm and master him.

"What do you want, monsieur," she said coldly. "The Count and Countess had the delicacy to respect my desire to keep quiet. I'm surprised to see you here."

He did not answer, but she discerned his dark shape nearer and repeated:

"What do you want?"

"I only want to say a few words to you," he murmured.

"Tomorrow—at the château will be soon enough."

"No; what I have to say can only be heard by you and me; and I can assure you, mademoiselle, that you can listen to it without being offended. In spite of the incomprehensible hostility that you have displayed towards me from the moment we met, I feel, for my part, nothing but friendliness, admiration, and the greatest respect for you. You need fear neither my words nor my actions. I am not addressing myself to the charming and attractive young girl, but to the woman who, all this afternoon, has dumfounded us by her intelligence. Now, listen to me—"

"No," she broke in. "I will not. Your proposals can only be insulting."

He went on, in a louder voice; and she could feel that gentleness and respectfulness did not come easy to him; he went on:

"Listen to me. I order you to listen to me... and to answer at once. I'm no maker of phrases and I'll come straight to the point, rather crudely if I must, at the risk of shocking you. Here it is: Chance has in a trice thrown you into an affair which I have every right to consider my business and no one else's. We are stuck with supernumeraries, of whom, when the time comes, I do not mean to take the slightest account. All these people are imbeciles who will never get anywhere. Chagny is a conceited ass... Davernoie a country bumpkin... so much dead weight that we've got to lug about with us, you and I. Then why work for them?... Let's work for ourselves, for the two of us. Will you? You and I partners, friends, what a job we should make of it! My energy and strength at the service of your intelligence and clearsightedness! Besides... besides, consider all I know! For I, I know the problem! What will take you weeks to discover, what, I'm certain, you'll never discover, I have at my fingers' ends. I know all the factors in the problem except one or two which I shall end by adding to them. Help me. Let us search together. It means a fortune, the discovery of fabulous wealth, boundless power... Will you?"

He bent a little too far over the young girl; and his fingers brushed the cloak she was wearing. Dorothy, who had listened in silence in order to learn the inmost thoughts of her adversary, started back indignantly at his touch.

"Be off!... Leave me alone!... I forbid you to touch me!... You a friend?... You? You?"

The repulsion with which he inspired Dorothy set him beside himself, and foaming with rage, he cried furiously:

"So... So... you refuse? You refuse, in spite of the secret I have surprised, in spite of what I can do... and what I'm going to do... For the stolen earrings: it is not merely a matter of Saint-Quentin. You were there, in the ravine, to watch over his expedition. And what is more, as his accomplice, you protected him. And the proof exists, terrible, irrefutable. The box is in the hands of the Countess. And you dare? You! A thief!"

He made a grab at her. Dorothy ducked and slipped along the parapet. But he was able to grip her wrists, and he was dragging her towards him, when of a sudden he let go of her, struck by a ray of light which blinded him.

Perched on the parapet Montfaucon had switched full on his face the clear light of an electric torch.

D'Estreicher took himself off. The ray followed him, cleverly guided.

"Dirty little brat!" he growled. "I'll get you... And you too, young woman! If tomorrow, at two o'clock, at the château, you do not come to heel, the box will be opened in the presence of the police. It's for you to choose."

He disappeared in the shrubbery.

Toward three o'clock in the morning, the trap, which looked down on the box from the interior of the caravan, was opened, as it had been opened the morning before. A hand reached out and shook Saint-Quentin, who was sleeping under his rugs.

"Get up. Dress yourself. No noise."

He protested.

"Dorothy, what you wish to do is absurd."

"Do as you're told."

Saint-Quentin obeyed.

Outside the caravan he found Dorothy, quite ready. By the light of the moon he saw that she was carrying a canvas bag, slung on a band running over her shoulder, and a coil of rope.

She led him to the spot at which the parapet touched the entrance gates. They fastened the rope to one of the bars and slid down it. Then Saint-Quentin climbed up to the parapet and unfastened the rope. They went down the slope into the ravine and along the foot of the cliff to the fissure up which Saint-Quentin had climbed the night before.

"Let us climb up," said Dorothy. "You will let down the rope and help me to ascend."

The ascent was not very difficult. The window of the pantry was open. They climbed in through it and Dorothy lit her bull's-eye lantern.

"Take that little ladder in the corner," she said.

But Saint-Quentin started to reason with her afresh:

"It's absurd. It's madness. We are running into the lion's maw."

"Get on!"

"But indeed, Dorothy."

He got a thump in the ribs.

"Stop it! And answer me," she snapped. "You're sure that d'Estreicher's is the last bedroom in the left-hand passage."

"Certain. As you told me to, I questioned the servants without seeming to do so, after dinner last night."

"And you dropped the powder I gave you into his cup of coffee?"

"Yes."

"Then he's sleeping like a log; and we can go straight to him. Not another word!"

On their way they stopped at a door. It was the dressing-room adjoining the boudoir of the Countess. Saint-Quentin set his ladder against it and climbed through the transom.

Three minutes later he came back.

"Did you find the cardboard box?" Dorothy asked.

"Yes. I found it on the table, took the earrings out of it, and put the box back in its place with the rubber ring round it."

They went on down the passage.

Each bedroom had a dressing-room and a closet which served as wardrobe attached to it. They stopped before the last transom; Saint-Quentin climbed through it and opened the door of the dressing-room for Dorothy.

There was a door between the dressing-room and the bedroom. Dorothy opened it an inch and let a ray from her lantern fall on the bed.

"He's asleep," she whispered.

She drew a large handkerchief from her bag, uncorked a small bottle of chloroform and poured some drops on the handkerchief.

Across the bed, in his clothes, like a man suddenly overcome by sleep, d'Estreicher was sleeping so deeply that the young girl switched on the electric light. Then very gently she placed the chloroformed handkerchief over his face.

The man sighed, writhed, and was still.

Very cautiously Dorothy and Saint-Quentin passed two slip-knots in a rope over both of his arms and tied the two ends of it round the iron uprights of the bed. Then quickly without bothering about him they wrapped the bedclothes round his body and legs, and tied them round him with the table-cloth and curtain-cords.

Then d'Estreicher did awake. He tried to defend himself—too late. He called out. Dorothy gagged him with a napkin.

Next morning the Count and Countess de Chagny were taking their coffee with Raoul Davernoie in the big dining-room of the château when the porter came to inform them that at daybreak the directress of Dorothy's Circus had asked him to open the gates and that the caravan had departed. The directress had left a letter addressed to the Count de Chagny. All three of them went upstairs to the Countess's boudoir. The letter ran as follows:

"My cousin"—offended by her brusqueness, the Count started—then he went on:

"My cousin: I took an oath, and I keep it. The man who was making excavations round the château and last night stole the earrings, is the same person who five years ago stole the medal and poisoned my father.

"I hand him over to you. Let justice take its course.

"DOROTHY, PRINCESS OF ARGONNE."

The Count and Countess and their cousin gazed at one another in amazement. What did it mean? Who was the culprit. How and where had she handed him over?

"It's a pity that d'Estreicher isn't down," said the Count. "He is so helpful."

The Countess took up the cardboard box which d'Estreicher had entrusted to her and opened it without more ado. The box contained exactly what Dorothy had told them, some white pebbles and shells. Then why did d'Estreicher seem to attach so much importance to his finding it?

Someone knocked gently at the boudoir door. It was the major-domo, the Count's confidential man.

"What is it, Dominique?"

"The château was broken into last night."

"Impossible!" the Count declared in a positive tone. "The doors were all locked. Where did they break in?"

"I don't know. But I've found a ladder against the wall by Monsieur d'Estreicher's bedroom; and the transom is broken. The criminals made their way into the dressing-room and when they had done the job, came out through the bedroom door."

"What job?"

"I don't know, sir. I didn't like to go further into the matter by myself. I put everything back in its place."

The Count de Chagny drew a hundred-franc note from his pocket.

"Not a word of this, Dominique. Watch the corridor and see that no one disturbs us."

Raoul and his wife followed him. The door between d'Estreicher's dressing-room and bedroom was half open. The smell of chloroform filled the room.

The Count uttered a cry.

On his bed lay d'Estreicher gagged and safely bound to it. His eyes were rolling wildly. He was groaning.

Beside him lay the muffler which Dorothy had described as belonging to the man who was engaged in making excavations.

On the table, well in sight, lay the sapphire earrings.

But a terrifying, overwhelming sight met the eyes of all three of them simultaneously—the irrefutable proof of the murder of Jean d'Argonne and the theft of the medal. His right arm, bare, was stretched out across the bed, fastened by the wrist. And on that arm they read, tattooed:

In robore fortuna.

VI

ON THE ROAD

Every day, at the easy walk or slack trot of One-eyed Magpie, Dorothy's Circus moved on. In the afternoon they gave their performance; after it they strolled about those old towns of France, the picturesque charm of which appealed so strongly to the young girl. Domfront, Mortain, Avranches, Fougères, Vitré, feudal cities, girdled in places by their fortifications, or bristling with their ancient keeps... Dorothy visited them with all the emotion of a creature who understands the past and evokes it with a passionate enthusiasm.

She visited them alone, even as she walked alone along the high roads, with so manifest a desire to keep to herself that the others, while watching her with anxious eyes and silently begging for a glance from their little mother, did not speak a word to her.

That lasted a week, a very dull week for the children. The pale Saint-Quentin walked at the head of One-eyed Magpie as he would have walked at the head of a horse drawing a hearse. Castor and Pollux fought no longer. As for the captain he buried himself in the perusal of his lesson-books and wore himself out over addition and subtraction, knowing that Dorothy, the school-mistress of the troupe, as a rule deeply appreciated these fits of industry. His efforts were vain. Dorothy was thinking of something else.

Every morning, at the first village they went through, she bought a newspaper, looked through it and crumpled it up with a movement of irritation, as if she had failed to find what she was looking for. Saint-Quentin at once picked it up and in his turn ran his eye through it. Nothing. Nothing about the crime of which she had informed him in a few words. Nothing about the arrest of that infamous d'Estreicher whom the two of them had trussed up on his bed.

At last on the eighth day, as the sun shines after unceasing rain, the smile appeared. It did not spring from any outside cause. It was that life recovered its grip on her. Dorothy's spirit was throwing off the distant tragedy in which her father lost his life. She became the light-hearted, cheerful, and affectionate Dorothy of old. Castor, Pollux, and the captain were smothered with kisses. Saint-Quentin was thumped and shaken warmly by the hand. At the performance they gave under the ramparts of Vitré she displayed an astonishing energy and gayety. And when the audience had departed, she hustled off her four comrades on one of those mad rounds which were for them the most exquisite of treats.

Saint-Quentin wept with joy:

"I thought you didn't love us any more," he said.

"Why shouldn't I love my four brats any more?"

"Because you're a princess."

"Wasn't I a princess before, idiot?"

In taking them through the narrow streets of old Vitré, amid the huddle of wooden houses, roofed with rough tiles, by fits and starts she told them for the first time about her early years.

She had always been happy, never having known shackles, boredom, or discipline, things which cramp the free instincts and deform the disposition. Not that she had been a rebel. She was quite ready to submit to rules and obligations, but she had

had to choose them herself; they had had to be such that her child's reason, already very clear and direct, could accept them as just and necessary.

It had been the same with the education she had given herself: she had only learnt from others that which it had pleased her to know, extracting from the village priest at Argonne all the Latin he knew, and letting him keep his catechism to himself; learning many things with the schoolmaster, many others from the books she borrowed, and very many more from the old couple who farmed her father's land, in whose charge her parents had left her.

"I owe most to those two," she said. "But for them I should not know what a bird is, or a plant, or a tree—the meaning of real things."

"It wasn't them, however, who taught you to dance on a tight rope and manage a circus," said Saint-Quentin, chaffing her.

"I've always danced on the tight rope. Some people are born poets. I was born a rope-dancer. Dancing is part of me. I get that from my mother who was by no means a theatrical star, but simply a fine little dancer, a dancing-girl of the music-halls and the English circus. I see her still. She was adorable; she could never keep still; and she loved stuffs of gorgeous colors... and beautiful jewels even more."

"Like you," said Saint-Quentin in a low voice.

"Like me," she said. "Yes: I take an extravagant pleasure in handling them and looking at them. I love things that shine. All these stones throw out flames which dazzle me. I should like to be very rich in order to have very fine ones that I should wear always—on my fingers and round my neck."

"And since you will never be rich?"

"Then I shall do without them."

For all that she had been brought up anyhow, deprived of mentors and good advice, having only before her eyes as example the frivolous life her parents led, she had acquired strong moral principles, always maintained a considerable natural dignity, and remained untroubled by the reproaches of conscience. That which is evil is evil—no traffic in it.

"One is happy," she said, "when one is in perfect agreement with good people. I am a good girl. If one lets one's self be guilty of a doubtful action, one repeats it without knowing it and one ends by yielding to temptation as one picks flowers and fruit over the hedge by the roadside."

Dorothy did not pick flowers and fruit over the hedge.

For a long while she went on telling them all about herself. Saint-Quentin listened open-mouthed.

"Goodness! Wherever did you learn all that? You're always surprising me, Dorothy. And then how do you guess what you do guess? Guess what is passing in people's minds? The other day at Roborey, I didn't understand what was going on, not a scrap of it."

"Ah, that's quite another matter. It's a need to combine, to organize, to command, a need to undertake and to succeed. When I was a child I gathered together all the urchins in the village and formed bands. I was always the chief of the band. Only the others used to rob the farmyards and kitchen-gardens, and go poaching. With me, it was quite the opposite. We used to form a league against an evil-doer and hunt for the sheep or duck stolen from an old woman, or again we exercised our wits in making inquiries. Oh those inquiries! They were my strong point. Before the police could be informed, I would unravel an affair in such a way that the country people roundabout came to consult the little girl of thirteen or fourteen that I was. 'A perfect little witch,' they used to say. Goodness, no! You know as well as I, Saint-Quentin, if I sometimes play the clairvoyant or tell fortunes by cards, everything I tell people I arrive at from facts which I observe and interpret. And I also arrive at those facts, I must admit, by a kind of intuition which shows me things under an aspect which does not at once appear to other people. Yes, very often I see, before comprehending. Then, most complicated affairs appear to me, at the first glance, very simple, and I am always astonished that no one has picked out such and such a detail which contains in it the whole of the truth."

Saint-Quentin, convinced, reflected. He threw back his head:

"That's it! That's it! Nothing escapes you; you think of everything. And that's how it came about that the earrings, instead of having been stolen by Saint-Quentin, were stolen by d'Estreicher. And it is d'Estreicher and not Saint-Quentin who will go to prison because you willed it so."

She began to laugh:

"Perhaps I did will it so. But Justice shows no sign of submitting to my will. The newspapers do not speak of anything happening. There is no mention of the drama of Roborey."

"Then what has become of that scoundrel?"

"I don't know."

"And won't you be able to learn?"

"Yes," she said confidently.

"How?"

"From Raoul Davernoie."

"You're going to see him then?"

"I've written to him."

"Where to?"

"At Roborey."

"He answered you."

"Yes—a telegram which I went to the Post Office to find before the performance."

"And he's going to meet us?"

"Yes. On leaving Roborey and returning home, he is to meet us at Vitré at about three o'clock. It's three now."

They had climbed up to a point in the city from which one had a view of a road which wound in and out among meadows and woods.

"There," she said. "His car ought not to be long coming into sight. That's his road."

"You really believe—"

"I really believe that that excellent young fellow will not miss an opportunity of seeing me again," she said, smiling.

Saint-Quentin, always rather jealous and easily upset, sighed:

"All the people you talk to are like that, obliging and full of attention."

They waited several minutes. A car came into sight between two hedges. They went forward and so came close to the caravan round which the three urchins were playing.

Presently the car came up the ascent and emerged from a turning, driven by Raoul Davernoie. Running to meet him and preventing him by a gesture from getting out of the car, Dorothy called out to him:

"Well, what has happened? Arrested?"

"Who? D'Estreicher?" said Raoul, a little taken aback by this greeting.

"D'Estreicher of course... He has been handed over to the police, hasn't he? He's under lock and key?"

"No."

"Why not?"

"He escaped."

The answer gave her a shock.

"D'Estreicher free!... Free to act!... It's frightful!"

And under her breath she muttered:

"Good heavens! Why—why didn't I stay? I should have prevented this escape."

But repining was of no avail and Dorothy was not the girl to waste much time on it. Without further delay she began to question the young man.

"Why did you stay on at the château?"

"To be exact—because of d'Estreicher."

"Granted. But an hour after his escape you ought to have started for home."

"For what reason?"

"Your grandfather... I warned you at Roborey."

Raoul Davernoie protested:

"First of all I have written to him to be on his guard for reasons which I would explain to him. And then, as a matter of fact, the risk that he runs is a trifle problematical."

"In what way? He is the possessor of that indispensable key to the treasure, the gold medal. D'Estreicher knows it. And you do not believe in his danger."

"But this key to the treasure, d'Estreicher also possesses it, since on the day he murdered your father, he stole the gold medal from him."

Dorothy stood beside the door of the car, her hand on the handle to prevent Raoul from opening it.

"Start at once, I beg you. I certainly don't understand the whole of the affair. Is d'Estreicher, who already is the possessor of the medal, going to try to steal a second? Has the one he stole from my father been stolen from him by an accomplice? As yet I don't know anything about it. But I am certain that from now on the real ground of the struggle is yonder, at your home. I'm so sure of it that I'm going there myself as well. Look: here is my road-map. Hillocks Manor near Clisson—still nearly a hundred miles to go—eight stages for the caravan. Be off; you will get there tonight. I shall be there in eight days."

Dominated by her, he gave way.

"Perhaps you're right. I ought to have thought of all this myself—especially since my father will be alone tonight."

"Alone?"

"Yes. All the servants are keeping holiday. One of them is getting married at a neighboring village."

She started.

"Does d'Estreicher know?"

"I think so. I fancy I spoke of this fête before him, during my stay at Roborey."

"And when did he escape?"

"The day before yesterday."

"So since the day before yesterday— "

She did not finish the sentence. She ran to the caravan, up the steps, into it. Almost on the instant she came out of it with a small suitcase and a cloak.

"I'm off," she said. "I'm coming with you. There isn't a moment to be lost!"

She cranked up the engine herself, giving her orders the while:

"I give the car and the three children into your charge, Saint-Quentin. Follow the red line I have drawn on the map. Double stages—no performances. You can be there in five days."

She took the seat beside Davernoie. The car was already starting when she caught up the captain who was stretching out his hands to her. She dropped him among the portmanteaux and bags in the tonneau.

"There—keep quiet. Au revoir, Saint-Quentin, Castor and Pollux—no fighting!"

She waved goodbye to them.

The whole scene had not lasted three minutes.

Raoul Davernoie's car was by way of being an old, old model. Therefore its pace was but moderate, and Raoul, delighted to be taking with him this charming creature, who was also his cousin, and his relations with whom, thanks to what had happened, were uncommonly intimate, was able to relate in detail what had taken place, the manner of their finding d'Estreicher, and the incidents of his captivity.

"What saved him," said he, "was a rather deep wound he had made in his head by striking it against the iron bed-head in his efforts to rid himself of his bonds. He lost a lot of blood. Fever declared itself; and my cousin de Chagny—you must have noticed that he is of a timid disposition—at once said to us:

"'That gives us time.'

"Time for what? I asked him.

"'Time to think things over. You understand clearly enough that all this is going to give rise to an unheard-of scandal, and one which, for the honor of our families, we might perhaps be able to avoid.'

"I opposed any delay. I wanted them to telephone at once to the police. But de Chagny was in his own house, you know. And the days passed waiting for him to come to a decision which he could not bring himself to make. They had told the servants that d'Estreicher was ill. Only the major-domo was in our confidence, brought him his food, and kept guard over him. Besides, the prisoner seemed so feeble. You would have declared that he had no strength left. How was one to distrust so sick a man?"

Dorothy asked:

"But what explanation of his conduct did he give?"

"None, because we didn't question him."

"Didn't he speak of me? Didn't he make any accusations against me?"

"No. He went on playing the part of a sick man, prostrated by pain and fever. During this time de Chagny wrote to Paris for information about him, for after all, his relations with his cousin only went back as far as 1915.

"Three days ago we received a telegram which said:

"'*A very dangerous man. Wanted by the police. Letters follows.*'

"At once de Chagny came to a decision and the day before yesterday, in the morning, he telephoned to the police. When the inspector arrived, he was too late. D'Estreicher had fled."

"Doubtless through the window of a pantry which looks down on the ravine?" said Dorothy.

"Yes, and down a fissure in the face of the cliff. How did you know?"

"It was the way Saint-Quentin and I took to get at d'Estreicher."

And forthwith, cutting short any questions, she added:

"Well, what was the information you got about him?"

"Extremely serious. Antoine d'Estreicher, formerly a naval officer, was dismissed from the service for theft. Later, prosecuted for being an accomplice in a case of murder, he was released for lack of evidence. At the beginning of the war he deserted. Evidence of it has come to hand and a fortnight ago an inquiry into the matter was begun. During the war he borrowed the personality of one of his relations, who had been dead some years; and it is actually under his new name of Maxime d'Estreicher that the police are hunting for him."

"What a pity! A scoundrel like that! To have him in one's hands and let him go!"

"We will find him again."

"Yes: always providing that it isn't too late."

Raoul quickened their pace. They were going at a fair rate, running through the villages without slackening their pace and bumping over the cobbles of the towns. The night was beginning to fall when they reached Nantes, where they had to stop to buy petrol.

"Still an hour's journey," said Raoul.

On the way she made him explain to her the exact topography of Hillocks Manor, the direction of the road which ran through the orchard to the house, the position of the hall and staircase. Moreover, he had to give her full information about his grandfather's habits, about the old man's age (he was seventy-five), and his dog Goliath—a huge beast, terrible to look at, with a terrific bark, but quite harmless and incapable of defending his master.

At the big market-town of Clisson, they entered La Vendée. When they had nearly reached the Manor Raoul would have liked to make a detour through the village where they would find the servants. They could take with them a couple of farm-laborers. Dorothy would not hear of it.

"But, after all," he exclaimed, "what are you afraid of?"

"Everything," she replied. "From that man—everything. We have no right to lose a minute."

They left the main road and turned down a lane which was more like a deep-rutted cart-track.

"There it is, over yonder," he said. "There is a light in the window of his room."

Almost at once he stopped the car and jumped out of it. A turreted gateway, relic of a far-removed epoch, rose in the high wall which encircled the estate. The gate was shut. While Raoul was engaged in opening it, they heard, dominating the dull noise of the engine, the barking of a dog.

From the clearness of the sound and the direction from which it came Raoul declared that Goliath was not inside the Manor, but outside it, at the foot of the steps, also that he was barking in front of a shut-up house.

"Well, are you never going to open that gate?" cried Dorothy.

He came back hurriedly to her.

"It's very disquieting. Someone has shot the bolt and turned the key in the lock."

"Don't they always?"

"Never. Some stranger has done it... And then you hear that barking."

"Well?"

"There's another gate two hundred yards further on."

"And suppose that's locked too. No: we must act at once."

She moved to the steering-wheel and drove the car close under the wall a little higher up, to the right of the gateway.

Then she piled the four cushions on the seat and stood on the top of them.

"Montfaucon!" she called.

The Captain understood. In half-a-dozen movements he climbed up Dorothy's back and stood upright on her shoulders. With that advantage his hands touched the top of the wall. Clinging to it, with Dorothy's help, he pulled himself up. When he was astride it, Raoul threw a rope to him. He tied one end round his waist, Dorothy held the other. In a few seconds the child touched the ground on the other side of the wall, and Raoul had barely got back to the gate before the key grated in the lock and the bolts were drawn.

Raoul did not get back to the car. He dashed across the orchard, followed by Dorothy and the Captain. As she ran she said to the child:

"Go round the house and if you see a ladder against it, pull it down!"

As they expected, they found Goliath on the steps scratching at the closed door. They made him stop barking and in the silence they heard above them outcries and the sound of a struggle.

Instantly, to frighten the assailant, Raoul fired off his revolver. Then with his latch-key he opened the door; and they ran up the stairs.

One of the rooms facing them was lighted by two lamps. On the floor, face downwards, Raoul's grandfather was writhing and uttering faint, hoarse cries.

Raoul dropped on his knees beside him. Dorothy seized one of the lamps and ran into the room on the opposite side of the corridor. She had noticed that the door of it was open.

The room was empty; through the open window stuck the top of a ladder.

She leant out:

"Montfaucon!"

"Here I am, mummy," the child replied.

"Did you see anyone come down the ladder and run away?"

"From a distance, mummy—as I came round the corner of the house."

"Did you recognize the man?"

"The man was two, mummy."

"Ah, there were two, were there?"

"Yes... another man... and the nasty gentleman."

Raoul's grandfather was not dead; he was not even in any danger of dying. From certain details of the conflict it looked as if d'Estreicher and his confederate had tried by threats and violence to force the old man to reveal what he knew, and doubtless to hand over the gold piece. In particular his throat showed red finger-marks where they had gripped it. Had the ruffian and his confederate succeeded at the last moment?

The servants were not very late getting back. The doctor was summoned and declared that there was no fear of any complications. But in the course of the next day they found that the old man did not answer any questions, did not appear to understand them, and only expressed himself by an incomprehensible stuttering.

The agitation, terror, and suffering had been too much for him... He was mad.

VII

THE HOUR DRAWS NEAR

In the flat country, in which stands Hillocks Manor, a deep gorge has been hollowed out by the river Maine. This gorge rings round the meadows and orchards and buildings of the Manor. Hillocks, humped with rocks and covered with fir-trees, rise in a semicircle at the back of the estate, and a backwater of the Maine, cutting the ring and isolating the hillocks, has formed a pleasant lake, which reflects the dark stones and red bricks and tiles of the ancient building.

Today that building is by way of being a farm. Part of the ground-floor is used for storerooms and barns, evidence of a wider cultivation, formerly flourishing, but very much fallen off since the days when Raoul's grandfather made it his business in life.

The old Baron, as they called him, had a right to the title and to the apostrophe since the property, before the Revolution, formed the barony d'Avernoie. A great sportsman, a fine figure of a man, and fond of wine and women, he had very little liking for work; and his son, Raoul's father, inheriting this distaste, had in his manner of life shown an equal lack of care for the future.

"I have done what I could, once I was demobilized," Raoul confided to Dorothy, "to restore prosperity here; and up-hill work it has been. But what would you? My father and my grandfather lived their lives in the assurance, which evidently sprang from those legends you have heard of: 'One of these days we shall be rich. So why worry?' And they did not worry. Actually we are in the hands of a money-lender who has bought up all our debts; and I have just heard that during my stay at Roborey my grandfather signed a bill of sale which gives that money-lender the power to turn us out of the house in six weeks."

He was an excellent young fellow, a trifle slow-witted, rather awkward in manner, but of an upright disposition, serious and thoughtful. The charm of Dorothy had made an instant conquest of him, and in spite of an invincible timidity which had always prevented him from putting into words his deeper feelings, he did not hide either his admiration or the fact that she had robbed him of his peace of mind. Everything that she said charmed him. Everything that she bade him do was done.

Following her advice he made no secret of the assault of which his grandfather had been the victim and lodged a complaint against this unknown criminal. To the people about him he talked openly about the fortune which he expected to come to him shortly and of the investigations on foot to discover a gold medal, the possession of which was the first condition of obtaining it. Without revealing Dorothy's name, he did not conceal the fact that she was a distant cousin, or the reasons which brought her to the Manor.

Three days later, having screwed double stages out of One-eyed Magpie, Saint-Quentin arrived in company with Castor and Pollux. Dorothy would not hear of any abode but her beloved caravan, which was installed in the middle of the courtyard; and once more the five comrades settled down to their happy, careless life. Castor and Pollux fought with less vigor. Saint-Quentin fished in the lake. The captain, always immensely consequential, took the old baron under his care and related to him and to Goliath interminable yarns.

As for Dorothy, she was observing. They found that she wore an air of mystery, keeping her thoughts and proceedings to herself. She spent hours playing with her comrades superintending their exercises. Then, her eyes fixed on the old baron, who, accompanied by his faithful dog, with tottering gait and dulled eyes, would go and lean against a tree in the orchard, she watched everything which might be a manifestation of instinct in him or of a survival of the past. At other times Raoul surprised her in some corner, motionless and silent. It seemed to him then as if the whole affair was confined to her brain, and that it was there, much more than on the estate of Hillocks Manor that she was looking for the guiding clue.

Several days in succession she spent the hours in the loft of a granary where there were some bookshelves, and on them, old newspapers, bundles of papers, pamphlets, printed during the last century, histories of the district, communal reports, and parish records.

"Well," asked Raoul, laughing. "Are we getting on? I have an impression that your eyes are beginning to see more clearly."

"Perhaps. I won't say that they aren't."

The eyes of Dorothy! In that combination of charming things on her face, it was they above everything which held one's attention. Large, almond-shaped and lengthened in the shadow of their black lashes, they surprised one by the inconceivable diversity of their coloring and expression: of the blue which changed like the blue of the sea according to the hour and the light; of a blue which seemed to vary with the successive thoughts which changed her expression. And these eyes, so delightful that it seemed that they must always be smiling or laughing, were in moments of meditation the gravest eyes that ever were, when she half-closed and fixed them on some image in her mind.

Raoul, now, only saw through them, and was only really interested in what they expressed. The fabulous story of the treasure and the medal was wholly summed up for him in the charming spectacle afforded by two beautiful eyes observant or thoughtful, troubled or joyful. And perhaps Dorothy allowed herself to be observed with a certain satisfaction. The love of this big, shy young fellow touched her by its respectfulness, she who had only known hitherto the brutal homage of desire.

One day she made him take a seat in the little boat which was moored to the shore of the lake, and letting it drift with the current she said to him:

"We are drawing near."

"Near what?" he asked, startled.

"The hour which so many things have so long foretold."

"You believe?"

"I believe that you made no mistake the day on which you saw in your grandfather's hands that gold medal in which all the traditions of the family seem to be summed up. Unfortunately the poor man lost his reason before you were put in possession of the facts; and the thread which bound the past to the future has been broken."

"Then what do you hope for, if we do not find that medal? We've searched everywhere, his room, his clothes, the house, the orchard, and found nothing."

"It is impossible that he should keep to himself forever the answer to the enigma. If his reason is dead, his instincts survive. And what an instinct that is that centuries have been forming! Doubtless he has put the coin within reach, or within sight. You may be sure that he has hidden it in such a way that no execrable piece of bad luck could rob him of it without his being aware of it. But don't worry: at the appointed hour some unconscious gesture will reveal the truth to us."

Raoul objected.

"But what if d'Estreicher took it from him?"

"He did not. If he had, we should not have heard the noise of the struggle. Your grandfather resisted to the end; and it was only our coming which put d'Estreicher to flight."

"Oh, that ruffian! If only I had him in my hands!" exclaimed Raoul.

The boat was drifting gently. Dorothy said in a very low voice, barely moving her lips:

"Not so loud! He can hear us."

"What! What do you mean?"

"I say that he is close by and that he doesn't lose a single word of what we say," she went on in the same low voice.

Raoul was dumfounded.

"But—but—what does it mean? Can you see him?"

"No. But I can feel his presence; and he can see us."

"Where from?"

"From some place among the hillocks. I have been thinking that this name of Hillocks Manor pointed to some inpenetrable hiding-place, and I've discovered a proof of it in one of those old books, which actually speaks of a hiding-place where the Vendéans lay hid, and says that it is believed to be in the neighborhood of Tiffauges and Clisson."

"But how should d'Estreicher have learnt of it?"

"Remember that the day of the assault your grandfather was alone, or believed himself to be alone. Strolling among the hillocks, he would have disclosed one of the entrances. D'Estreicher was watching him at the time. And since then the rascal had been using it as a refuge.

"Look at the ground, all humps and ravines. On the right, on the left, everywhere, there are places in the rock for observations, so to speak, from which one can hear and see everything that takes place inside the boundaries of the estate. D'Estreicher is there."

"What is he doing?"

"He's searching and, what's more, he is keeping an eye on my investigations. He also—for all that I can't guess exactly the reason—wants the gold medal. And he is afraid that I shall get it before him."

"But we must inform the police!"

"Not yet. This underground hiding-place should have several issues, some of which perhaps run under the river. If we give the ruffian warning, he will escape."

"Then what's your plan?"

"To get him to come out of this lair and trap him."

"How?"

"I'll tell you at the appointed time, and that will not be long. I repeat: the hour draws near."

"What proof have you?"

"This," she said. "I have seen the money-lender, Monsieur Voirin, and he showed me the bill of sale. If by five o'clock on July 31st Monsieur Voirin, who has desired all his life to acquire the Manor, has not received the sum of three hundred thousand francs in cash or government securities, the Manor becomes his property."

"I know," said he. "And it will break my heart to go away from here."

She protested:

"There's no question of your going away from here."

"Why not? There's no reason why I should become rich in a month."

"Yes, there is a reason, the reason which has always sustained your grandfather, the reason which made him act as he did on this occasion, which made him say to old Voirin—I repeat the money-lender's words: 'Don't get bucked about this, Voirin. On the 31st of July I shall pay you in cash.' This is the first time that we are face to face with a precise fact. Up to now words and a confused tradition. Today a fact. A fact which proves that, according to your grandfather all the legends which turn round these promised riches come to a head on a certain day in the month of July."

The boat touched the bank. Dorothy sprang lightly ashore and cried without fear of being heard:

"Raoul, today's the 27th of June. In a few weeks you will be rich; and I too. And d'Estreicher will be hanged high and dry as I predicted to his face."

That very evening Dorothy slipped out of the Manor and furtively made her way to a lane which ran between very tall hedges. After an hour's walking she came to a little garden at the bottom of which a light was shining.

Her private investigations had brought to her knowledge the name of an old lady, Juliet Assire, whom the gossip of the countryside declared to be one of the old flames of the Baron. Before his attack, the Baron paid her a visit, for all that she was deaf, in poor health, and rather feeble-witted. Moreover, thanks to the lack of discretion of the maid who looked after her and whom Saint-Quentin had questioned, Dorothy had learnt that Juliet Assire was the possessor of a medal of the kind they were searching for at the Manor.

Dorothy had formed the plan of taking advantage of the maid's weekly evening out to knock at the door and question Juliet Assire. But Fortune decided otherwise. The door was not locked, and when she stepped over the threshold of the low and comfortable sitting-room, she perceived the old lady asleep in the lamplight, her head bent over the canvas which she was engaged in embroidering.

"Suppose I look for it?" thought Dorothy. "What's the use of asking her questions she won't answer?"

She looked round her, examined the prints hanging on the wall, the clock under its glass case, the candlesticks.

Further on an inner staircase led up to the bedrooms. She was moving towards it when the door creaked. On the instant she was certain that d'Estreicher was about to appear. Had he followed her?... Had he by any chance brought her there by a combination of machinations? She was frightened and thought only of flight... The staircase? The rooms on the first floor... She hadn't the time! Near her was a glass door... Doubtless it led to the kitchen... And from there to the back door through which she could escape.

She went through it and at once found out her mistake. She was in a dark closet, a cupboard rather, against the boards of which she had to flatten herself before she could get the door shut. She found herself a prisoner.

At that moment the door of the room opened, very quietly. Two men came cautiously into it; and immediately one of them whispered:

"The old woman's asleep."

Through the glass, which was covered by a torn curtain, Dorothy easily recognized d'Estreicher, in spite of his turned-up coat-collar and the flaps of his cap, which were tied under his chin. His confederate in like manner had hidden half his face in a muffler.

"That damsel does make you play the fool," he said.

"Play the fool? Not a bit of it!" growled d'Estreicher. "I'm keeping an eye on her, that's all."

"Rot! You're always shadowing her. You're losing your head about her... You'll go on doing it till the day she helps you to lose it for good."

"I don't say, no. She nearly succeeded in doing it at Roberey. But I need her."

"What for?"

"For the medal. She's the only person capable of laying her hands on it."

"Not here—in any case. We've already searched the house twice."

"Badly, without a doubt, since she is coming to it. At least when we caught sight of her she was certainly coming in this direction. The chatter of the maid has sent her here; and she has chosen the night when the old woman would be alone."

"You are stuck on your little pet."

"I'm stuck on her," growled d'Estreicher. "Only let me lay my hands on her, and I swear the little devil won't forget it in a hurry!"

Dorothy shivered. There was in the accents of this man a hate and at the same time a violence of desire which terrified her.

He was silent, posted behind the door, listening for her coming.

Several minutes passed. Juliet Assire still slept, her hand hanging lower and lower over her work.

At last d'Estreicher muttered:

"She isn't coming. She must have turned off somewhere."

"Ah well, let's clear out," said his accomplice.

"No."

"Have you got an idea?"

"A determination—to find the medal."

"But since we've already searched the house twice—"

"We went about it the wrong way. We must change our methods... All the worse for the old woman!"

He banged the table at the risk of waking Juliet Assire.

"After all, it's too silly! The maid distinctly said: 'There's a medal in the house, the kind of thing they're looking for at the Manor.' Then let's make use of the opportunity, what? What failed in the case of the Baron may succeed today."

"What? You'd—"

"Make her speak—yes. As I tried to make the Baron speak. Only, she's a woman, she is."

D'Estreicher had taken off his cap. His evil face wore an expression of savage cruelty. He went to the door, locked it, and put the key in his pocket. Then he came back to the arm-chair in which the good lady was sleeping, gazed at her a moment and of a sudden fell upon her, gripping her throat, and thrust her backwards against the back of the chair.

His confederate chuckled:

"You needn't give yourself all that trouble. If you squeeze too hard, you'll kill the poor old thing."

D'Estreicher opened his fingers a little. The old woman opened her eyes wide and uttered a low groan.

"Speak!" d'Estreicher commanded. "The Baron intrusted a medal to you. Where have you put it?"

Juliet Assire did not clearly understand what was happening to her. She struggled. Exasperated, he shook her.

"Will you prattle? Hey? Where's your old sweetheart's medal? He gave it to you all right. Don't say he didn't, you old hag! Your maid's telling everybody who cares to listen to her. Come, speak up. If you don't—"

He picked one of the iron fire-dogs with copper knobs from the hearthstone and brandished it crying:

"One... two... three... At twenty I'll crack your skull!"

VIII

ON THE IRON WIRE

The door behind which Dorothy was hiding herself shut badly. Having pushed it to gently, she not only saw but heard everything that took place, except that the face of Juliet Assire remained hidden from her. The ruffian's threat did not trouble her much, for she knew that he would not put it into execution. In fact d'Estreicher counted up to twenty without the old woman having uttered a word. But her resistance infuriated him to such a degree that, dropping the mass of iron, he seized the hand of Juliet Assire and twisted it violently. Juliet Assire yelled with pain.

"Ah, you're beginning to understand, are you?" he said. "Perhaps you'll answer... Where is the medal?"

She was silent.

He gave her hand another twist.

The old woman fell on her knees and begged for mercy incoherently.

"Speak!" he cried. "Speak! I'll go on twisting till you speak!"

She stammered several syllables.

"What's that you say? Speak more distinctly, will you? Do you want me to give it another twist?"

"No... no," she implored. "It's there... at the Manor... in the river."

"In the river? What nonsense! You threw it into the river? You're laughing at me!"

He held her down with one knee on her chest, their hands clenched round one another. From her post of observation Dorothy watched them, horror-stricken, powerless against these two men, but nevertheless unable to resign herself to inaction.

"Then I'll twist it, what?" growled the ruffian. "You prefer it to speaking?"

He made a quick movement which drew a cry from Juliet Assire. And all at once she raised herself, showed her face convulsed with terror, moved her lips, and succeeded in stuttering:

"The c—c—cupboard... the cupboard... the flagstones."

The sentence was never finished, though the mouth continued to move, but a strange thing happened: her frightful face little by little grew calm, assumed an ineffable serenity, became happy, smiling; and of a sudden Juliet Assire burst out laughing. She no longer felt the torture of her twisted wrist and she laughed gently, not jerkily, with an expression of beatitude.

She was mad.

"You've no luck," said his confederate in a mocking tone. "Directly you try to make people speak, they collapse—the Baron, cracked; his sweetheart, mad as a hatter. You're doing well."

The exasperated d'Estreicher thrust away the old woman who stumbled and turning fell down behind an arm-chair quite close to Dorothy, and cried furiously.

"You're right, my luck's out. But this time perhaps we've found a lode. Before her brain gave she spoke of a cupboard and flagstones. Which? This one or that? They're both paved with flags?"

He pointed first to the kind of closet in which Dorothy was hiding and then to a cupboard on the other side of the fireplace.

"I'll begin with this cupboard. You start on that one," he said. "Or rather, no—come and help me; we'll go through this one thoroughly first."

He knelt down near the fireplace, opened the cupboard door, and with the poker got to work on one of the cracks between the flags of its floor which his accomplice tried to raise.

Dorothy lost no time. She knew that they were coming to the closet and that she was lost if she did not fly. The old woman, stretched out close to her, was laughing gently and then grew silent as the men worked on.

Hidden by the arm-chair, Dorothy slipped noiselessly out of the cupboard, took off the lace cap which covered the hair of Juliet Assire and put it on her own head. Then she took her spectacles, then her shawl, put it round her shoulders, and succeeded in hiding her figure with a big table-cloth of black serge. At that moment Juliet fell silent. On the instant Dorothy took up her even, joyous laughter. She rose, and stooping like an old woman, ambled across the room.

D'Estreicher growled: "What's the old lunatic up to? Mind she doesn't get away."

"How *can* she get away?" asked his confederate. "You've got the key in your pocket."

"The window."

"Much too high. Besides she doesn't want to leave the cottage."

Dorothy slipped in front of the window, the sill of which, uncommonly high up, was on a level with her eyes. The shutters were not closed. With a slow movement she succeeded in turning the catch. Then she paused. She knew that directly it was opened the window would let in the fresh air and the noises outside, and give the ruffians warning. In a few seconds she calculated and analyzed the movements she would need to make. Sure of herself and relying on her extraordinary agility, she took a look at her enemies; then swiftly, without a single mistake or a second's hesitation, she threw the window wide, jumped on to the sill, and from it into the garden.

There came two shouts together, then a hubbub of cries. But it took the two men time to understand, to stumble upon the body of the real Juliet and discover it was she, to unlock the door. Dorothy made use of it. Too clever to escape down the garden and through the gate, she ran round the cottage, jumped down a slope, scratched herself among the thorns of a hedge, and came out into the fields.

As she did so pistol-shots rang out. D'Estreicher and his confederate were firing at the shadows.

When Dorothy had rejoined Raoul and the children, who, alarmed by her absence, were waiting for her at the door of the caravan, and had told them briefly about her expedition, she ended:

"And now we're going to make an end of it. The final hand will be played in exactly a week from today."

These few days were very sweet to the two young people. While still remaining shy, Raoul grew bolder in his talks with her and let her see more clearly the depths of his nature, at once serious and impassioned. Dorothy abandoned herself with a certain joy to this love, of the sincerity of which she was fully conscious. Deeply disturbed, Saint-Quentin and his comrades grew uncommonly gloomy.

The captain tossed his head and said:

"Dorothy, I think I like this one less than the nasty gentleman, and if you'd listen to me..."

"What should we do, my lamb?"

"We'd harness One-eye' Magpie and go away."

"And the treasure? You know we're hunting for treasure."

"You're the treasure, mummy. And I'm afraid that they'll take you away from us."

"Don't you worry, my child. My four children will always come first."

But the four children did worry. The sense of danger weighed on them. In this confined space, between the walls of Hillocks Manor they breathed a heavy atmosphere which troubled them. Raoul was the chief danger: but another danger was little by little taking form in their minds: twice they saw the outline of a man moving stealthily among the thickets of the hillocks in the dusk.

On the 30th of June, Dorothy begged Raoul to give all his staff a holiday next day. It was the day of the great religious fête at Clisson. Three of the stoutest of the servants, armed with guns, were ordered to come back surreptitiously at four in the afternoon and wait near a little inn, Masson Inn, a quarter of a mile from the Manor.

Next day Dorothy seemed in higher spirits than ever. She danced jigs in the courtyard and sang English songs. She sang others in the boat, in which she had asked Raoul to row her, and then behaved so wildly, that several times they just missed capsizing. In this way it came about that in juggling with three coral bracelets she let one of them fall into the water. She wanted to recover it, dipped her bare arm in the water as high as the shoulder, and remained motionless, her head bent over the lake, as if she was considering carefully something she saw on its bottom.

"What are you looking at like that?" said Raoul.

"There has been no rain for a long while, the lake is low, and one can see more distinctly the stones and pebbles on the bottom. Now I've already noticed that some of the stones are arranged in a certain pattern. Look."

"Undoubtedly," he said. "And they've hewn stones, shaped. One might fancy that they formed huge letters. Have you noticed it?"

"Yes. And one can guess the words that those letters form: '*In robore fortuna.*' At the mayor's office I've studied an old map of the neighborhood. Here, where we are, was formerly the principal lawn of a sunken garden, and on this very lawn one of your ancestors had this device inscribed in blocks of stone. Since then someone has let in the water of the Maine over the sunken garden. The pool has taken the place of the lawn. The device is hidden."

And she added between her teeth:

"And so are the few words and the figures below the device, which I have not yet been able to see. And it's that which interests me. Do you see them?"

"Yes. But indistinctly."

"That's just it. We're too near them. We need to look at them from a height."

"Let's climb up on the hillocks."

"No use. The slope—the water would blur the image."

"Then," said he, laughing, "we must mount above them in an aëroplane."

At lunch-time they parted. After the meal, Raoul superintended the departure of the *char-à-bancs*, which were taking all the staff of the Manor to Clisson, then he took his way to the pool where he saw Dorothy's little troupe hard at work on the bank. The captain, always the man of affairs, was running to and fro somewhat in the manner of a Gugusse. The others were carrying out exactly Dorothy's instructions.

When it was all over, a sufficiently thick iron wire was stretched above the lake at a height of ten or twelve feet, fastened at one end to the gable of a barn, at the other to a ring affixed to a rock among the hillocks.

"Hang it all!" he said. "It looks to me as if you'd made preparations for one of your circus turns."

"You're right," she replied gayly. "Having no aëroplane I fall back on my aërial rope-walking."

"What? Is that what you intend to do?" he exclaimed in anxious accents. "But you're bound to fall."

"I can swim."

"No, no. I refuse to allow it."

"By what right?"

"You haven't even a balancing-pole."

"A balancing-pole?" she said, running off. "And what next? A net? A safety-rope?"

She climbed up the ladder inside the barn and appeared on the edge of the roof. She was laughing, as was her custom when she began her performance before a crowd. She was dressed in a silk frock, with broad white and red stripes, a scarlet silk handkerchief was crossed over her chest.

Raoul was in a state of feverish excitement.

The captain went to him.

"Do you want to help mummy, Dorothy?" he said in a confidential tone.

"Certainly I do."

"Well, go away, monsieur."

Dorothy stretched out her leg. Her foot, which was bare in a cloth sandal divided at the big toe, tried the wire, as a bather's foot tries the coldness of the water. And then she quickly stepped on to it, made several steps, sliding, and stopped.

She saluted right and left, pretending to believe herself in the presence of a large audience, and came sliding forward again with a regular, rhythmic movement of her legs and a swaying of her bust and arms which balanced her like the beating of the wings of a bird. So she arrived above the pool. The wire, slackened, bent under her weight and jerked upwards. A second time she stopped, when she was over the middle of the pool.

This was the hardest part of her undertaking. She was no longer able to hook, so to speak, her gaze on a fixed point among the hillocks, and lend her balance the support of something stable. She had to lower her eyes and try to read, in the moving and glittering water, repelling the fascination of the sun's reflection, the words and the figures. A terribly dangerous task! She had to essay it several times and to rise upright the very moment she found herself bending over the void. A minute or two passed, minutes of veritable anguish. She brought them to an end by a salute with both arms, stretching them out with even gracefulness, and a cry of victory; then she at once walked on again.

Raoul had crossed the bridge which spans the end of the pool and he was already on a kind of platform among the hillocks, at which the wire ended. She was struck by his paleness and touched by his anxiety on her account.

"Goodness," she said, gripping his hand. "Were you as frightened as that on my account?... If I'd only known!... And yet, no": she went on. "Even if I had known, I should have made the experiment, so certain was I of the result."

"Well?" he said.

"Well, I read the device distinctly, and the date under it, which we couldn't make out—the 12th of July, 1921. We know now that the 12th of July of this year is the great day foretold so many years ago. But there's something better, I fancy."

She called Saint-Quentin to her and said some words to him in a low voice. Saint-Quentin ran to the caravan and a few minutes came out of it in his acrobat's tights. He stepped into the boat with Dorothy, who rowed it to the middle of the pool. He slipped quickly into the water and dived. Twice he came up to receive more exact instructions from Dorothy. At last, the third time he came up, he cried:

"Here it is, mummy!"

He tossed into the boat a somewhat heavy object. Dorothy snatched it up, examined it, and when they reached the bank, handed it to Raoul. It was a metal disc, of rusted iron or copper, of the size of a saucer, and convex—like an enormous watch.

It must have been formed of two plates joined together, but the edges of these plates had been soldered together so that one could not open it.

Dorothy rubbed one of its faces and pointed out to Raoul with her finger the deeply engraved word: "Fortuna."

"I was not mistaken," she said, "and poor old Juliet Assire was speaking the truth, in speaking first of the river. During one of their last meetings the Baron must have thrown in here the gold medal in its metal case."

"But why?"

"Didn't you write to him from Roborey, after I left, to be on his guard?"

"Yes."

"In that case what better hiding-place could he find for the medal till the day came for him to use it than the bottom of the pool? The first boy who came along could fish it out for him."

Joyously she tossed the disc in the air and juggled with it and three pebbles. Then she caught hold of the shivering Saint-Quentin, very scraggy in his wet tights, and with the other three boys danced round the platform, singing the lay of "The Recovered Medal."

At the end of his breath the captain made the observation that there was a fête at Clisson and that they might very well go there to celebrate their success.

"Let's harness One-eye' Magpie."

Dorothy approved of it.

"Excellent! But One-eyed Magpie's too slow. What about your car, Raoul?"

They hurried back to the Manor. Saint-Quentin went to change his costume. Raoul set his engine going and brought the car out of the garage. While the three boys were getting into it, he went to Dorothy, who had sat down at a little table on the terrace which ran the length of the building.

"Are you ready?" he asked.

She said:

"But I never had any intention of going with you. Today you're going to be nursemaid."

He was not greatly surprised. Since early morning he had had an odd feeling that everything that happened was not quite natural. The incidents followed one another in such perfect sequence and with a logic and exactness foreign to actuality. One might have said that they were scenes in a too-well-made play, of which it would have been easy, with a little experience of the playwright's art, to analyze the construction and the tricks. Certainly, without knowing Dorothy's game, he guessed the dénouement she proposed to bring about—the capture of d'Estreicher. But by means of what stratagem?

"Don't question me," she said. "We are watched. So no heroics, no remonstrances. Listen."

She was amusing herself by spinning the disk on the table and quite calmly she outlined her plan and her maneuvers.

"It's like this. A day or two ago I wrote, in your name, to the Public Prosecutor, advising him that our friend d'Estreicher, for whom the police are hunting, guilty of attempts to murder Baron Davernoie and Madame Juliet Assire, would be at Hillocks Manor today. I asked him to send two detectives who would find you at Masson Inn at four o'clock. It's now a quarter to four. Your three servants will be there too. So off you go."

"What am I to do?"

"Come back quickly with the two detectives and your three servants, not by the main road, but by the paths Saint-Quentin and the three boys will point out to you. At the end of them you will find ladders ready. You will set them up against the wall. D'Estreicher and his confederate will be there. You will cover them with your guns while the detectives arrest them."

"Are you sure that d'Estreicher will come out of the hillocks—if it's the fact that the hillocks are his hiding-place?"

"Quite sure. Here is the medal. He knows that it is in my hands. How can he help seizing the opportunity of taking it now that we are on the eve of the great event."

She expressed herself with a disconcerting calmness. For all that she was exposing herself alone to all the menace of a combat which promised to be formidable, she had not the faintest air of being in danger. Indeed, such was her indifference to the risk she was running that, when the old Baron went past them and into the Manor, followed by his faithful Goliath, she imparted to Raoul some results of her observations.

"Have you noticed that for the last day or two that your grandfather has been ill at ease? He too is instinctively aware that the great event is at hand, and he wants to act. He is pulling himself together and struggling against the disease which paralyzes him in the very hour of action."

In spite of everything, Raoul hesitated. The idea of leaving her to face d'Estreicher alone was infinitely painful to him.

"One question," he said.

"Only one then, for you've no time to lose."

"You made all your preparations for today. The police are informed, the servants warned, the rendezvous fixed. Good. But nevertheless you couldn't know that the discovery of this disc would take place just an hour before that rendezvous."

"Excellent, Raoul; I congratulate you. You've put your finger on the weak point in my explanation. But I can't tell you anything more at the moment."

"Nevertheless—"

"Do as I ask you, Raoul. You know that I don't act at random."

Dorothy's confidence, her boldness, the simplicity of her plan, her quiet smile, all inspired him with such trust in her judgment that he raised no more objections.

"Very well," he said. "I'll go."

"That's right," she said, laughing. "You have faith. In that case make haste and come back quickly, for d'Estreicher will come here not only to get hold of the medal but also for something on which perhaps he is equally keen."

"What's that?"

"Me."

This was a suggestion which hastened the young man's decision. The car started and crossed the orchard. Saint-Quentin opened the big gate and shut it again as soon as the car had gone through it.

Dorothy was alone; and she was to remain alone and defenceless for as long she reckoned, if her calculations were correct, as twelve to fifteen minutes.

Keeping her back turned to the hillocks, she did not stir from her chair. She appeared to be very busy with the disc, testing the soldering, like one who seeks to discover the secret or the weak point of a piece of mechanism. But with her ears, all her nerves on edge, she tried to catch every sound or rustle that the breeze might bring her.

By turns she was sustained by an unshakable certainty, or attacked by discouraging doubts. Yes: d'Estreicher was bound to come. She could not admit to herself that he might not come. The medal would draw him to her with an irresistible enticement.

"And yet, no," she said to herself. "He will be on his guard. My little maneuver is really too puerile. This case, this medal which we find at the fateful moment, this departure of Raoul and the children, and then my staying alone in the empty farm, when my one care on the contrary would be to protect my find against the enemy—all this is really too far-fetched. An old fox like d'Estreicher will shun the trap."

And then the other side of the problem presented itself:

"He *will* come. Perhaps he has already left his lair. Manifestly the danger will be clear to him, but afterwards, when it is too late. At the actual moment he is not free to act or not to act. He obeys."

So once more Dorothy was guided by her keen insight into the trend of events, in spite of what her reason might tell her. The facts grouped themselves before her intelligence in a logical sequence and with strict method, she saw their accomplishment while they were yet in process of becoming. The motives which actuated other people were always perfectly clear to her. Her intuition revealed them; her quick intelligence instantly fitted them to the circumstances.

Besides, as she had said, d'Estreicher was drawn by a double temptation. If he succeeded in resisting the temptation to try to seize the medal, how could he help succumbing to the temptation to seize that marvelous prize, right within his reach, Dorothy herself?

She sat upright with a smile. The sound of footsteps had fallen on her ears. It must come from the wooden bridge which spanned the end of the pool.

The enemy was coming!

But almost at the same moment she heard another sound on her right and then another on her left. D'Estreicher had *two* confederates. She was hemmed in!

The hands of her watch pointed to five minutes to four.

IX

FACE TO FACE

"If they seize me," she thought. "If it's d'Estreicher's intention to kidnap me without more ado, there's nothing to be done. Before I could be rescued, they would carry me off to their underground lair, and from there I don't know where!"

And why should it be otherwise? Master of the medal and of Dorothy, the ruffian had only to fly.

On the instant she saw all the faults of her plan. In order to compel d'Estreicher to risk a sortie that she might capture him during that sortie, she had invented a too subtle ruse, which actual developments of Fortune's spite might turn to her undoing. A conflict which turns on the number of seconds gained or lost is extremely doubtful.

She went quickly into the house and pushed the disc under a heap of discarded things in a small lumber-room. The necessary hunt for it would delay for a while the enemy's flight. But when she came back to go out of the house, d'Estreicher, grimacing ironically behind his spectacles and under his thick beard, stood on the threshold of the front door.

Dorothy never carried a revolver. All her life she never cared to trust to anything but her courage and intelligence. She regretted it at this horrible moment when she found herself face to face with the man who had murdered her father. Her first act would have been to blow out his brains.

Divining her vengeful thought, he seized her arm quickly and twisted it, as he had twisted the arm of old Juliet Assire. Then bending over her, he snapped:

"Where have you put it?... Be quick!"

She did not even dream of resisting, so acute was the pain, and took him to the little room, and pointed to the heap. He found the disc at once, weighed it in his hand, examining it with an air of immense satisfaction and said:

"That's all right. Victory at last! Twenty years of struggle come to an end. And over and above what I bargained for, you, Dorothy—the most magnificent and desirable of rewards."

He ran his hand over her frock to make sure that she was not armed, then seized her round the body, and with a strength which no one would have believed him to possess, swung her over his shoulder on to his back.

"You make me feel uneasy, Dorothy," he chuckled. "What? No resistance? What pretty behavior, my dear! There must be something in the way of a trap under it all. So I'll be off."

Outside she caught sight of the two men, who were on guard at the big gate. One of them was the confederate she knew, from having seen him at Juliet Assire's cottage. The other, his face flattened against the bars of a small wicket, was watching the road.

D'Estreicher called to them:

"Keep your eyes skinned, boys. You mustn't be caught in the sheepfold. And when I whistle, bucket off back to the hillocks."

He himself made for them with long strides without weakening under his burden. She could smell the odor of a damp cellar with which his subterranean lair had impregnated his garments. He held her by the neck with a hard hand that bruised it.

They came to the wooden bridge and were just about to cross it. No more than a hundred yards from it, perhaps, among the bushes and rocks, was one of the entrances to his underground lair. Already the man was raising his whistle to his lips.

With a deft movement, Dorothy snatched the disc, which was sticking up above the top of the pocket into which he had stuffed it, and threw it towards the pool. It ran along the ground, rolled down the bank, and disappeared under the water.

"You little devil!" growled the ruffian throwing her roughly to the ground. "Stir, and I'll break your head!"

He went down the bank and floundered about in the viscid mud of the river, keeping an eye on Dorothy and cursing her.

She did not dream of flying. She kept looking from one to another of the points at the top of the wall above which she expected the heads of the farm-servants or the detectives to rise. It was certainly five or six minutes past the hour, yet none of them appeared. Nevertheless she did not lose hope. She expected d'Estreicher, who had evidently lost his head, to make some mistake of which she could take advantage.

"Yes, yes," he snarled: "You wish to gain time, my dear. And suppose you do? Do you think I'll let go of you? I've got you both, you and the medal; and your bumpkin of a Raoul isn't the man to loosen my grip. Besides, if he does come, it'll be all the worse for him. My men have their orders: a good crack on the head—"

He was still searching; he stopped short, uttered a cry of triumph and stood upright, the disc in his hand.

"Here it is, ducky. Certainly the luck is with me; and you've lost. On we go, cousin Dorothy!"

Dorothy cast a last look along the walls. No one. Instinctively, at the approach of the man she hated, she made as if to thrust him off. It made him laugh—so absurd did any resistance seem. Violently he beat down her outstretched arms, and again swung her on to his shoulder with a movement in which there was as much hate as desire.

"Say goodbye to your sweetheart, Dorothy, for the good Raoul is in love with you. Say goodbye to him. If ever you see him again, it will be too late."

He crossed the bridge and strode in among the hillocks.

It was all over. In another thirty seconds, even if he were attacked, no longer being in sight of the points on the wall at which the men armed with guns were to rise up, he would have time to reach the mouth of the entrance to his lair. Dorothy had lost the battle. Raoul and the detectives would arrive too late.

"You don't know how nice it is to have you there, all quivering, and to carry you away with me, against me, without your being able to escape the inevitable," whispered d'Estreicher. "But what's the matter with you? Are you crying? You mustn't, my dear. After all why should you? You would certainly let yourself be lulled one of these days on the bosom of the handsome Raoul. Then there's no reason why I should be more distasteful to you than he, is there? But—hang it!" he cried angrily, "Haven't you done sobbing yet?"

He turned her on his shoulder and caught hold of her head.

He was dumfounded.

Dorothy was laughing.

"What—what's this? What are you laughing at? Is it p-p-possible that you dare to laugh? What on earth do you mean by it?"

This laughter frightened him as a threat of danger? The slut! What was she laughing at? A sudden fury rose in him, and setting her down clumsily against a tree, he struck her with his clenched fist, out of which a ring stuck, on the forehead, among her hair, with such force that the blood spurted out.

She was still laughing, as she stammered:

"You b-b-brute! What a brute you are!"

"If you laugh, I'll bite your mouth, you hussy," he snarled, bending over her red lips.

He did not dare to carry out the threat, respecting her in spite of himself, and even a little intimidated. She was frightened, however, and laughed no more.

"What is this? What is it?" he repeated. "You should be crying, and you're laughing. Why?"

"I was laughing because of the plates," she said.

"What plates?"

"Those which form the case of the medal."

"These?"

"Yes."

"What about them?"

"They're the plates of Dorothy's Circus. I used to juggle with them."

He looked utterly flabbergasted.

"What's this rot you're talking?"

"It is rot, isn't it? Saint-Quentin and I soldered them together; I engraved the motto on them with a knife; and last night we threw them into the pool."

"But you're mad. I don't understand. With what object did you do it?"

"Since poor old Juliet Assire babbled some admissions about the river when you tortured her, I was pretty sure you'd fall into the trap."

"What do you mean? What trap?"

"I wanted to get you to come out of here."

"You knew that I was here then?"

"Rather! I knew that you were watching us fish up the case; and I knew for certain what would happen after that. Believing that this case, found at the bottom of the pool under your very eyes, contained the medal, and seeing moreover that Raoul had gone and I was alone at the Manor, you wouldn't be able to come. But you have come."

He stuttered:

"The g-g-gold medal... It isn't in this case then?"

"No. It's empty."

"And Raoul?... Raoul?... You're expecting him?"

"Yes."

"Alone?"

"With some detectives. He went to meet them."

He clenched his fists and growled:

"You little beast, you denounced me."

"I denounced you."

Not for a second did d'Estreicher think she might be lying. He held the metal disc in his hand; and it would have been easy enough to force it open with his knife. To what end? The disc was empty. He was sure of it. Of a sudden he grasped the full force of the comedy she had played on the pool; it explained to him the odd uneasiness and disquiet he had felt while he was watching that series of actions the connection of which seemed to him strange.

However he had come. He had plunged blindly, with his head down, into the trap she had audaciously laid for him before his very eyes. Of what miraculous power was she mistress? And how was he going to slip through the meshes of the net which was being drawn tighter and tighter round him?

"Let's be getting away," he said, eager to get out of danger.

But he was suffering from a lassitude of will, and instead of picking up his victim, he questioned her.

"The disc is empty. But you know where the medal is?" he questioned.

"Of course I know," said Dorothy, who only thought of gaining time and whose furtive eyes were scanning the top of the wall.

The man's eyes sparkled:

"Ah, you do, do you?... You must be a fool to admit it!... Since you know, you're going to tell, my dear. If not—"

He drew his revolver.

She said mockingly:

"Just as with Juliet Assire? Twenty's what you count, isn't it? You may as well save your breath; it doesn't work with me."

"I swear, dammit!—"

"Words!"

No: the battle was certainly not lost. Dorothy, though exhausted, her face smeared with blood, clung to every possible incident with grim tenacity. She felt strongly that, in his fury, d'Estreicher was capable of killing her. But she was quite as clearly aware of his confusion of ideas and of her power over him. He hadn't the strength to depart and abandon the medal for which he had struggled so desperately. If only his hesitation lasted a few minutes longer, Raoul was bound to appear on the scene.

At this moment an incident occurred which appeared to excite her keenest interest, for she leant forward to follow it more closely. The old Baron came out of the Manor, carrying a bag, not dressed, as usual, in a blouse, but in a cloth suit, and wearing a felt hat. That showed that he had made a choice, that is to say, an effort of thought. Then there was another such effort. Goliath was not with him. He waited for him, stamped his foot, and when the dog did come, caught him by the collar, looked about him, and took his way to the gate.

The two confederates barred his path; he muttered some grumbling complaints and tried to get past them. They shoved him back and at last he went off among the trees, without losing Goliath, but leaving his bag behind him.

His action was easy to understand; and Dorothy and d'Estreicher alike grasped the fact that the old fellow had wanted to go off on the quest of the treasure. In spite of his madness, he had not forgotten the enterprise. The appointed date was engraved on his memory; and on the day he had fixed, he strapped up his bag and started out like a piece of mechanism which one has wound up and which goes off at the moment fixed.

D'Estreicher called out to his confederates:

"Search his bag!"

Since they found nothing, no medal, no clue, he walked up and down in front of Dorothy for a moment, undecided what course to take and then stopped beside her:

"Answer me. Raoul loves you. You don't love him. Otherwise I should have put a stop to your little flirtation a fortnight ago. But all the same you feel some obligations towards him in the matter of the medal and the treasure; and you've joined forces. It's just foolishness, my dear, and I'm going to set your mind at rest about the matter, for there's a thing you don't know and I'm going to tell it you. After which I'm sure you'll speak. Answer me then. With regard to this medal, you must be wondering how I come to be hunting for it, since, as you very well know, I stole it from your father. What do you suppose?"

"I suppose somebody took it from you."

"You're right. But do you know who it was?"

"No."

"Raoul's father, George Davernoie."

She started and exclaimed:

"You lie!"

"I do not!" he declared firmly. "You remember your father's last letter which cousin Octave read to us at Roborey? The Prince of Argonne related how he heard two men talking under his window and saw a hand slip through it towards the table and sneak the medal. Well, the man who had accompanied the other on the expedition and was waiting below, was George Davernoie. And that rogue, Dorothy, the very next night robbed his comrade."

Dorothy was shaking with indignation and abhorrence:

"It's a lie! Raoul's father take to such a trade? A thief?"

"Worse than that. For the enterprise had not only robbery for its aim... And if the man who poured the poison into the glass and whose tattooed arm was seen by the Prince of Argonne, does not deny his acts, he doesn't forget that the poison was provided by the other."

"You lie! You lie! You alone are the culprit! You alone murdered my father!"

"You don't really believe that. And look: here's a letter from him to the old Baron, to his father, that is. I found it among the Baron's papers. Read it:

"'I have at last laid my hand on the indispensable gold piece. On my next leave I'll bring it to you.'

"And look at the date. A week after the death of the Prince of Argonne! Do you believe me now, eh? And don't you think that we might come to an understanding between ourselves, apart from this milksop Raoul?"

This revelation had tried Dorothy sorely. However, she pulled herself together and putting a good face on it, she asked:

"What do you mean?"

"I mean that the gold medal, brought to the Baron, intrusted by him to his old flame for a while, then hidden I don't know where, belongs to you. Raoul has no right to it. I'll buy it from you."

"At what price?"

"Any price you like—half the treasure, if you demand it."

Dorothy saw on the instant how she could make the most of the situation. Here again was a way of gaining some minutes, decisive minutes perhaps, a painful and costly way, since she risked handing over to him the key to the treasure. But dare she hesitate? D'Estreicher was nearly at the end of his patience. He was beside himself at the notion of the imminent attack with which he was threatened. Let him get carried away by an access of panic and all would be lost by his taking flight.

"A partnership between us? Never! A sharing of the treasure which would make me your ally? A thousand times, no! I detest you. But an agreement for a few moments? Perhaps."

"Your conditions?" he said. "Be quick! Make the most of my allowing you to impose conditions!"

"That won't take long. You have a double object—the medal and me. You must choose between them. Which do you want most?"

"The medal."

"If you let me go free, I'll give it to you."

"Swear to me on your honor that you know where it is."

"I swear it."

"How long have you known?"

"For about five minutes. A little while ago I did not know. A little fact has just come under my observation which has informed me."

He believed her. It was impossible for him to disbelieve her. Everything that she said in that fashion, looking you straight in the face, was the exact truth.

"Speak."

"It's for you to speak first. Swear that as soon as my promise is fulfilled, I shall be free."

The ruffian blinked. The idea of keeping an oath appeared comic to him; and Dorothy was quite aware that his oath had no value of any kind.

"I swear it," he said.

Then he repeated: "Speak. I can't quite make out what you are faking; but it doesn't strike me as being gospel truth. So I don't put much faith in it; and don't you forget it."

The conflict between them was now at its height; and what gave that conflict its peculiar character was that both of them saw clearly the adversary's game. Dorothy had no doubt that Raoul, after an unforeseen delay, was on his way to the Manor, and d'Estreicher, who had no more doubt of it than she, knew that all her actions were based on her expectation of immediate intervention. But there was one trifling fact which rendered their chances of victory equal. D'Estreicher believed himself to be in perfect security because his two confederates, glued to the wicket, were watching the road for the coming of the car; while the young girl had taken the admirable precaution of instructing Raoul to abandon the car and take the paths which were out of sight of the gate. All her hope sprang from this precaution.

She made her explanation quietly, all the while bearing in mind her keen desire to drag out the interview.

"I've never ceased to believe," she said "—and I'm sure that you are of the same opinion that the Baron has never, so to speak, quitted the medal."

"I hunted everywhere," d'Estreicher objected.

"So did I. But I don't mean that he kept it on him. I meant that he kept it and still keeps it within reach."

"You do?"

"Yes. He has always managed in such a way that he has only to stretch out his hand to grasp it."

"Impossible. We should have seen it."

"Not at all. Only just now you failed to see anything."

"Just now?"

"Yes. When he was going off, compelled by the bidding of his instinct—when he was going off on the very day he had fixed before he fell ill—"

"He was going off without the medal."

"With the medal."

"They searched his bag."

"The bag wasn't the only thing he was taking with him."

"What else was there? Hang it all! You were more than a hundred yards away from him! You saw nothing."

"I saw that he was holding something besides his bag."

"What?"

"Goliath."

D'Estreicher was silent, struck by that simple word and all it signified.

"Goliath," Dorothy went on, "Goliath who *never quitted him*, Goliath always *within reach of his hand*, and whom he was holding, whom he is holding at this moment. Look at him. His five fingers are clenched round the dog's collar. Do you understand? *Round its collar!*"

Once more d'Estreicher had no doubt. Dorothy's declaration immediately appeared to him to meet all the circumstances of the case. Once more she threw light on the affair. Beyond that light: nothing but darkness and contradictions.

He recovered all his coolness. His will to act instantly revived; and at the same time he saw clearly all the precautions to be taken to minimize the risks of the attempt.

He drew from his pocket a thin piece of rope, with which he bound Dorothy, and a handkerchief which he tied across her mouth.

"If you've made a mistake, darling, all the worse for you. You'll pay for it."

And he added in a sarcastic tone:

"Moreover, if you haven't made a mistake, all the worse for you just the same. I'm not the man to lose my prey."

He hailed his confederates:

"Hi, boys! Is there anyone on the road?"

"Not a soul!"

"Keep your eyes open! We'll be off in three minutes. When I whistle, bucket off to the entrance to the caves. I'll bring the young woman along."

The threat, terrible as it was, did not effect Dorothy. For her the whole drama was unfolding itself down below, between d'Estreicher and the Baron. D'Estreicher ran down from the hillocks, crossed the bridge, and ran towards the old man who was sitting on a bench on the terrace, with Goliath's head on his knee.

Dorothy felt her heart beating wildly. Not that she doubted that he would find the medal. It would be found in the dog's collar—of that she was sure. But it must be that this supreme effort to snatch a last delay could not fail.

"If the barrel of a gun doesn't appear above the top of the wall before a minute is up, d'Estreicher is my master."

And since she would rather kill herself than submit to that degradation, during that minute her life was at stake.

The respite accorded by circumstances was longer than that. D'Estreicher, having flung himself on the dog, met with an unexpected resistance from the Baron. The old man thrust him off furiously, while the dog barked and dragged himself free from the ruffian's grip. The struggle was prolonged. Dorothy followed its phases with alternating fear and hope, backing up Raoul's grandfather with all the force of her will, cursing the energy and stubbornness of the ruffian. In the end the old Baron grew tired and appeared all at once to lose interest in what might happen. One might have thought that Goliath must have suddenly fallen a victim to the same sense of lassitude. He sat down at his master's feet and let himself be handled with a kind of indifference. With trembling fingers d'Estreicher caught hold of the collar, and ran his fingers along the nail-studded leather under the dog's thick coat. His fingers found the buckle.

But he got no further. The dramatic surprise came at last. A man's bust rose above the wall, and a voice cried:

"Hands up!"

At last Dorothy smiled with an indescribable sensation of joy and deliverance. Her plan, delayed by some obstacle, was a success. Near Saint-Quentin who had been the first to appear, another figure rose above the wall, leveled a gun, and cried:

"Hands up!"

Instantly d'Estreicher abandoned his search and looked about him with an air of panic. Two other shouts rang out:

"Hands up! Hands up!"

From the points chosen by the young girl two more guns were leveled at him, and the men who aimed, aimed straight at d'Estreicher only. Nevertheless he hesitated. A bullet sang over his head. His hands went up. His confederates were already half-way to the hillocks in their flight. No one paid any attention to them. They ran across the bridge and disappeared in the direction of an isolated hillock which was called the Labyrinth.

The big gate flew open. Raoul rushed through it, followed by two men whom Dorothy did not know, but who must be the detectives dispatched on his information.

D'Estreicher did not budge; he kept his hands up; and doubtless he would not have made any resistance, if a false move of the police had not given him the chance. As they reached him they closed round him, covering him for two or three seconds from the fire of the servants on the wall. He took advantage of their error to whip out his revolver and shoot. Four times it cracked. Three bullets went wide. The fourth buried itself in Raoul's leg; and he fell to the ground with a groan.

It was a futile outburst of rage and savagery. On the instant the detectives grappled with d'Estreicher, disarmed him, and reduced him to impotence.

They handcuffed him; and as they did so his eyes sought Dorothy, who was almost out of sight, for she had slipped behind a clump of bushes; and as they sought her they filled with an expression of appalling hate.

It was Saint-Quentin, followed by the captain, who found Dorothy; and at the sight of her blood-smeared face, they were nearly beside themselves.

"Silence," she commanded, to cut short their questions. "Yes, I'm wounded. But it's a mere nothing. Run to the Baron, captain; catch hold of Goliath, pat him, and take off his collar. In the collar, you will find behind the metal plate, on which his name is engraved, a pocket, forming a lining to it and containing the metal we're looking for. Bring it to me."

The boy hurried off.

"Saint-Quentin," Dorothy continued. "Have the detectives seen me?"

"No."

"You must give everyone to understand that I left the Manor some time ago and that you're to meet me at the market-town, Roche-sur-Yon. I don't want to be mixed up with the inquiry. They'll examine me; and it will be a sheer waste of time."

"But Monsieur Davernoie?"

"As soon as you get the chance, tell him. Tell him that I've gone for reasons which I will explain later, and that I beg him to keep silent about everything that concerns us. Besides, he is wounded, and his mind is confused, and nobody will think about me. They're going to hunt through the hillocks, I expect, to get hold of d'Estreicher's confederates. They mustn't see me. Cover me with branches."

"That's all right," she said when he had done so, "As soon as it is getting dark, come, all four of you, and carry me down to the caravan; and we'll start as soon as it's daylight. Perhaps I shall be out of sorts for a few days. Rather too much overwork and excitement—nothing for you to worry about. Do you understand, my boy?"

"Yes, Dorothy."

As she had foreseen, the two detectives, having shut up d'Estreicher at the Manor, passed at no great distance from her, guided by one of the farm-servants. She presently heard them calling out and guessed that they had discovered the entrance to the caves of the Labyrinth, down which d'Estreicher's confederates had fled.

"Pursuit is useless," murmured Dorothy. "The quarry has too long a start."

She felt exhausted. But for nothing in the world would she have yielded to her lassitude before the return of the captain. She asked Saint-Quentin how the attack had come to be so long delayed.

"An accident, wasn't it?"

"Yes," said he. "The detectives made a mistake about the inn; and the farm-servants were late getting back from the fête. It was necessary to collect the whole lot; and the car broke down."

Montfaucon came running up. Dorothy went on:

"Perhaps, Saint-Quentin, there'll be the name of a town, or rather of a château, on the medal. In that case, find out all you can about the route and take the caravan there. Did you find it, captain?"

"Yes, mummy."

"Give it to me, pet."

What emotion Dorothy felt when she touched the gold medal so keenly coveted by them all, which one might reckon the most precious of talismans, as the guarantee even of success!

It was a medal twice the size of a five-franc piece, and above all much thicker, less smoothly cut than a modern medal, less delicately modeled, and of duller gold that did not shine.

On the face was the motto:

In robore fortuna,

On the reverse these lines:

July 12, 1921.

At noon. Before the clock of the Château of Roche-Périac.

"The twelfth of July," muttered Dorothy. "I have time to faint."

She fainted.

X

TOWARDS THE GOLDEN FLEECE

It was not till nearly three days afterwards that Dorothy got the better of the physical torpor, aggravated by fever, which had overwhelmed her. The four boys gave a performance on the outskirts of Nantes. Montfaucon took the place of the directress in the leading rôle. It was a less taking spectacle; but in it the captain displayed such an animated comicality that the takings were good.

Saint-Quentin insisted that Dorothy should take another two days' rest. What need was there to hurry? The village of Roche-Périac was at the most sixty-five miles from Nantes so that there was no need for them to set out till six days before the time appointed.

She allowed herself to be ordered about by him, for she was still suffering from a profound lassitude as a result of so many ups and downs and such violent emotions. She thought a great deal about Raoul Davernoie, but in a spirit of angry revolt against the feeling of tenderness towards the young man with which those weeks of intimacy had inspired her. However little he might be connected with the drama in which the Prince of Argonne had met his death, he was none the less the son of the man who had assisted d'Estreicher in the perpetration of the crime. How could she forget that? How could she forgive it?

The quiet pleasantness of the journey soothed the young girl. Her ardent and happy nature got the better of painful memories and past fatigues. The nearer she drew to her goal, the more fully her strength of mind and body came back to her, her joy in life, her childlike gayety, and her resolve to bring the enterprise to a successful end.

"Saint-Quentin," she said, "we are advancing to the capture of the Golden Fleece. Are you bearing in mind the solemn importance of the days that are passing? Four days yet... three days... two days; and the Golden Fleece is ours. Baron de Saint-Quentin, in a fortnight you will be dressed like a dandy."

"And you like a princess," replied Saint-Quentin, to whom this prospect of fortune, promising a less close intimacy with his great friend, did not seem to give any great pleasure.

She was strongly of the opinion that other trials awaited her, that there would still be obstacles to surmount and perhaps enemies to fight. But for the time being there was a respite and a truce. The first part of the drama was finished. Other adventures were about to begin. Curious and of a daring spirit, she smiled at the mysterious future which opened before her.

On the fourth day they crossed the Vilaine, the right bank of which they were henceforth to follow, along the top of the slopes which run down to the river. It was a somewhat barren country, sparsely inhabited, over which they moved slowly under a scorching sun which overwhelmed One-eyed Magpie.

At last, next day, the 11th of July, they saw on a sign-post:

Roche-Périac 12-1/2 Miles

"We shall sleep there tonight," declared Dorothy.

It was a painful stage of the journey... The heat was suffocating. On the way they picked up a tramp who lay groaning on the dusty grass. A woman and a club-footed child were walking a hundred yards ahead of them without One-eyed Magpie being able to catch them up.

Dorothy and the four boys took it in turn to sit with the tramp in the caravan. He was a wretched old man, worn out by poverty, whose rags were only held together by pieces of string. In the middle of his bushy hair and unkempt beard his eyes, however, still had a certain glow, and when Dorothy questioned him about the life he led, he confounded her by saying:

"One mustn't complain. My father, who was a traveling knife-grinder always said to me: 'Hyacinth—that's my name—Hyacinth, one isn't miserable while one's brave: Fortune is in the firm heart.'"

Dorothy concealed her amazement and said:

"That's not a weighty legacy. Did he only leave you this secret?"

"Yes," said the tramp quite simply. "That and a piece of advice: to go on the 12th of July every year, and wait in front of the church of Roche-Périac for somebody who will give me hundreds and thousands. I go there every year. I've never received anything but pennies. All the same, it keeps one going, that idea does. I shall be there tomorrow, as I was last year... and as I shall be next."

The old man fell back upon his own thoughts. Dorothy said no more. But an hour later she offered the shelter of the box to the woman and the club-footed child, whom they had at last overtaken. And questioning this woman, she learnt that she was a factory hand from Paris who was going to the church of Roche-Périac that her child's foot might be healed.

"In my family," said the woman, "in my father's time and my grandfather's too, one always did the same thing when a child was ill, one took it on the 12th of July into the chapel of Saint Fortunat at Roche-Périac. It's a certain cure."

So, by these two other channels, the legend had passed to this woman of the people and this tramp, but a deformed legend, of which there only remained a few shreds of the truth:

the church took the place of the château, Saint Fortunat of the fortune. Only the day of the month mattered; there was no question of the year. There was no mention at all of the medal. And each was making a pilgrimage towards the place from which so many families had looked for miraculous aid.

That evening the caravan reached the village, and at once Dorothy obtained information about the Château de la Roche-Périac. The only château of that name that was known was some ruins six miles further on situated on the shore of the ocean on a small peninsula.

"We'll sleep here," said Dorothy, "and we'll start early in the morning."

They did not start early in the morning. The caravan was drawn into a barn for the night; and soon after midnight Saint-Quentin was awakened by the pungent fumes of smoke and a crackling. He jumped up. The barn was on fire. He shouted and called for help. Some peasants, passing along the high road by a happy chance, ran to his assistance.

It was quite time. They had barely dragged the caravan out of the barn when the roof fell in. Dorothy and her comrades were uninjured. But One-eyed Magpie half roasted, refused firmly to let himself be harnessed; the shafts chafed her burns. It was not till seven o'clock that the caravan tottered off, drawn by a wretched horse they had hired, and followed by One-eyed Magpie. As they crossed the square in front of the church, they saw the woman and her child kneeling at the end of the porch, and the tramp on his quest. For them the adventure would go no further.

There were no further incidents. Except Saint-Quentin on the box, they went to sleep in the caravan, leaning against one another. At half-past nine they stopped. They had come to a cottage dignified with the name of an inn, on the door of which they read "Widow Amoureux. Lodging for man and beast." A few hundred yards away, at the bottom of a slope which ended in a low cliff, the little peninsula of Périac stretched out into the ocean five promontories which looked like the five fingers of a hand. On their left was the mouth of the Vilaine.

For the children it was the end of the expedition. They made a meal in a dimly lighted room, furnished with a zinc counter, in which coffee was served. Then while Castor and Pollux fed One-eyed Magpie, Dorothy questioned the widow Amoureux, a big, cheerful, talkative country-woman about the ruins of Roche-Périac.

"Ah, you're going there too, are you, my dear?" the widow exclaimed.

"I'm not the first then?" said Dorothy.

"Goodness, no. There's already an old gentleman and his wife. I've seen the old gentleman before at this time of year. Once he slept here. He's one of those who seek."

"Who seek what?"

"Who can tell? A treasure, according to what they say. The people about here don't believe in it. But people come from a long way off who hunt in the woods and turn over the stones."

"It's allowed then, is it?"

"Why not? The island of Périac—I call it an island because at high tide the road to it is covered—belongs to the monks of the monastery of Sarzeau, a couple of leagues further on. It seems, indeed, that they're ready to sell the ruins and all the land. But who'd buy them? There's none of it cultivated; it's all wild."

"Is there any other road to it but this?"

"Yes, a stony road which starts at the cliff and runs into the road to Vannes. But I tell you, my dear, it's a lost land—deserted. I don't see ten travelers a year—some shepherds, that's all."

At last at ten o'clock, the caravan was properly installed, and in spite of the entreaties of Saint-Quentin who would have liked to go with her and to whom she intrusted the children,

Dorothy, dressed in her prettiest frock and adorned with her most striking fichu, started on her campaign.

The great day had begun—the day of triumph or disappointment, of darkness or light. Whichever it might be, for a girl like Dorothy with her mind always alert and of an ever quivering sensitiveness, the moment was delightful. Her imagination created a fantastic palace, bright with a thousand shining windows, people with good and bad genies, with Prince Charmings and beneficent fairies.

A light breeze blew from the sea and tempered the rays of the sun with its freshness. The further she advanced the more distinctly she saw the jagged contours of the five promontories and of the peninsula in which they were rooted in a mass of bushes and green rocks. The meager outline of a half demolished tower rose above the tops of the trees; and here and there among them one caught sight of the gray stones of a ruin.

But the slope became steeper. The Vannes' road joined hers where it ran down a break in the cliff, and Dorothy saw that the sea, very high up at the moment, almost bathed the foot of this cliff, covering with calm, shallow water the causeway to the peninsula.

On the top were standing, upright, the old gentleman and the lady of whom the widow Amoureux had told her. Dorothy was amazed to recognize Raoul's grandfather and his old flame Juliet Assire. The old Baron! Juliet Assire! How had they been able to get away from the Manor, to escape from Raoul, to make the journey, and reach the threshold of the ruins?

She came right up to them without their even seeming to notice her presence. Their eyes were vague; and they were gazing in dull surprise at this sheet of water which hindered their progress.

Dorothy was touched. Two centuries of chimerical hopes had bequeathed to the old Baron instructions so precise that they survived the extinction of his power to think. He had come here from a distance, in spite of terrible fatigues and superhuman efforts to attain the goal, groping his way, in the dark, and accompanied by another creature, like himself, demented. And behold both of them stopped dead before a little water as before an obstacle there was no surmounting.

She said to him gently:

"Will you follow me? It's a mere nothing to go through."

He raised his head and looked at her and did not reply. The woman also was silent. Neither he nor she could understand. They were automata rather than living beings, urged on by an impulse which was outside them. They had come without knowing what they were doing; they had stopped and they would go back without knowing what they were doing.

There was no time to lose. Dorothy did not insist. She pulled up her frock and pinned it between her legs. She took off her shoes and stockings and stepped into the water which was so shallow that her knees were not wet.

When she reached the further shore the old people had not budged. With a dumfounded air they still gazed at the unforeseen obstacle. In spite of herself, with a compassionate smile, she stretched out her arms towards them. The old Baron again threw back his head. Juliet Assire was as still as a statue.

"Goodbye," said Dorothy, almost happy at their inaction and at being alone to prosecute the enterprise.

The approach to the peninsula of Périac is made very narrow by two marshes, according to the widow Amoureux reputed to be very dangerous, between which a narrow band of solid ground affords the only path. This path mounted a wooded ravine, which some faded writing on an old board described as "Bad Going" and came out to a plateau covered with gorse and heather. At the end of twenty minutes Dorothy crossed the débris of part of the old wall which ran round the château.

She slackened her pace. At every step it seemed to her that she was penetrating into a more and more mysterious region in which time had accumulated more silence and more solitude. The trees hugged one another more closely. The shade of the brushwood was so thick that no flowers grew beneath it. Who then had lived here formerly and planted these trees, some of which were of rare species and foreign origin?

The road split into three paths, goat-tracks, along which one had to walk in a stooping posture under the low branches. She chose at random the middle track of the three and passed through a series of small enclosures marked out by small walls of crumbling stone. Under heavy draperies of ivy she saw rows of buildings. She did not doubt that her goal was close at hand, and her emotion was so great that she had to sit down like a pilgrim who is about to arrive in sight of the sacred spot towards which he has been advancing ever since his earliest days.

And of her inmost self she asked this question:

"Suppose I have made a mistake? Suppose all this means nothing at all? Yes: in the little leather bag I have in my pocket, there is a medal, and on it the name of a château, and a given day in a given year. And here I am at the château at the appointed time; but all the same what is there to prove that my reasoning is sound, or that anything is going to happen? A hundred and fifty or two hundred years is a very long time, and any number of things may have happened to sweep away the combinations of which I believe I have caught a glimpse."

She rose. Step by step she advanced slowly. A pavement of different-colored bricks, arranged in a design, covered the ground. The arch of an isolated gateway, quite bare, opened high above. She passed through it, and at once, at the end of a large courtyard, she saw—and it was all she did see—the face of a clock.

A glance at her watch showed her that it was half-past eleven. There was no one else in the ruins.

And truly it seemed as if there never could be anyone else in this last corner of the world, whither chance could only bring ignorant wayfarers or shepherds in quest of pasturage for their flocks. Indeed, there were only fragments of ruins, rather than actual ruins, covered with ivy and briars—here a porch, there a vault, further on a chimney-piece, further still the skeleton of a summer-house—alone, venerable witnesses to a time at which there had been a house, with a courtyard in front, wings on both sides, surrounded by a park. Further off there stood, in groups or in fragments of avenues, fine old trees, chiefly oaks, wide-spreading, venerable, and majestic.

At one side of the courtyard, the shape of which she could make out by the position of the buildings which had crumbled to ruins, part of the front, still intact, and backed by a small hill of ruins, held, at the top of a very low first story, this clock which had escaped by a miracle man's ravages. Across its face stretched its two big hands, the color of rust. Most of the hours, engraved contrary to the usual custom in Roman figures, were effaced. Moss and wall-pellitory were growing between the gaping stones of the face. Right at the bottom of it, under cover in a small niche, a bell awaited the stroke of the hammer.

A dead clock, whose heart had ceased to beat. Dorothy had the impression that time had stopped there for centuries, suspended from these motionless hands, from that hammer which no longer struck, from that silent bell in its sheltering niche. Then she espied underneath it, on a marble tablet, some scarcely legible letters, and mounting a pile of stones, she could decipher the words: *In robore fortuna!*

In robore fortuna! The beautiful and noble motto that one found everywhere, at Roborey, at the Manor, at the Château de la Roche-Périac, and on the medal! Was Dorothy right then? Were the instructions given by the medal still valid? And was it truly a meeting-place to which one was summoned, across time and space, in front of this dead clock?

She gained control of herself and said, laughing:

"A meeting-place to which I alone shall come."

So keen was this conviction of hers that she could hardly believe that those who, like herself, had been summoned would come. The formidable series of chances, thanks to which, little by little, she had come to the very heart of this enigmatic adventure, could not logically be repeated in the case of some other privileged being. The chain of tradition must have been broken in the other families, or have ended in fragments of the truth, as the instances of the tramp and the factory hand proved.

"No one will come," she repeated. "It is five and twenty to twelve. Consequently—"

She did not finish the sentence. A sound came from the land side, a sound near at hand, distinct from those produced by the movements of the sea or the wind. She listened. It came with an even beat which grew more and more distinct.

"Some peasant... some wood-cutter," she thought.

No. It was something else. She made it out more clearly the nearer it came: it was the slow and measured step of a horse whose hoofs were striking the harder soil of the path. Dorothy followed its progress through one after the other of the inclosures of the old estate, then along the brick pavement. A clicking of the tongue of a rider, urging on his mount, at intervals came to her ears.

Her eyes fixed on the yawning arch Dorothy waited almost shivering with curiosity.

And suddenly a horseman appeared. An odd-looking horseman, who looked so large on his little horse, that one was rather inclined to believe that he was advancing by means of those long legs which hung down so far, and pulling the horse along like a child's toy. His check suit, his knickerbockers, his thick woolen stockings, his clean-shaven face, the pipe between his teeth, his phlegmatic air, all proclaimed his English nationality.

On seeing Dorothy he said to himself and without the slightest air of astonishment:

"Oh."

And he would have continued his journey if he had not caught sight of the clock. He pulled in his horse.

To dismount he had only to stand on tip-toe and his horse slipped from under him. He knotted the bridle round a root, looked at his watch, and took up his position not far from the clock.

"Here is a gentleman who doesn't waste words," thought Dorothy. "An Englishman for certain."

She presently discovered that he kept looking at her, but as one looks at a woman one finds pretty and not at all as one looks at a person with whom circumstances demand that one should converse. His pipe having gone out, he lit it again; and so they remained three or four minutes, close to one another, serious, without stirring. The breeze blew the smoke from his pipe towards her.

"It's too silly," said Dorothy to herself. "For after all it's very likely that this taciturn gentleman and I have an appointment. Upon my word, I'm going to introduce myself. Under which name?"

This question threw her into a state of considerable embarrassment. Ought she to introduce herself to him as Princess of Argonne or as Dorothy the rope-dancer? The solemnity of the occasion called for a ceremonious presentation and the revelation of her rank. But on the other hand her variegated costume with its short skirt called for less pomp. Decidedly "Rope-dancer" sufficed.

These considerations, to the humor of which she was quite alive, had brought a smile to her face. The young man observed it. He smiled too. Both of them opened their mouths, and they were about to speak at the same time when an incident stopped them on the verge of utterance. A man came out of the path into the courtyard, a pedestrian with a clean shaven face, very pale, one arm in a sling under a jacket much too large for him, and a Russian soldier's cap.

The sight of the clock brought him also to a dead stop. Perceiving Dorothy and her companion, he smiled an expansive smile that opened his mouth from ear to ear, and took off his cap, uncovering a completely shaven head.

During this incident the sound of a motor had been throbbing away, at first at some distance. The explosions grew louder, and there burst, once more through the arch, into the courtyard a motor-cycle which went bumping over the uneven ground and stopped short. The motor-cyclist had caught sight of the clock.

Quite young, of a well set-up, well-proportioned figure, tall, slim, and of a cheerful countenance, he was certainly, like the first-comer, of the Anglo-Saxon race. Having propped up his motor-cycle, he walked towards Dorothy, watch in hand as if he were on the point of saying:

"You will note that I am not late."

But he was interrupted by two more arrivals who came almost simultaneously. A second horseman came trotting briskly through the arch on a big, lean horse, and at the sight of the group gathered in front of the clock, drew rein sharply, saying in Italian:

"Gently—gently."

He had a fine profile and an amiable face, and when he had tied up his mount, he came forward hat in hand, as one about to pay his respects to a lady.

But, mounted on a donkey, appeared a fifth individual, from a different direction from any of the others. On the threshold of the court he pulled up in amazement, staring stupidly with wide-open eyes behind his spectacles.

"Is it p-p-possible?" he stammered. "Is it possible? They've come. The whole thing isn't a fairy-tale!"

He was quite sixty. Dressed in a frock-coat, his head covered with a black straw hat, he wore whiskers and carried under his arm a leather satchel. He did not cease to reiterate in a flustered voice:

"They have come!... They have come to the rendezvous!... It's unbelievable!"

Up to now Dorothy had been silent in the face of the exclamations and arrivals of her companions. The need of explanations, of speech even, seemed to diminish in her the more they flocked round her. She became serious and grave. Her thoughtful eyes expressed an intense emotion. Each apparition seemed to her as tremendous an event as a miracle. Like the gentleman in the frock-coat with the satchel, she murmured:

"Is it possible? They have come to the rendezvous!"

She looked at her watch.

Noon.

"Listen," she said, stretching out her hand. "Listen. The Angelus is ringing somewhere... at the village church..."

They uncovered their heads, and while they listened to the ringing of the bell, which came to them in irregular bursts, one would have said that they were waiting for the clock to start going and connect with the minute that was passing the thread of the minutes of long ago.

Dorothy fell on her knees. Her emotion was so deep that she was weeping.

XI

THE WILL OF THE MARQUIS DE BEAUGREVAL

Tears of joy, tears which relieved her strained nerves and bathed her in an immense peacefulness. The five men were greatly disturbed, knowing neither what to do nor what to say.

"Mademoiselle?... What's the matter, mademoiselle?"

They seemed so staggered by her sobs and by their own presence round her, that Dorothy passed suddenly from tears to laughter, and yielding to her natural impulse, she began forthwith to dance, without troubling to know whether she would appear to them to be a princess or a rope-dancer. And the more this unexpected display increased the embarrassment of her companions the gayer she grew. Fandango, jig, reel, she gave a snatch of each, with a simulated accompaniment of castanets, and a genuine accompaniment of English songs and Auvergnat ritornelles, and above all of bursts of laughter which awakened the echoes of Roche-Périac.

"But laugh too, all five of you!" she cried. "You look like five mummies. It's I who order you to laugh, I, Dorothy, rope-dancer and Princess of Argonne. Come, Mr. Lawyer," she added, addressing the gentleman in the frock-coat. "Look more cheerful. I assure you that there's plenty to be cheerful about."

She darted to the good man, shook him by the hand, and said, as if to assure him of his status: "You are the lawyer, aren't you? The notary charged with the execution of the provisions of a will. That's much clearer than you think... We'll explain it to you... You are the notary?"

"That is the fact," stammered the gentleman. "I am Maître Delarue, notary at Nantes."

"At Nantes? Excellent; we know where we are. And it's a question of a gold medal, isn't it?... A gold medal which each has received as a summons to the rendezvous?"

"Yes, yes," he said, more and more flustered. "A gold medal—a rendezvous."

"The 12th of July, 1921."

"Yes, yes—1921."

"At noon?"

"At noon."

He made as if to look at his watch. She stopped him:

"You needn't take the trouble, Maître Delarue; we've heard the Angelus. You are punctual at the rendezvous... We are too... Everything is in order... Each has his gold medal... They're going to show it to you."

She drew Maître Delarue towards the clock, and said with even greater animation:

"This is Maître Delarue, the notary. You understand? If you don't, I can speak English—and Italian—and Javanese."

All four of them protested that they understood French.

"Excellent. We shall understand one another better. Then this is Maître Delarue; he is the notary, the man who has been instructed to preside at our meeting. In France notaries represent the dead. So that since it is a dead man who brings us together, you see how important Maître Delarue's position is in the matter. You don't grasp it? How funny that is! To me it is all so clear—and so amusing. So strange! It's the prettiest adventure I ever heard of—and the most thrilling. Think now!

We all belong to the same family... We're by way of being cousins. Then we ought to be joyful like relations who have come together. And all the more because—yes: I'm right—all four of you are decorated... The French Croix de Guerre. Then all four of you have fought?... Fought in France?... You have defended my dear country?"

She shook hands with all of them, with an air of affection, and since the American and the Italian displayed an equal warmth, of a sudden, with a spontaneous movement, she rose on tip-toe and kissed them on both cheeks.

"Welcome cousin from America... welcome cousin from Italy... welcome to my country. And to you two also, greetings. It's settled that we're comrades—friends—isn't it?"

The atmosphere was charged with joy and that good humor which comes from being young and full of life. They felt themselves to be really of the same family, scattered members brought together. They no longer felt the constraint of a first meeting. They had known one another for years and years—for ages! cried Dorothy, clapping her hands. So the four men surrounded her, at once attracted by her charm and lightheartedness, and surprised by the light she brought into the obscure story which so suddenly united them to one another. All barriers were swept away. There was none of that slow infiltration of feeling which little by little fills you with trust and sympathy, but the sudden inrush of the most unreserved comradeship. Each wished to please and each felt that he did please.

Dorothy separated them and set them in a row as if about to review them.

"I'll take you in turn, my friends. Excuse me, Monsieur Delarue, I'll do the questioning and verify their credentials. Number one, the gentleman from America, who are you? Your name?"

The American answered:

"Archibald Webster, of Philadelphia."

"Archibald Webster, of Philadelphia. You received from your father a gold medal?"

"From my mother, mademoiselle. My father died many years ago."

"And from whom did your mother receive it?"

"From her father."

"And he from his and so on in succession, isn't that it?"

Archibald Webster confirmed her statement in excellent French, as if it was his duty to answer her questions:

"And so on in succession, as you say, mademoiselle. A family tradition, which goes back to we don't know when, ascribes a French origin to her family, and directs that a certain medal should be transmitted to the eldest son, without more than two persons ever knowing of its existence."

"And what do you understand this tradition to mean?"

"I don't know what it means. My mother told me that it gave us a right to a share of a treasure. But she laughed as she told me and sent me to France rather out of curiosity."

"Show me your medal, Archibald Webster."

The American took the gold medal from his waistcoat pocket. It was exactly like the one Dorothy possessed—the inscription, the size, the dull color were the same. Dorothy showed it to Maître Delarue, then gave it back to the American, and went on with her questioning:

"Number two—English, aren't you?"

"George Errington, of London."

"Tell us what you know, George Errington, of London."

The Englishman shook his pipe, emptied it, and answered in equally good French.

"I know no more. An orphan from birth, I received the medal three days ago from the hands of my guardian, my father's brother. He told me that, according to my father, it was a matter of collecting a bequest, and according to himself, there was nothing in it, but I ought to obey the summons."

"You were right to obey it, George Errington. Show me your medal. Right: you're in order... Number three—a Russian, doubtless?"

The man in the soldier's cap understood; but he did not speak French. He smiled his large smile and gave her a scrap of paper of doubtful cleanliness, on which was written: "Kourobelef, French war, Salonica. War with Wrangel."

"The medal?" said Dorothy. "Right. You're one of us. And the medal of number four—the gentleman from Italy?"

"Marco Dario, of Geneva," answered the Italian, showing his medal. "I found it on my father's body, in Champagne, one day after we had been fighting side by side. He had never spoken to me about it."

"Nevertheless you have come here."

"I did not intend to. And then, in spite of myself, as I had returned to Champagne—to my father's tomb, I took the train to Vannes."

"Yes," she said: "like the others you have obeyed the command of our common ancestor. What ancestor? And why this command? That is what Monsieur Delarue is going to reveal to us. Come Monsieur Delarue: all is in order. All of us have the token. It is now in order for us to call on you for the explanation."

"What explanation?" asked the lawyer, still dazed by so many surprises. "I don't quite know..."

"How do you mean you don't know?... Why this leather satchel... And why have you made the journey from Nantes to Roche-Périac? Come, open your satchel and read to us the documents it must contain."

"You truly believe—"

"Of course I believe! We have, all five of us, these gentlemen and myself, performed our duty in coming here and informing you of our identity. It is your turn to carry out your mission. We are all ears."

The gayety of the young girl spread around her such an atmosphere of cordiality that even Maître Delarue himself felt its beneficent effects. Besides, the business was already in train; and he entered smoothly on ground over which the young girl had traced, in the midst of apparently impenetrable brushwood, a path which he could follow with perfect ease.

"But certainly," said he. "But certainly... There is nothing else to do... And I must communicate what I know to you... Excuse me... But this affair is so disconcerting."

Getting the better of the confusion into which he had been thrown, he recovered all the dignity which befits a lawyer. They set him in the seat of honor on a kind of shelf formed by an inequality of the ground, and formed a circle round him. Following Dorothy's instructions, he opened his satchel with the air of importance of a man used to having every eye fixed on him and every ear stretched to catch his every word, and without waiting to be again pressed to speak, embarked on a discourse evidently prepared for the event of his finding himself, contrary to all reasonable expectation, in the presence of someone at the appointed rendezvous.

"My preamble will be brief," he said, "for I am eager to come to the object of this reunion. On the day—it is fourteen years ago—on which I installed myself at Nantes in the office of a notary whose practice I had bought, my predecessor, after having given me full information about the more complicated cases in hand, exclaimed: 'Ah, but I was forgetting... not that it's of any importance... But all the same... Look, my dear confrère, this is the oldest set of papers in the office... And a measly set too, since it only consists of a sealed letter with a note of instructions, which I will read to you:

Missive intrusted to the strict care of the Sire Barbier, scrivener, and of his successors, to be opened on the 12th of July, 1921, at noon, in front of the clock of the Château of Roche-Périac, and to be read in the presence of all possessors of a gold medal struck at my instance.

"There! No other explanations. My predecessor did not receive any from the man from whom he had bought the practice. The most he could learn, after researches among the old registers of the parish of Périac, was that the Sire Barbier (Hippolyte Jean), scrivener, lived at the beginning of the eighteenth century. At what epoch was his office closed? For what reasons were his papers transported to Nantes? Perhaps we may suppose that owing to certain circumstances, one of the lords of Roche-Périac left the country and settled down at Nantes with his furniture, his horses, and his household down to the village scrivener. Anyhow, for nearly two hundred years the letter intrusted to the strict care of the scrivener Barbier and his successors, lay at the bottom of drawers and pigeon-holes, without anyone's having tried to violate the secrecy enjoined by the writer of it. And so it came about that in all probability it would fall to my lot to break the seal!"

Maître Delarue made a pause and looked at his auditors. They were, as they say, hanging on his lips. Pleased with the impression he had produced, he tapped the leather satchel, and continued:

"Need I tell you that my thoughts have very often dwelt on this prospect and that I have been curious to learn the contents of such a letter? A journey even which I made to this château gave me no information, in spite of my searches in the archives of the villages and towns of the district. Then the appointed time drew near. Before doing anything I went to consult the president of the civil court. A question presented itself. If the letter was to be considered a testamentary disposition, perhaps I ought not to open it except in the presence of that magistrate. That was my opinion. It was not his. He was of the opinion that we were confronted by a display of fantasy (he went so far as to murmur the word 'humbug') which was outside the scope of the law and that I should act quite simply. 'A trysting-place beneath the elm,' he said, joking, 'has been fixed for you at noon on the 12th of July. Go there, Monsieur Delarue, break the seal of the missive in accordance with the instructions, and come back and tell me all about it. I promise you not not to laugh if you come back looking like a fool.' Accordingly, in a very sceptical state of mind, I took the train to Vannes, then the coach, and then hired a donkey to bring me to the ruins. You can imagine my surprise at finding that I was not alone under the elm—I mean the clock—at the rendezvous but that all of you were waiting for me."

The four young people laughed heartily. Marco Dario, of Genoa, said:

"All the same the business grows serious."

George Errington, of London, added:

"Perhaps the story of the treasure is not so absurd."

"Monsieur Delarue's letter is going to inform us," said Dorothy.

So the moment had come. They gathered more closely round the notary. A certain gravity mingled with the gayety on the young faces; and it grew deeper when Maître Delarue displayed before the eyes of all one of those large square envelopes which formerly one made oneself out of a thick sheet of paper. It was discolored with that peculiar shine which only the lapse of time can give to paper. It was sealed with five seals, once upon a time red perhaps, but now of a grayish violet seamed by a thousand little cracks like a network of wrinkles. In the left-hand corner at the top, the formula of transmission must have been renewed several times, traced afresh with ink by the successors of the scrivener Barbier.

"The seals are quite intact," said Monsieur Delarue. "You can even manage to make out the three Latin words of the motto."

"*In robore fortuna*," said Dorothy.

"Ah, you know?" said the notary, surprised.

"Yes, Monsieur Delarue, yes, they are the same as those engraved on the gold medals, and those I discovered just now, half rubbed out, under the face of the clock."

"We have here an indisputable connection," said the notary, "which draws together the different parts of the affair and confers on it an authenticity—"

"Open the letter—open it, Monsieur Delarue," said Dorothy impatiently.

Three of the seals were broken; the envelope was unfolded. It contained a large sheet of parchment, broken into four pieces which separated and had to be put together again.

From top to bottom and on both sides the sheet of parchment was covered with large handwriting with bold down-strokes, which had evidently been written in indelible ink. The lines almost touched and the letters were so close together that the whole had the appearance of an old printed page in a very large type.

"I'm going to read it," murmured Monsieur Delarue.

"Don't lose a second—for the love of God!" cried Dorothy.

He took a second pair of glasses from his pocket and put them on over the first, and read:

> "'*Written this day, the 12th of July, 1721 ...*'"
>
> "Two centuries!" gasped the notary and began again:
>
> "'*Written this day, the 12th of July, 1721, the last day of my existence, to be read the 12th of July, 1921, the first day of my resurrection.*'"

The notary stopped short. The young people looked at one another with an air of stupefaction.

Archibald Webster, of Philadelphia, observed:

"This gentleman was mad."

"The word resurrection is perhaps used in a symbolic sense," said Maître Delarue. "We shall learn from what follows: I will continue:

"'*My children*'..."

He stopped again and said:

"'*My children*'... He is addressing you."

"For goodness sake, Maître Delarue, do not stop again, I beg you!" exclaimed Dorothy. "All this is thrilling."

"Nevertheless..."

"No, Maître Delarue, comment is useless. We're eager to know, aren't we, comrades?"

The four young men supported her vehemently.

Thereupon the notary resumed his reading, with the hesitation and repetitions imposed by the difficulties of the text:

> "'*My children,*
>
> "'*On leaving a meeting of the Academy of the sciences of Paris, to which Monsieur de Fontenelle had had the goodness to invite me, the illustrious author of the "Discourses on the Plurality of Worlds," seized me by the arm and said:*
>
> "'*Marquis, would you mind enlightening me on a point about which, it seems, you maintain a shrinking reserve? How did you get that wound on your left hand, get your fourth finger cut off at the very root? The story goes that you left that finger at the bottom of one of your retorts, for you have the reputation, Marquis, of being something of an alchemist, and of seeking, inside the walls of your Château of Roche-Périac, the elixir of life.*'

"'I do not seek it, Monsieur de Fontenelle,' I answered, 'I possess it.'

"'Truly?'

"'Truly, Monsieur de Fontenelle, and if you will permit me to put you in possession of a small phial, the pitiless Fate will certainly have to wait till your hundredth year.'

"'I accept with the greatest pleasure,' he said, laughing—'on condition that you keep me company. We are of the same age—which gives us another forty good years to live.'

"'For my part, Monsieur de Fontenelle, to live longer does not greatly appeal to me. What is the good of sticking stubbornly to a world in which no new spectacle can surprise and in which the day that is coming will be the same as the day that is done. What I wish to do is to come to life again, to come to life again in a century or two, to make the acquaintance of my grandchildren's children, and see what men have done since our time. There will be great changes here below, in the government of empires as well as in everyday life. I shall learn about them.'

"'Bravo, Marquis!' exclaimed Monsieur de Fontenelle, who seemed more and more amused. 'Bravo! It is another elixir which will give you this marvelous power.'

"'Another,' I asserted. 'I brought it back with me from India, where, as you know, I spent ten years of my youth, becoming the friend of the priests of that marvelous country, from which every revelation and every religion came to us. They initiated me into some of their chief mysteries.'

"'Why not into all?' asked Monsieur de Fontenelle, with a touch of irony.

"'There are some secrets which they refused to reveal to me, such as the power to communicate with those other worlds, about which you have just discoursed so admirably, Monsieur de Fontenelle, and the power to live again.'

"'Nevertheless, Marquis, you claim—'

"'That secret, Monsieur de Fontenelle, I stole; and to punish me for the theft they sentenced me to the punishment of having all my fingers torn off. After pulling off the first finger, they offered to pardon me, if I consented to restore the phial I had stolen. I told them where it was hidden. But I had taken the precaution beforehand to change the contents, having poured the elixir into another phial.'

"'So that, at the cost of one of your fingers, you have purchased a kind of immortality... Of which you propose to make use. Eh, Marquis,' said Monsieur de Fontenelle.

"'As soon as I shall have put my affairs in order,' I answered; 'that is to say, in about a couple of years.'

"'You're going to make use of it to live again?'

"'In the year of grace 1921.'

"My story caused Monsieur de Fontenelle the greatest amusement; and in taking leave of me, he promised to relate it in his Memoirs as a proof of my lively imagination—and doubtless, as he said to himself, of my insanity."

Maître Delarue paused to take breath and looked round the circle with questioning eyes.

Marco Dario, of Genoa, threw back his head and laughed. The Russian showed his white teeth. The two Anglo-Saxons seemed greatly amused.

"Rather a joke," said George Errington, of London, with a chuckle.

"Some farce," said Archibald Webster, of Philadelphia.

Dorothy said nothing; her eyes were thoughtful.

Silence fell and Maître Dalarue continued:

"Monsieur de Fontenelle was wrong to laugh, my children. There was no imagination or insanity about it. The great Indian priests know things that we do not know and never shall know; and I am the master of one of the most wonderful of their secrets. The time has come to make use of it. I am resolved to do so. Last year, my wife was killed by accident, leaving me in bitter sorrow. My four sons, like me of a venturesome spirit, are fighting or in business in foreign lands. I live alone. Shall I drag on to the end an old age that is useless and without charm?

No. Everything is ready for my departure... and for my return. My old servants, Geoffrey and his wife, faithful companions for thirty years, with a full knowledge of my project, have sworn to obey me. I say goodbye to my age.

"Learn, my children, the events which are about to take place at the Château of Roche-Périac. At two o'clock in the afternoon I shall fall into a stupor. The doctor, summoned by Geoffrey, will ascertain that my heart is no longer beating. I shall be quite dead as far as human knowledge goes; and my servants will nail me up in the coffin which is ready for me. When night comes, Geoffrey and his wife will take me out of that coffin and carry me on a stretcher, to the ruins of Cocquesin tower, the oldest donjon of the Lords of Périac. Then they will fill the coffin with stones and nail it up again.

"For his part, Master Barbier, executor of my will and administrator of my property, will find in my drawer instructions, charging him to notify my four sons of my death and to convey to each of the four his share of his inheritance. Moreover by means of a special courier he will dispatch to each a gold medal which I have had struck, engraved with my motto and the date the 12th of July, 1921, the day of my resurrection. This medal will be transmitted from hand to hand, from generation to generation, beginning with the eldest son or grandson, in such a manner that not more than two persons shall know the secret at one time. Lastly Master Barbier will keep this letter, which I am going to seal with five seals, and which will be transmitted from scrivener to scrivener till the appointed date.

"When you read this letter, my children, the hour of noon on the 12th of July, 1921, will have struck. You will be gathered together under the clock of my château, fifty yards from old Cocquesin tower, where I shall have been sleeping for two centuries. I have chosen it as my resting-place, calculating that, if the revolutions which I foresee destroy the buildings in use, they will leave alone that which is already a crumbling ruin.

Then, going along the avenue of oaks, which my father planted, you will come to this tower, which will doubtless be much the same as it is today. You will stop under the arch from which the drawbridge was formerly raised, and one of you counting to the left, from the groove of the portcullis, the third stone above it, will push it straight before him, while another, counting on the right, always from the groove, the third stone above it, will do as the first is doing. Under this double pressure, exercised at the same time, the middle of the right wall will swing back inwards and form an incline, which will bring you to the bottom of a stone staircase in the thickness of the wall.

"Lighted by a torch, you will ascend a hundred and thirty-two steps, they will bring you to a partition of plaster which Geoffrey will have built up after my death. You will break it down with a pick-ax, waiting for you on the last step, and you will see a small massive door, the key of which only turns if one presses at the same time the three bricks which form part of that step.

"Through that door you will enter a chamber in which there will be a bed behind curtains. You will draw aside those curtains. I shall be sleeping there.

"Do not be surprised, my children, at finding me younger perhaps than the portrait of me which Monsieur Nicolas de Largillière, the King's painter, painted last year, and which hangs at the head of my bed. Two centuries' sleep, the resting of my heart, which will scarcely beat, will, I have no doubt, have filled up my wrinkles and restored youth to my features. It will not be an old man you will gaze upon.

"My children, the phial will be on a stool beside the bed, wrapped in linen, corked with virgin wax. You will at once break the neck of the phial. While one of you opens my teeth with the point of a knife, another will pour the elixir, not drop by drop but in a thin trickle, which should flow down to the bottom of my throat. Some minutes will pass. Then little by little life will return. The beating of my heart will grow quicker. My breast will rise and fall; and my eyes will open.

"Perhaps, my children, it will be necessary for you to speak in low voices, and not light up the room with too bright a light, that my eyes and ears may not suffer any shock. Perhaps on the other hand I shall only see you and hear you indistinctly, with enfeebled organs. I do not know. I foresee a period of torpor and uneasiness, during which I shall have to collect my thoughts as one does on awaking from sleep. Moreover I shall make no haste about it, and I beg you not to try to quicken my efforts. Quiet days and a nourishing diet will insensibly restore me to the sweetness of life.

"Have no fear at all that I shall need to live at your expense. Unknown to my relations I brought back from the Indies four diamonds of extraordinary size, which I have hidden in a hiding-place there is no finding. They will easily suffice to keep me in luxury befitting my station.

"Since I have to take into consideration that I may have forgotten the secret hiding-place of the diamonds, I have set forth the secret in some lines enclosed herein in a second envelope bearing the designation 'The Codicil.'

"Of this codicil I have not breathed a word, not even to my servant Geoffrey and his wife. If out of human weakness they bequeath to their children an account revealing my secret history, they will not be able to reveal the hiding-place of those four marvelous diamonds, which they have often admired and which they will seek in vain after I am gone.

"The enclosed envelope then will be handed over to me as soon as I return to life. In the event—to my thinking impossible, but which none the less your interests compel me to take into account—of destiny having betrayed me and of your finding no trace of me, you will yourselves open the envelope and learning the whereabouts of the hiding-place, take possession of the diamonds. Then and thereafter I declare that the ownership of the diamonds is vested in those of my descendants who shall present the gold medal, and that no person shall have the right to intervene in the fair partition of them, on which they shall agree among themselves, and I beg them to make that partition themselves as their consciences shall direct.

"I have said what I have to say, my children. I am about to enter into the silence and await your coming. I do not doubt that you will come from all the corners of the earth at the imperious summons of the gold medal. Sprung from the same stock, be as brothers and sisters among yourselves. Approach with serious minds him who sleeps, and deliver him from the bonds which keep him in the kingdom of darkness.

"Written by my own hand, in perfect health of mind and body, this day, the 12th of July, 1721. Delivered under my hand and seal.

"Jean-Pierre-Augustin de la Roche, Marquis de —"

Maître Delarue was silent, bent nearer to the paper, and murmured:

"The signature is scarcely legible: the name begins with a B or an R... the flourish muddles up all the letters."

Dorothy said slowly:

"Jean-Pierre-Augustin de la Roche, Marquis de Beaugreval."

"Yes, yes: that's it!" cried the notary at once. "Marquis de Beaugreval. How did you know?"

XII

THE ELIXIR OF RESURRECTION

Dorothy did not answer. She was still quite absorbed in the strange will of the Marquis. Her companions, their eyes fixed on her, seemed to be waiting for her to express an opinion; and since she remained silent, George Earrington, of London, said:

"Not a bad joke. What?"

She shook her head:

"Is it quite certain, cousin, that it is a joke?"

"Oh, mademoiselle! This resurrection... the elixir... the hidden diamonds!"

"I don't say that it isn't," said Dorothy, smiling. "The old fellow does seem to me a trifle cracked. Nevertheless the letter he has written to us is certainly authentic; at the end of two centuries we have come, as he foresaw that we should, to the rendezvous he appointed, and above all we are certainly members of the same family."

"I think that we might start embracing all over again, mademoiselle."

"I'm sure, if our ancestor permits it, I shall be charmed," said Dorothy.

"But he does permit it."

"We'll go and ask him."

Maître Delarue protested:

"You'll go without me, mademoiselle. Understand once and for all that I am not going to see whether Jean-Pierre-Augustin de la Roche, Marquis de Beaugreval, is still alive at the age of two hundred and sixty-two years!"

"But he isn't as old as all that, Maître Delarue. We need not count the two hundred years' sleep. Then it's only a matter of sixty-two years; that's quite normal. His friend, Monsieur de Fontenelle, as the Marquis predicted and thanks to an elixir of life, lived to be a hundred."

"In fact you do not believe in it, mademoiselle?"

"No. But all the same there should be something in it."

"What else can there be in it?"

"We shall know presently. But at the moment I confess to my shame that I should like before—"

She paused; and with one accord they cried:

"What?"

She laughed.

"Well, the truth is I'm hungry—hungry with a two-hundred-year-old hunger—as hungry as the Marquis de Beaugreval must be. Has any of you by any chance—"

The three young men darted away. One ran to his motorcycle, the other two to their horses. Each had a haversack full of provisions which they brought and set out on the grass at Dorothy's feet. The Russian Kourobelef, who had only a slice of bread, dragged a large flat stone in front of her by way of table.

"This is really nice!" she said, clapping her hands. "A real family lunch! We invite you to join us, Maître Delarue, and you also, soldier of Wrangel."

The meal, washed down by the good wine of Anjou, was a merry one. They drank the health of the worthy nobleman who had had the excellent idea of bringing them together at his château; and Webster made a speech in his honor.

The diamonds, the codicil, the survival of their ancestor and his resurrection had become so many trifles to which they paid no further attention. For them the adventure came to an end with the reading of the letter and the improvised meal. And even so it was amazing enough!

"And so amusing!" said Dorothy, who kept laughing. "I assure you that I have never been so amused—never."

Her four cousins, as she called them, hung on her lips and never took their eyes off her, amused and astonished by everything she said. At first sight they had understood her and she had understood them, without the five of them having to pass through the usual stages of becoming intimate, through which people who are thrown together for the first time generally have to pass. To them she was grace, beauty, spirit and freshness. She represented the charming country from which their ancestors had long ago departed; they found in her at once a sister of whom they were proud and a woman they burned to win.

Already rivals, each of them strove to appear at his best.

Errington, Webster, and Dario organized contests, feats of strength, exhibitions of balancing; they ran races. The only prize they asked for was that Dorothy, queen of the tourney, should regard them with favor with those beautiful eyes, of which they felt the profound seduction, and which appeared to them the most beautiful eyes they had ever seen.

But the winner of the tournament was Dorothy herself. Directly she took part in it, all that the others could do was to sit down, look on, and wonder. A fragment of wall, of which the top had crumbled so thin that it was nearly a sharp edge, served her as a tight-rope. She climbed trees and let herself drop from branch to branch. Springing upon the big horse of Dario she forced him through the paces of a circus horse. Then, seizing the bridle of the pony, she did a turn on the two of them, lying down, standing up, or astride.

She performed all these feats with a modest grace, full of reserve, without a trace of coquetry. The young men were no less enthusiastic than amazed. The acrobat delighted them. But the young girl inspired them with a respect from which not one of them dreamt of departing. Who was she? They called her princess, laughing; but their laughter was full of deference. Really they did not understand it.

It was not till three in the afternoon that they decided to carry the adventure to its end. They all started to do so in the spirit of picnickers. Maître Delarue, to whose head the good wine of Anjou had mounted in some quantity, with his broad bow unknotted and his tall hat on the back of his head, led the way on his donkey, chanting couplets about the resurrection of Marquis Lazarus. Dario, of Genoa, imitated a mandolin accompaniment. Errington and Webster held over Dorothy's head, to keep the sun off it, an umbrella made of ferns and wild flowers.

They went round the hillock, which was composed of the débris of the old château, behind the clock and along a beautiful avenue of trees centuries old, which ended in a circular glade in the middle of which rose a magnificent oak.

Maître Delarue said in the tone of a guide:

"These are the trees planted by the Marquis de Beaugreval's father. You will observe their vigor. Venerable trees, if ever there were any! Behold the oak king! Whole generations have taken shelter under his boughs. Hats off, gentlemen!"

Then they came to the woody slopes of a small hill, on the summit of which in the middle of a circular embankment, formed by the ruins of the wall that had encircled it, rose a tower oval in shape.

"Cocquesin tower," said Maître Delarue, more and more cheerful. "Venerable ruins, if ever there were any! Remnants of the feudal keep! That's where the sleeping Marquis of the enchanted wood is waiting for us, whom we're going to resuscitate with a thimbleful of foaming elixir."

The blue sky appeared through the empty windows. Whole masses of wall had fallen down. However, the whole of the right side seemed to be intact; and if there really was a staircase and some kind of habitation, as the Marquis had stated, it could only be in that part of the tower.

And now the arch, against which the drawbridge had formerly been raised opened before them. The approach to it was so blocked by interlaced briars and bushes, that it took them a long time to reach the vault in which were the stones indicated by the Marquis de Beaugreval.

Then, another barrier of fallen stones, and another effort to clear a double path to the two walls.

"Here we are," said Dorothy at last. She had directed their labors. "And we can be quite sure that no one has been before us."

Before beginning the operation which had been enjoined on them they went to the end of the vault. It opened on to the immense nave formed by the interior of the keep, its storeys fallen away, its only roof the sky. They saw, one above the other, the embrasures of four fireplaces, under chimney-pieces of sculptured stone, full now of wild plants.

One might have described it as the oval of a Roman amphitheater, with a series of small vaulted chambers above, of which one perceived the gaping openings, separated by passages into distinct groups.

"The visitors who risk coming to Roche-Périac can enter from this side," said Dorothy. "Wedding parties from the neighborhood must come here now and then. Look: there are greasy pieces of paper and sardine-tins scattered about on the ground."

"It's odd that the drawbridge vault hasn't been cleared out," said Webster.

"By whom? Do you think that picnickers are going to waste their time doing what we have done, when on the opposite side there are easy entrances?"

They did not seem in any hurry to get to work to verify the statements of the Marquis; and it was rather to have their consciences clear and to be able to say to themselves without any equivocation, "The adventure is finished," that they attacked the walls of the vault.

Dorothy, sceptical as the others, again carelessly took command, and said: "Come on, cousins. You didn't come from America and Russia to stand still with folded arms. We owe our ancestor this proof of our goodwill before we have the right to throw our medals into drawers. Dario, of Genoa—Errington, be so good as to push, each on the side you are, the third stone at the top. Yes: those two, since this is the groove in which the old portcullis worked."

The stones were a good height above the ground, so that the Englishman and the Italian had to raise their arms to reach them. Following Dorothy's advice, they climbed on to the shoulders of Webster and Kourobelef.

"Are you ready?"

"We're ready," replied Errington and Dario.

"Then push gently with a continuous pressure. And above all have faith! Maître Delarue has no faith. So I am not asking him to do anything."

The two young men set their hands against the two stones and pushed hard.

"Come: a little vigor!" said Dorothy in a tone of jest. "The statements of the Marquis are gospel truth. He has written that the stone on the right will slip back. Let the stone on the right slip back."

"Mine *is* moving," said the Englishman, on the left.

"So is mine," said the Italian, on the right.

"It isn't possible!" cried Dorothy incredulously.

"But it is! But it is!" declared the Englishman. "And the stone above it, too. They are slipping back from the top."

The words were hardly out of his mouth, when the two stones, forming one piece, slipped back into the interior of the wall and revealed in the semi-darkness the foot of a staircase and some steps.

The Englishman uttered a cry of triumph:

"The worthy gentleman did not lie! There's the staircase!"

For a moment they remained speechless. Not that there was anything extraordinary in the affair so far; but it was a confirmation of the first part of the Marquis de Beaugreval's statement; and they asked themselves if the rest of his predictions would not be fulfilled with the same exactness.

"If it turns out that there are a hundred and thirty-two steps, I shall declare myself convinced," said Errington.

"What?" said Maître Delarue, who also appeared deeply impressed. "Do you mean to assert that the Marquis—"

"That the Marquis is awaiting us like a man who is expecting our visit."

"You're raving," growled the notary. "Isn't he, mademoiselle?"

The young men hauled themselves on to the landing formed by the stones which had slipped back. Dorothy joined them. Two electric pocket-lamps took the place of the torch suggested by the Marquis de Beaugreval, and they set about mounting the high steps which wound upwards in a very narrow space.

"Fifteen—sixteen—seventeen," Dario counted.

To hearten himself, Maître Delarue sang the couplets of "da Tour, prende garde." But at the thirtieth step he began to save his breath.

"It's a steep climb, isn't it?" said Dorothy.

"Yes it is. But it's chiefly the idea of paying a visit to a dead man. It makes my legs a bit shaky."

At the fiftieth step a hole in the wall let in some light. Dorothy looked out and saw the woods of La Roche-Périac; but a cornice, jutting out, prevented her from seeing the ground at the foot of the keep.

They continued the ascent. Maître Delarue kept singing in a more and more shaky voice, and towards the end it was rather a groaning than a singing.

"A hundred... a hundred and ten... a hundred and twenty."

At a hundred and thirty-two he made the announcement:

"It is indeed the last. A wall blocks the staircase. About this also our ancestor was telling the truth."

"And are there three bricks let into the step?"

"There are."

"And a pick-ax?"

"It's here."

"Come: on getting to the top of the staircase and examining what we find there, every detail agrees with the will, so that we have only to carry out the good man's final instructions." She said: "Break down the wall, Webster. It's only a plaster partition."

At the first blow in fact the wall crumbled away, disclosing a small, low door.

"Goodness!" muttered the lawyer, who was no longer trying to dissemble his uneasiness. "The program is indeed being carried out item by item."

"Ah, you're becoming a trifle less sceptical, Maître Delarue. You'll be declaring next that the door will open."

"I do declare it. This old lunatic was a clever mechanician and a scenical producer of the first order."

"You speak of him as if he were dead," observed Dorothy.

The notary seized her arm.

"Of course I do! I'm quite willing to admit that he's behind this door. But alive? No, no! Certainly not!"

She put her foot on one of the bricks. Errington and Dario pressed the two others. The door jerked violently, quivered, and turned on its hinges.

"Holy Virgin!" murmured Dario. "We're confronted by a genuine miracle. Are we going to see Satan?"

By the light of their lamps they perceived a fair-sized room with an arched ceiling. No ornament relieved the bareness of the stone walls. There was nothing in the way of furniture in it. But one judged that there was a small, low room, which formed an alcove, from the piece of tapestry, roughly nailed to a beam, which ran along the left side of it.

The five men and Dorothy did not stir, silent, motionless. Maître Delarue, extremely pale, seemed very ill at ease indeed.

Was it the fumes of wine, or the distress inspired by mystery?

No one was smiling any longer. Dorothy could not withdraw her eyes from the piece of tapestry. So the adventure did not come to an end with the astonishing meeting of the Marquis' heirs, nor with the reading of his fantastic will. It went as far as the hollow stairway in the old tower, to which no one had ever penetrated, to the very threshold of the inviolable retreat in which the Marquis had drunk the draft which brings sleep... Or which kills. What was there behind the tapestry? A bed, of course... some garments which kept perhaps the shape of the body they had covered... and besides, a handful of ashes.

She turned her head to her companions as if to say to them: "Shall I go first?"

They stood motionless—undecided, ill at ease.

Then she took a step forward—then two. The tapestry was within reach. With a hesitating hand she took hold of the edge of it, while the young men drew nearer.

They turned the light of their lamps into the alcove.

At the back of it was a bed. On that bed lay a man.

This vision was, in spite of everything, so unexpected, that for a few seconds Dorothy's legs almost failed her, and she let the tapestry fall. It was Archibald Webster who, deeply perturbed, raised it quickly, and walked briskly to this sleeping man, as if he were about to shake him and awake him forthwith. The others tumbled into the alcove after him. Archibald stopped short at the bed, with his arm raised, and dared not make another movement.

One might have judged the man on the bed to be sixty years old.

But in the strange paleness of that wholly colorless skin, beneath which flowed no single drop of blood, there was something that was of no age. A face absolutely hairless. Not an eyelash, no eyebrows. The nose, cartilage and all, transparent like the noses of some consumptives. No flesh. A jaw, bones, cheek-bones, large sunken eyelids. That was the face between two sticking-out ears; and above it was an enormous forehead running up into an entirely bald skull.

"The finger—the finger!" murmured Dorothy.

The fourth finger of the left hand was missing, cut exactly level with the palm as the will had stated.

The man was dressed in a coat of chestnut-colored cloth, a black silk waistcoat, embroidered in green, and breeches. His stockings were of fine wool. He wore no shoes.

"He *must* be dead," said one of the young men in a low voice.

To make sure, it would have been necessary to bend down and apply one's ear to the breast above the heart. But they had an odd feeling that, at the slightest touch, this shape of a man would crumble to dust and so vanish like a phantom.

Besides, to make such an experiment, would it not be to commit sacrilege? To suspect death and question a corpse: none of them dared.

Dorothy shivered, her womanly nerves strained to excess. Maître Delarue besought her:

"Let's get away... It's got nothing to do with us... It's a devilish business."

But George Errington had an idea. He took a small mirror from his pocket and held it close to the man's lips. After the lapse of some seconds there was a film on it.

"Oh! I b-b-believe he's alive!" he stammered.

"He's alive! He's alive!" muttered the young people, keeping with difficulty their excitement within bounds.

Maître Delarue's legs were so shaky that he had to sit down on the foot of the bed. He murmured again and again:

"A devilish business! We've no right—"

They kept looking at one another with troubled faces. The idea that this dead man was alive—for he was dead, undeniably dead—the idea that this dead man was alive shocked them as something monstrous.

And yet was not the evidence that he was alive quite as strong as the evidence that he was dead? They believed in his death because it was impossible that he should be alive. But could they deny the evidence of their own eyes because that evidence was against all reason?

Dorothy said:

"Look: his chest rises and falls—you can see it—ever so slowly and ever so little. But it does. Then he is *not* dead."

They protested.

"No... It's out of the question. Such a phenomenon would be inexplicable."

"I'm not so sure... I'm not so sure. It might be a kind of lethargy... a kind of hypnotic trance," she murmured.

"A trance which lasted two hundred years?"

"I don't know... I don't understand it."

"Well?"

"Well, we must act."

"But how?"

"As the will tells us to act. The instructions are quite definite. Our duty is to execute them blindly and without question."

"How?"

"We must try to awaken him with the elixir of which the will speaks."

"Here it is," said Marco Dario, picking up from the stool a small object wrapped in linen. He unfolded the wrapping and displayed a phial, of antique shape, heavy, of crystal, with a round bottom and long neck which terminated in a large wax cork.

He handed it to Dorothy, who broke off the top of the neck with a sharp tap against the edge of the stool.

"Has any of you a knife?" she asked. "Thank you, Archibald. Open the blade and introduce the point between the teeth as the will directs."

They acted as might a doctor confronted by a patient whom he does not know exactly how to handle, but whom he nevertheless treats, without the slightest hesitation, according to the formal prescription in use in similar cases. They would see what happened. The essential thing was to carry out the instructions.

Archibald Webster did not find it easy to perform his task. The lips were tightly closed, the upper teeth, for the most part black and decayed, were so firmly wedged against the lower that the knife-point could not force its way between them. He had to introduce it sideways, and then raise the handle to force the jaws apart.

"Don't move," said Dorothy.

She bent down. Her right hand, holding the phial, tilted it gently. A few drops of a liquid of the color and odor of green Chartreuse fell between the lips; then an even trickle flowed from the phial, which was soon empty.

"That's done," she said, straightening herself.

Looking at her companions, she tried to smile. All of them were staring at the dead man.

She murmured: "We've got to wait. It doesn't work straightaway."

And as she uttered the words she thought:

"And then what? I am ready to admit that it will have an effect and that this man will awake from sleep! Or rather from death... For such a sleep is nothing but death. No: really we are the victims of a collective hallucination... No: there was no film on the mirror. No: the chest does not rise and fall. No—a thousand times no! One does *not* come to life again!"

"Three minutes gone," said Marco Dario.

And watch in hand, he counted, minute by minute, five more minutes—then five more.

The waiting of these six persons would have been incomprehensible, had its explanation not been found in the fact that all the events foretold by the Marquis de Beaugreval had followed one another with mathematical precision. There had been a series of facts which was very like a series of miracles, which compelled the witnesses of those facts to be patient—at least till the moment fixed for the supreme miracle.

"Fifteen minutes," said the Italian.

A few more seconds passed. Of a sudden they quivered. A hushed exclamation burst from the lips of each. *The man's eyelids had moved.*

In a moment the phenomenon was repeated, and so clearly and distinctly that further doubt was impossible. It was the twitching of two eyes that tried to open. At the same time the arms stirred. The hands quivered.

"Oh!" stuttered the distracted notary. "He's alive! He's alive!"

XIII

LAZARUS

Dorothy gazed; her eyes missed no slightest movement. Like her, the young men remained motionless, with drawn faces. The Italian, however, just sketched the sign of the cross.

"He's alive!" broke in Maître Delarue. "Look; he's looking at us."

A strange gaze. It did not shift; it did not try to see. The gaze of the newly born, animated by no thought. Vague, unconscious, it shunned the light of the lamps and seemed ready to be extinguished in a new sleep. On the other hand the rest of the body became instinct with life, as if the blood resumed its normal course under the impulsion of a heart which again began to beat. The arms and the hands moved with purposed movements. Then suddenly the legs slipped off the bed. The bust was raised. After several attempts the man sat up.

Then they saw him face to face; and since one of the young men raised his lamp that its light might not shine in his eyes, that lamp lit up on the wall of the alcove above the bed the portrait of which the Marquis had made mention. They could then perceive that it was indeed the portrait of the man. The same enormous brow, the same eyes deeply sunk in their orbits, the same high cheekbones, the same bony jaw, the same projecting ears. But the man, contrary to the prediction in the letter, had greatly aged and grown considerably thinner, for the portrait represented a nobleman of good appearance and sufficiently plump.

Twice he tried to stand upright without succeeding. He was too weak; his legs refused to support him. He seemed also to be laboring under a heavy oppression and to breathe with difficulty, either because he had lost the habit or because he needed more air. Dorothy observed two planks nailed to the wall, pointed them out to Dario and Webster, and signed to them to pull them down. It was easy to do so, for they were not nailed very firmly to the wall; and they uncovered a small round window, a bull's-eye rather, not more than a foot or fifteen inches across.

A whiff of fresh air blew into the room all round the man sitting on the bed; and for all that he appeared to have no understanding of anything, he turned towards the window, and opening his mouth, drew in great breaths.

All these trifling incidents were spread over a considerable time. The astonished witnesses of them had a feeling that they were taking part in the mysterious phases of a resurrection which they were wholly unable to consider final. Every minute gained by this living dead man appeared to them a new miracle which passed all imagining, and they hoped for the inevitable event which would restore things to their natural order, and which would be as it were the disarticulation and crumbling away of this incredible automaton.

Dorothy stamped her foot impatiently, as if she were struggling against herself and trying to shake off a torpor.

She turned away from this sight which fascinated her, and her face took on an expression of such profound thought, that her companions withdrew their eyes from the man to watch her. Her eyes were seeking something. Their blue irises became of a deeper blue. They seemed to see beyond what ordinary eyes see and to pursue the truth into more distant regions.

At the end of a minute or two she said:

"We must try."

She went firmly to the bed. After all here was a clear and definite phenomenon; it had to be taken into account: this man was alive. It was necessary therefore to treat him as a living being, who has ears to hear and a mouth to speak with, and who distinguishes the things about him by a personal existence. This man had a name. Every circumstance pointed directly to the fact that his presence in this sealed chamber was the result not of a miracle—a hypothesis which they need only examine as a last resort—but of an experiment that had succeeded—a hypothesis which one had no right to set aside for *a priori* reasons, however astonishing it might appear to be.

Then why not question him?

She sat down beside him, took his hands, which were cold and moist, in hers and said gravely:

"We have hastened hither at your summons... We are they to whom the gold medal—"

She stopped. The words were not coming easily to her. They seemed to her absurd and childish; and she was quite certain that they must appear so to those who heard them. But she must make an effort to continue:

"In our families the gold medal has passed from hand to hand right down to us... It is now for two centuries that the tradition has been forming and that your will—"

But she was incapable of continuing on these pompous lines. Another voice within her murmured:

"Goodness, how idiotic what I am saying is!"

However, the hands of the man were growing warm from their contact with hers. He almost wore an air of hearing the noise of her words and of understanding that they were addressed to him. And so, dropping the phrase-making, she brought herself to speak to him simply, as to a poor man whom his resurrection did not set apart from human necessities:

"Are you hungry?... Do you want to eat?... to drink? Answer. What would you like?... My friends and I will try..."

The old man, with the light full on his face, his mouth open, his lower lip hanging down, preserved a dull and stupid countenance, animated by no expression, no desire.

Without turning away from him, Dorothy called out to the notary:

"Don't you think we ought to offer him the second envelope, Maître Delarue, the codicil? His understanding may perhaps awake at the sight of this paper which formerly belonged to him, and which, according to the instructions in the will, we're to hand over to him."

Maître Delarue agreed with her and passed the envelope to her. She held it out to the old man, saying:

"Here are the directions for finding the diamonds, written by yourself. No one knows these directions. Here they are."

She stretched out her hand. It was clear that the old man tried to respond with a similar movement. She accentuated the gesture. He lowered his eyes towards the envelope; and his fingers opened to receive it.

"You quite understand?" she asked. "You are going to open this envelope. It contains the secret of the diamonds—a fortune."

Once more she stopped abruptly, as if struck by a sudden thought, something she had unexpectedly observed.

Webster said to her:

"He certainly understands. When he opens the letter and reads it, the whole of the past will come back to his memory. We may give it to him."

George Errington supported him.

"Yes, mademoiselle, we may give it to him. It's a secret which belongs to him."

Dorothy however did not perform the action she had suggested. She looked at the old man with the most earnest attention. Then she took the lamp, moved it away, then near, examined the mutilated hand, and then suddenly burst into a fit of wild laughter; it burst out with all the violence of laughter long restrained.

Bent double, holding her ribs, she laughed till it hurt her. Her pretty head shook her wavy hair in a series of jerks. And it was a laugh so fresh and so young, of such irresistible gayety that the young men burst out laughing in their turn. Maître Delarue, on the other hand, irritated by a hilarity which seemed to him out of place in the circumstances protested in a tone of annoyance:

"Really, I'm amazed... There's nothing to laugh at in all this... We are in the presence of a really extraordinary occurrence..."

His shocked air re-doubled Dorothy's merriment. She stammered:

"Yes—extraordinary—a miracle! Goodness, how funny it is! And what a pleasure it is to let one's self go! I had been holding myself in quite long enough. Yes, I was manifestly serious... uneasy... But all the same I did want to laugh!... It is all so funny!"

The notary muttered:

"I don't see anything funny in it... The Marquis—"

Dorothy's delight passed all bounds. She repeated, wringing her hands, with tears in her eyes:

"The Marquis!... The friend of Fontenelle! The revivified Marquis! Lazarus de Beaugreval! Then you didn't see?"

"I saw the film on the mirror... the eyes open."

"Yes, yes: I know. But the rest?"

"What rest?"

"In his mouth?"

"What on earth is it?"

"There's a..."

"A what? Out with it!"

"A false tooth!"

Maître Delarue repeated slowly:

"There's a false tooth?"

"Yes, a molar... a molar all of gold!"

"Well, what about it?"

Dorothy did not immediately reply. She gave Maître Delarue plenty of time to collect his wits and to grasp the full value of this discovery.

He said again in a less assured tone:

"Well?"

"Well, there you are?" she said, very much out of breath. "I ask myself, with positive anguish: did they make gold teeth in the days of Louis XIV and Louis XV?... Because, you see, if the Marquis was unable to get his gold tooth before he died, he must have had his dentist come here—to this tower—while he was dead. That is to say, he must have learnt from the newspapers, or from some other source, that he could have a false tooth put in the place of the one which used to ache in the days of Louis XIV."

Dorothy had finally succeeded in repressing the ill-timed mirth which had so terribly shocked Maître Delarue. She was merely smiling—but smiling with an extremely mischievous and delighted air. Naturally the four strangers, grouped closely round her, were also smiling with the air of people amused beyond words.

On his bed, the man, always impassive and stupid, continued his breathing exercises. The notary drew his companions out of the alcove, into the outer room so that they formed a group with their backs to the bed, and said in a low voice:

"Then, according to you, mademoiselle, this is a mystification?"

"I'm afraid so," she said, tossing her head with a humorous air.

"But the Marquis?"

"The Marquis has nothing to do with the matter," she said. "The adventure of the Marquis came to an end on the 12th of July, 1721, when he swallowed a drug which put an end to his brilliant existence for good and all. All that remains of the Marquis, in spite of his hopes of a resurrection, is: firstly, a pinch of ashes mingled with the dust of this room; secondly, the authentic and curious letter which Maître Delarue read to us; thirdly, a lot of enormous diamonds hidden somewhere or other; fourthly, the clothes he was wearing at the supreme hour when he voluntarily shut himself up in his tomb, that is to say in this room."

"And those clothes?"

"Our man is dressed in them—unless he bought others, since the old ones must have been in a very bad state."

"But how could he get here? This window is too narrow; besides it's inaccessible. Then how?..."

"Doubtless the same way we did."

"Impossible! Think of all the obstacles, the difficulties, the wall of briars which barred the road."

"Are we sure that this wall was not already pierced in some other place, that the plaster partition had not been broken down and reconstructed, that the door of this room had not been opened before we came?"

"But it would have been necessary for this man to know the secret combinations of the Marquis, the mechanical device of the two stones and so on."

"Why not? Perhaps the Marquis left a copy of his letter... or a draft of it. But no... Of course!... Better than that! We know the truth from the Marquis de Beaugreval himself... He foresaw it, since he alludes to an always possible defection of his old servant, Geoffrey, and takes into account the possibility of the good fellow's writing a description of what had taken place. This description the good fellow did write, and along different lines it has come down to our time."

"It's a simple supposition."

"It's a supposition more than probable, Maître Delarue, since besides us, besides these four young men and myself, there are other families in which the history, or a part of the history of Beaugreval, has been handed down; and as a consequence for some months I've been fighting for the possession of the indispensable gold medal stolen from my father."

Her words made a very deep impression. She entered into details:

"The family of Chagny-Roborey in the Orne, the family of Argonne in the Ardennes, the family of Davernoie in Vendée, are so many focuses of the tradition. And around it dramas, robberies, assassinations, madness, a regular boiling up of passion and violence."

"Nevertheless," observed Errington, "here there is no one but us. What are the others doing?"

"They're waiting. They're waiting for a date of which they are ignorant. They are waiting for the medal. I saw in front of the church of Roche-Périac a tramp and a factory hand, a woman, from Paris. I saw two poor mad people who came to the rendezvous and are waiting at the edge of the water. A week ago I handed over to the police a dangerous criminal of the name of d'Estreicher, a distant connection of my family, who had committed a murder to obtain possession of the gold medal. Will you believe me now when I tell you that we are dealing with an impostor?"

Dario said:

"Then the man who is here has come to play the same part as the Marquis expected to play two hundred years after his death?"

"Of course."

"With what object?"

"The diamonds, I tell you—the diamonds!"

"But since he knew of their existence, he had only to search for them and appropriate them."

"You can take it from me that he has searched for them and without ceasing, but in vain. A fresh proof that the man only knew Geoffrey's story, since Geoffrey had not been informed by his master of their hiding-place. And it is in order to learn where this hiding-place is, to be present at the meeting of the descendants of the Marquis de Beaugreval, that he is playing today, the 12th of July, 1921, after months and years of preparation, the part of the Marquis."

"A dangerous part! An impossible part!"

"Possible for at least some hours, which would be enough. What do I say, some hours? But just think: at the end of ten minutes we were all of one mind about giving him the second envelope which contains the key to the enigma, and which was probably the actual object of his enterprise. He must have known of the existence of a codicil, of a document giving directions. But where to find that document. No longer any scrivener Barbier—no longer any successors. But where to find it? Why here! At the meeting on the 12th of July. Logically, the codicil must be brought to that meeting. Logically, it would be handed over to him. And as a matter of fact I had it in my hand. I held it out to him. A second later he would have obtained from it the information he wanted. After that, goodbye. The Marquis de Beaugreval, once possessor of the diamonds of the Marquis de Beaugreval, would retire into the void, that is to say he would bolt at full speed."

Webster asked:

"Why didn't you give him the envelope? Did you guess?"

"Guess? No. But I distrusted him. In offering it to him I was above all things making an experiment. What evidence it would be against him, if he accepted my offer by a gesture of acceptance, inexplicable at the end of such a short period? He did accept. I saw his hand tremble with impatience. I knew where I was. But at the same time Fortune was kind to me; I saw that little bit of gold in his mouth."

It was all linked together in a flawless chain of reasoning. Dorothy had set forth the coördination of events, causes and effects, as one displays a piece of tapestry in which the complicated play of design and color produces the most harmonious unity.

The four young men were astounded; not one of them threw any doubt on her statement.

Archibald Webster said:

"One would think that you had been present throughout the whole adventure."

"Yes," said Dario. "The revivified Marquis played a whole comedy before you."

"What a power of observation and what terrible logic!" said Errington, of London.

And Webster added:

"And what intuition!"

Dorothy did not respond to the praise with her habitual smile. One would have said that events were happening in a manner far from pleasing to her, which seemed to promise others which she distrusted in advance. But what events? What was there to fear?

In the silence Maître Delarue suddenly cried:

"Well, for my part, I assert that you're making a mistake. I'm not at all of your opinion, mademoiselle."

Maître Delarue was one of those people who cling the more firmly to an opinion the longer they have been adopting it. The resurrection of the Marquis suddenly appeared to him a dogma he was bound to defend.

He repeated:

"Not at all of your opinion! You are piling up unfounded hypotheses. No: this man is not an impostor. There is evidence in his favor which you do not take into account."

"What evidence?" she asked.

"Well, his portrait! His indisputable resemblance to the portrait of the Marquis de Beaugreval, executed by Largillière!"

"Who tells you that this is the portrait of the Marquis, and not the portrait of the man himself? It's a very easy way of resembling anyone."

"But this old frame? This canvas which dates from earlier days?"

"Let us admit that the frame remained. Let us admit that the old canvas, instead of having been changed, has simply been painted over in such a way as to represent the false Marquis here present."

"And the cut-off finger?" exclaimed Maître Delarue triumphantly.

"A finger can be cut off."

The notary became vehement:

"Oh, no! A thousand times, no! Whatever be the attraction of the benefit to be derived, one does not mutilate oneself. No, no: your contention falls to the ground. What? You represent this fellow as ready to cut off his finger! This fellow with his dull face, his air of stupidity! But he is incapable of it! He's weak and a coward..."

The argument struck Dorothy. It threw light on the most obscure part of the business; and she drew from it exactly the conclusions it warranted.

"You're right," she said. "A man like him is incapable of mutilating himself."

"In that case?"

"In that case, someone else has charged himself with this sinister task."

"Someone else has cut off the finger? An accomplice?"

"More than an accomplice, his chief? The brain which has devised these combinations is not his. He is not the man who has staged the adventure. He is only an instrument, some common rogue chosen for his fleshless aspect. The man who holds the threads remains invisible; and he is formidable."

The notary shivered.

"One would say you knew him."

After a pause she answered slowly:

"It is possible that I do know him. If my instinct does not deceive me, the master criminal is the man who I handed over to justice, this d'Estreicher of whom I spoke just now. While he is in prison his accomplices—for there are several of them—have taken up the work he began and are trying to carry it through... Yes, yes," she added, "one can well believe that it is d'Estreicher who has arranged the whole business. He has been engaged in the affair for years; and such a machination is entirely in accord with his cunning and wily spirit. We must be on our guard against him. Even in prison he is a dangerous adversary."

"Dangerous... dangerous..." said the notary, trying to reassure himself. "I don't see what threatens us. Besides, the affair draws to its end. As regards the precious stones, open the codicil. And as far as I am concerned, my task is performed."

"It isn't a matter of knowing whether your task is performed, Maître Delarue," Dorothy answered in the same thoughtful tone. "It's a matter of escaping a danger which is not quite clear to me but which permits me to expect anything, which I foresee more and more clearly. Where will it come from? I don't know. But it exists."

"It's terrible," groaned Maître Delarue. "How are we to defend ourselves? What are we to do?"

"What are we to do?"

She turned towards the little room which served as alcove. The man no longer stirred, his head and face buried in the shadow.

"Question him. You quite understand that this super did not come here alone. They have intrusted him with this post, but the others are on the watch, the agents of d'Estreicher. They are waiting in the wings for the result of the comedy. They are spying on us. Perhaps they hear us. Question him. He is going to tell us the measures to be taken against us in case of a check."

"He will not speak."

"But he will—he will. He is in our hands; and it is entirely to his interest to win our forgiveness for the part he has played. He is one of those people who are always on the side of the stronger... Look at him."

The man remained motionless. Not a gesture. However his attitude did not look natural. Sitting as he was, half bent over, he should have lost his balance.

"Errington... Webster... light him up," Dorothy ordered.

Simultaneously the rays from the two electric lamps fell on him.

Some seconds passed.

"Ah!" sighed Dorothy, who was the first to grasp the terrible fact; and she started back.

All six of them were shocked by the same sight, at first inexplicable. The bust and the head which they believed to be motionless, were bending a little forward, with a movement which was hardly perceptible, but which did not cease. At the bottom of the orbits rose the eyes, quite round, eyes full of terror, which gleamed, like carbuncles, in the concentric fires of the two lamps. His mouth moved convulsively as if to utter a cry which did not issue from it. Then the head settled down on to the chest, dragging the bust with it. They saw for some seconds the ebony hilt of a dagger, the blade of which half buried in the right shoulder, at the junction with the neck, was streaming with blood. And finally the whole body huddled on to itself. Slowly, like a wounded beast, the man sank to his knees on the stone floor, and suddenly fell in a heap.

XIV

THE FOURTH MEDAL

Violent though this sensational turn was, it provoked from those who witnessed it neither outcries nor disorder. Something mastered their terror, smothered their words, and restrained their gestures: the impossibility of conceiving how this murder had been committed. The impossible resurrection of the Marquis was transformed into a miracle of death quite as impossible; but they could not deny this miracle since it had taken place before their eyes. In truth, they had the impression, since no living being had entered, that death itself had stepped over the threshold, crossed the room to the man, struck him in their presence with its invisible hand, and then gone away, leaving the murderous weapon in the corpse. None but a phantom could have passed. None but a phantom could have killed.

"Errington," said Dorothy, who had recovered her coolness more quickly than her companions, "there's no one on the staircase, is there? Dario, surely the window is too small for any one to slip through? Webster and Kourobelef look to the walls of the alcove."

She stooped and took the dagger from the wound. No convulsion stirred the victim's body. It was indeed a corpse. An examination of the dagger and the clothes gave no clue.

Errington and Dario rendered an account of their mission. The staircase? Empty. The window? Too narrow.

They joined the Russian and the American, as did Dorothy also; and all five of them examined and sounded the walls of the alcove with such minuteness that Dorothy expressed the absolute conviction of all of them when she declared in a tone of finality:

"No entrance. It is impossible to admit that anyone passed that way."

"Then?" stuttered the notary, who was sitting on the stool and had not moved for the excellent reason that his legs refused to be of the slightest use to him. "Then?"

He asked the question with a kind of humility as if he regretted not having admitted without opposition all Dorothy's explanations, and promised to accept all she should consent to give him. Dorothy, who had so clearly announced the peril which threatened them, and so clearly elucidated all the problems of this obscure affair, suddenly appeared to him to be a woman who makes no mistake, who cannot make any mistake. And owing to that fact he saw in her a powerful protection against the attacks which were about to ensue.

Dorothy for her part felt confusedly that the truth was prowling round her, that she was on the point of perceiving with perfect clearness that which had no form, and that it was a thing which must moreover astonish her infinitely. Why could she not guess what was hidden in the shadow? It appeared almost as if she was afraid to guess it and that she was deliberately turning away from a danger which her intelligence would have pointed out to her at once, if her womanly instincts had not suffered her to blind herself for several minutes.

Indeed, those several minutes, she lost them. Like one whom dangers surround and who does not know against which he must first defend himself, she shuffled about on one spot. She wasted time on futile phrases, keeping herself simply to the actual facts of the situation, in the hope perhaps that one of her words might strike the enlightening spark out of its flint.

"Maître Delarue, there's a death and a crime. We must therefore inform the police. However... however I think we could put it off for a day or two."

"Put it off?" he protested. "That's a step I won't take. That is a formality which admits of no delay."

"You will never get back to Périac."

"Why not?"

"Because the band which had been able to get rid under our very eyes of a confederate who was in its way, must have taken precautions, and the road which leads to Périac must be guarded."

"You believe that?... You believe that?" stuttered Maître Delarue.

"I believe it."

She answered in a hesitating fashion. At the moment she was suffering bitterly, being one of those creatures to whom uncertainty is torture. She had a profound impression that an essential element of the truth was lacking. Protected as she was in that tower, with four resolute men beside her, it was not she who directed events. She was under the constraint of the law of the enemy who was oppressing and in a way directing her as his fancy took him.

"But it's terrible," lamented Maître Delarue. "I cannot stay here forever... My practice demands my attention... I have a wife... children."

"Go, Maître Delarue. But first of all hand over to us the envelope of the codicil that I gave back to you. We will open it in your presence."

"Have you the right?"

"Why not? The letter of the Marquis is explicit: 'In the event of Destiny having betrayed me and your finding no trace of me, you will yourselves open the envelope, and learning their hiding-place, take possession of the diamonds.' That's clear, isn't it? And since we know that the Marquis is dead and quite dead, we have the right to take possession of the four diamonds of which we are the proprietors—all five of us... all five."

She stopped short. She had uttered words which, as the saying goes, clashed curiously. The contradiction of the terms she had used—four diamonds, five proprietors—was so flagrant that the young men were struck by them, and that Maître Delarue himself, absorbed as he was in other matters, received a considerable shock.

"As a matter of fact that's true: you are five. How was it we didn't notice that detail? You are five and there are only four diamonds."

Dario explained.

"Doubtless that arises from the fact that there are four men and that we have only paid attention to this number four, four strangers in contrast with you, mademoiselle, who are French."

"But you can't get away from the fact that you are five," said Maître Delarue.

"And what about it?" said Webster.

"Well, you're five; and the Marquis, according to his letter, had only four sons to whom he left four gold medals. You understand, four gold medals?"

Webster made the objection:

"He could have bequeathed four... and left five."

He looked at Dorothy. She was silent. Was she going to find in this unexpected incident the solution of the enigma which escaped him? She said thoughtfully:

"Always supposing that a fifth medal has not been fabricated since on the model of the others and then transmitted to us by a process of fraud."

"How are we to know it?"

"Let us compare our medals," she said. "An examination of them will enlighten us perhaps."

Webster was the first to present his medal:

It showed no peculiarity which gave them to believe that it was not one of the four original pieces struck by the instructions of the Marquis and controlled by him. An examination of the medals of Dario, Kourobelef, and Errington showed the same. Maître Delarue who had taken all four of them and was examining them minutely, held out his hand for Dorothy's medal.

She had taken out the little leather purse which she had slipped into her bodice. She untied the strings and stood amazed. The purse was empty.

She shook it, turned it inside out. Nothing.

"It's gone... It's gone," she said in a hushed voice.

An astonished silence followed her declaration. Then the notary asked:

"You haven't lost it by any chance?"

"No," she said. "I can't have lost it. If I had, I should have lost the little bag at the same time."

"But how do you explain it?" said the notary.

Dario intervened a trifle dryly:

"Mademoiselle has no need to explain. For you don't pretend..."

"Of course none of us supposes that mademoiselle has come here without having the right," said the notary. "In the place of four medals there are five, that's all I meant to say."

Dorothy said again in the most positive tones: "I have not lost it. From the moment it was missing—"

She was on the point of saying:

"From the moment it was missing from this purse it had been stolen from me."

She did not finish that sentence. Her heart was wrung by a sudden anguish, as she suddenly grasped the full meaning of such an accusation; and the problem presented itself to her in all its simplicity and with its only possible and exact solution:

"The four pieces of gold are there. One of them has been stolen from me. Then one of these four men is a thief."

And this undeniable fact brought her abruptly to such a vision of the facts, to a certainty so unforeseen and so formidable that she needed almost super-human energy to restrain herself. It was needful that no one should be on their guard against her, before she had considered the matter and fully taken in the tragic aspect of the situation. She accepted therefore the notary's hypothesis and murmured:

"After all... yes... that's it. You must be right, Maître Delarue, I've lost that medal... But how? I can't think in what way I could have lost it... at what moment."

She spoke in a very low voice, an absent-minded voice. The parted curls showed her forehead furrowed by anxiety. Maître Delarue and the four strangers were exchanging futile phrases; not one of them seemed worth her consideration. Then they were silent. The silence lengthened. The lamps were switched off. The light from the little window was concentrated on Dorothy. She was very pale, so pale that she was aware of it and hid her face in her hands in order to prevent them from perceiving the effects of the emotions which were racking her.

Violent emotions, which proceeded from that truth that she had had such difficulty in attaining and which was disengaging itself from the shadows. It was not by scraps that she was gathering up the revealing clues but in a mass so to speak. The clouds had been swept away. In front of her, before her closed eyes, she saw... she saw... Ah! What a terrifying fact!

However she stubbornly kept herself silent and motionless, while to her mind there presented themselves in quick succession during the course of a few seconds all the questions and all the answers, all the arguments and all the proofs.

She recalled the fact that the night before at the village of Périac the caravan had nearly been destroyed by fire. Who had started that fire? And with what motive? Might she not suppose that one of those unhoped-for helpers, who had appeared so suddenly in the very nick of time, had taken advantage of the confusion to slip into the caravan, ransack her sleeping berth, and open the little leather purse hanging from a nail.

Possessor of the medal, the chief of the gang returned in haste to the ruins of Roche-Périac and disposed his men in that peninsula, the innermost recesses of which must be known to him, and in which he had everything arranged in view of the fateful day, the 12th of July, 1921. Doubtless he had had a dress rehearsal with his confederate cast for the part of the sleeping Marquis. Final instructions. Promises of reward in the event of success. Menaces in the event of failure. And at noon he arrived quietly in front of the clock, like the other strangers, presented the medal, the only certificate of identity required, and was present at the reading of the will. Then came the ascent of the tower and the resurrection of the Marquis. In another instant she would have handed over the codicil to him; and he reached his goal. The great plot which d'Estreicher had been so long weaving attained its end. And how could she fail to observe that up to the very last minute, there had been in the working out of that plan, in the performance of unforeseen actions, necessitated by the chances, the same boldness, the same vigor, the same methodical decision? There are battles which are only won when the chief is on the battlefield.

He is here, she thought, distracted. He has escaped from prison and *he is here*. His confederate was going to betray him and join us; he killed him. *He is here*. Rid of his beard and spectacles, his skull shaved, his arm in a sling, disguised as a Russian soldier, not speaking a word, changing his bearing, he was unrecognizable. But it is certainly d'Estreicher. Now he has his eyes fixed on me. He is hesitating. He is asking himself have I penetrated his disguise... Whether he can go on with the comedy... or whether he should unmask and compel us, revolver in hand, to hand over the codicil, that is to say the diamonds.

Dorothy did not know what to do. In her place a man of her character and temper would have settled the question by throwing himself on the enemy. But a woman?... Already her legs were failing her; she was in the grip of terror—of terror also for the three young men whom d'Estreicher could lay low with three shots.

She withdrew her hands from her face. Without turning she was aware that they were waiting, *all four of them*. D'Estreicher was one of the group, his eyes fixed on her... yes, fixed on her... She felt the savage glare which followed her slightest movement and sought to discover her intentions.

She slid a step towards the door. Her plan was to gain that door, bar the enemy's way, face him, and throw herself between him and the three young men. Blockaded against the walls of the room, with escape impossible, there were plenty of chances that he would be forced to yield to the will of three strong and resolute men.

She moved yet another step, imperceptibly... then another. Ten feet separated her from the door. She saw on her right its heavy mass, studded with nails.

She said, as if the disappearance of the medal still filled her mind:

"I must have lost it... a day or two ago... I had it on my knee... I must have forgotten to put it back—"

Suddenly she made her spring.

Too late. At the very moment that she drew herself together, d'Estreicher, foreseeing it, leapt in front of the door, a revolver in either outstretched hand.

This sudden act was masked by no single word. There was no need of words indeed for the three young men to grasp the fact that the murderer of the false Marquis stood before them. Instinctively they recoiled from the menace; then on the instant pulled themselves together, and ready for the counterstroke, they advanced.

Dorothy stopped them at the moment that d'Estreicher was on the point of shooting. Drawn to her full height in front of them, she protected them, certain that the scoundrel would not pull the trigger. But he was aiming straight at her bosom; and the young men could not stir, while, his right arm outstretched, with his left hand still holding the other revolver, he felt for the lock.

"Leave it to us, mademoiselle!" cried Webster, beside himself.

"A single movement and he kills me," she said.

The scoundrel did not utter a word, he opened the door behind him, flattened himself against the wall, then slipped quickly out.

The three young men sprang forward like unleashed hounds—only to dash themselves against the obstacle of the heavy door.

XV

THE KIDNAPING OF MONTFAUCON

For a minute or two extreme confusion reigned in the room. Errington and Webster struggled furiously with the old lock. Almost past use, it worked badly from the inside. Exasperated and maddened at having let the enemy escape, they got in one another's way and their efforts only ended in their jamming it.

Marco Dario raged at them.

"Get on! Get on! What are you messing about like that for?... It's d'Estreicher, isn't it, mademoiselle? The man you spoke of? He murdered his confederate?... He stole the medal from you? Holy Virgin, hurry up, you two!"

Dorothy tried to reason with them:

"Wait, I implore you. Think. We must work together... It's madness to act at random!"

But they did not listen to her; and, when the door did open, they rushed down the staircase, while she called out to them:

"I implore you... They're below... They're watching you."

Then a whistle, strident and prolonged, rent the air. It came from without.

She ran to the window. Nothing was to be seen from it, and in despair she asked herself:

"What does that mean? He isn't calling his confederates. They're with him now. Then, why that signal?"

She was about to go down in her turn when she found herself caught by her petticoat. From the beginning of the scene, in front of d'Estreicher and his leveled revolvers, Maître Delarue had sunk down in the darkest corner, and now he was imploring her, almost on his knees:

"You aren't going to abandon me—with the corpse?... And then that scoundrel might come back!... His confederates!"

She pulled him to his feet.

"No time to lose... We must go to the help of our friends..."

"Go to their help? Stout young fellows like them?" he cried indignantly.

Dorothy drew him along by the hand as one leads a child. They went, anyhow, half-way down the staircase. Maître Delarue was sniveling, Dorothy muttering:

"Why that signal? To whom was it given? And what are they to do?"

An idea little by little took hold of her. She thought of the four children who had remained at the inn, of Saint-Quentin, of Montfaucon. And this idea so tormented her that three parts of the way down the staircase she stopped at the hole which pierced the wall, which she had noticed as they came up. After all what could an old man and a young girl do to help three young men?

"What is it?" stammered the notary. "Can one hear the f-f-f-fight?"

"One can't hear anything," she said bending down.

She squeezed herself into the narrow passage and crawled to the opening. Then, having looked more carefully than she had done in the afternoon, she perceived on her right, on the cornice, a good-sized bundle, thrust down into a crack, screened in front by wild plants. It was a rope-ladder. One of its ends was fastened to a hook driven into the wall.

"Excellent," she said. "It's evident that on occasions d'Estreicher uses this exit. In the event of danger it's an easy way to safety, since this side of the tower is opposite the entrance in the interior."

The way to safety was less easy for Maître Delarue, who began by groaning.

"Never in my life! Get down that way?"

"Nonsense!" she said. "It isn't thirty-five feet—only two storeys."

"As well commit suicide."

"Do you prefer a knife stuck in you? Remember that d'Estreicher has only one aim—the codicil. And you have it."

Terrified, Maître Delarue made up his mind to it, on condition that Dorothy descended first to make sure that the ladder was in a good state and that no rungs were missing.

Dorothy did not bother about rungs. She gripped the ladder between her legs and slid from the top to bottom. Then catching hold of the two ropes she kept them as stiff as she could. The operation was nevertheless painful and lengthy; and Maître Delarue expended so much courage on it that he nearly fainted at the lower rungs. The sweat trickled down his face and over his hands in great drops.

With a few words Dorothy restored his courage.

"You can hear them... Don't you hear them?"

Maître Delarue could hear nothing. But he set out at a run, breathless from the start, mumbling:

"They're after us!... In a minute they'll attack us!"

A side-path led them through thick brushwood to the main path, which connected the keep with the clearing in which the solitary oak stood. No one behind them.

More confident, Maître Delarue threatened:

"The blackguards! At the first house I send a messenger to the nearest police station... Then I mobilize the peasants—with guns, forks and anything handy. And you, what's your plan?"

"I haven't one."

"What? No plan? You?"

"No," she said. "I've acted rather at random, I'm afraid."

"Ah, you see clearly—"

"I'm not afraid for myself."

"For whom?"

"For my children."

Maître Delarue exclaimed:

"Gracious! You've got children?"

"I left them at the inn."

"But how many have you?"

"Four."

The notary was flabbergasted.

"Four children! Then you're married?"

"No," admitted Dorothy, not perceiving the good man's mistake. "But I wish to secure their safety. Fortunately Saint-Quentin is not an idiot."

"Saint-Quentin?"

"Yes, the eldest of the urchins... an artful lad, cunning as a monkey."

Maître Delarue gave up trying to understand. Besides, nothing was of any importance to him but the prospect of being overtaken before he had passed that narrow, devilish causeway.

"Let's run! Let's run!" he said, for all that his shortness of breath compelled him to go slower every minute. "And then catch hold, mademoiselle! Here's the second envelope! There's no reason why I should carry such a dangerous paper on me; and after all it's no business of mine."

She took the envelope and put it in her purse just as they came into the court of the clock. Maître Delarue who could move only with great difficulty, uttered a cry of joy on perceiving his donkey in the act of browsing in the most peaceful fashion in the world, at some distance from the motor-cycle and the two horses.

"You'll excuse me, mademoiselle."

He scrambled on to his mount. The donkey began by backing; and it threw the good man into such a state of exasperation that he belabored its head and belly with thumps and kicks. The donkey suddenly gave in and went off like an arrow.

Dorothy called out to him:

"Look out, Maître Delarue! The confederates have been warned!"

The notary heard the words, on the instant leaned back in the saddle, and tugged desperately at the reins. But nothing could stop the brute. When Dorothy got clear of the ruins of the outer wall, she saw him a long way off, still going hard.

Then she began to run again, in a growing disquiet: d'Estreicher's whistle had been meant for confederates posted on the mainland at the entrance to the peninsula the access to which they were guarding. She said to herself:

"In any case if I don't get through, Maître Delarue will; and it is clear that Saint-Quentin will be warned and be on his guard."

The sea, very blue and very calm, had ebbed to right and left, forming two bays on the other side of which rose the cliff of the coast. The path down the gorge was distinguishable by the dark cutting she saw in the mass of trees which covered the plateau. Here and there it rose to some height. Twice she caught sight of the flying notary.

But as in her turn she reached the line of the trees, a report rang out ahead, and a little smoke rose in the air above what must have been the steepest point in the path.

There came cries and shouts for help; then silence. Dorothy doubled her speed in order to help Maître Delarue; undoubtedly he had been attacked. But after running for some minutes at such a pace that no sound could have reached her ears, she had barely time to spring out of the path to get out of the way of the furiously galloping donkey whose rider was crouching forward on its back with his arms knotted round its neck. Maître Delarue, since his head was glued to the further side of its neck, did not even see her.

More anxious than ever, since it was clear that Saint-Quentin and his comrades would not be warned if she did not succeed in getting through the path down the gorge and over the causeway, she started to run again. Then she caught sight of the figures of two men on one of the high points of the path in front, coming towards her. They were the confederates. They had barred the road to Maître Delarue and were now acting after the manner of beaters.

She flung herself into the bushes, dropped into a hollow full of dead leaves, and covered herself with them.

The confederates passed her in silence. She heard the dull noise of their hobnailed boots, which went further and further off in the direction of the ruins; and when she raised herself, they had disappeared.

Forthwith, having no further obstacle before her, Dorothy made her way down the path, so correctly described by the board as bad going, and came to the causeway which joined the peninsula to the mainland, observed that the Baron Davernoie and his old flame were no longer on the edge of the water, mounted the slope, and hurried towards the inn. A little way from it she called out:

"Saint-Quentin!... Saint-Quentin."

Getting no answer, her forebodings re-doubled. She passed in front of the house and saw no one. She crossed the orchard, went to the barn, and jerked open the caravan door. There once more—no one. Nothing but the children's bags and the usual things.

"Saint-Quentin!... Saint-Quentin!" she cried again.

She returned to the house and this time she entered.

The little room which formed the café and in which stood the zinc counter, was empty. Overturned benches and chairs lay about the floor. On a table stood three glasses, half full, and a bottle.

Dorothy called out:

"Madame Amoureux!"

She thought she heard a groan and went to the counter. Behind it, doubled up, her legs and arms bound, the landlady was lying with a handkerchief covering her mouth.

"Hurt?" asked Dorothy when she had freed her from the gag.

"No... no..."

"And the children?" said the young girl in a shaky voice.

"They're all right."

"Where are they?"

"Down on the beach, I think."

"All of them?"

"All but one, the smallest."

"Montfaucon."

"Yes."

"Good heavens! What has become of him?"

"They've carried him off."

"Who?"

"Two men—two men who came in and asked for a drink. The little boy was playing near us. The others must have been amusing themselves at the bottom of the orchards behind the barns. We couldn't hear them. And then of a sudden one of the men, with whom I was drinking a glass of wine, seized me by the throat while the second caught hold of the little boy.

"'Not a word,' said they. 'If you speak, we'll squeeze your throttle. Where are the other nippers?'

"It occurred to me to say that they were down on the beach fishing among the rocks.

"'It's true, that, is it, old 'un?' said they. 'If you're lying, you're taking a great risk. Swear it.'

"'I swear it.'

"'And you too, nipper, answer. Where are your brothers and sisters?'

"I was terribly afraid, madam. The little boy was crying. But all the same he said, and well he knew it wasn't true:

"'They're playing down below—among the rocks.'

"Then they tied me up and said:

"'You stay there. We're coming back. And if we don't find you here, look out, mother.'

"And off they went, taking the little boy with them. One of them had rolled him up in his jacket."

Dorothy, very pale, was considering. She asked:

"And Saint-Quentin?"

"He came in about half an hour afterwards to look for Montfaucon. He ended by finding me. I told him the story: 'Ah,' said he, the tears in his eyes. 'Whatever will mummy say?' He wanted to cut my ropes. I refused. I was afraid the men would come back. Then he took down an old broken gun from above the chimney-piece, a chassepot which dates from the time of my dead father, without any cartridges, and went off with the two others."

"But where was he going?" said Dorothy.

"Goodness, I don't know. I gathered they were going along the seashore."

"And how long ago is that?"

"A good hour at least."

"A good hour," murmured Dorothy.

This time the landlady did not refuse to have her bonds untied. As soon as she was free she said to Dorothy who wished to dispatch her to Périac in search of help:

"To Périac? Six miles! But, my poor lady, I haven't the strength. The best thing you can do is to get there yourself as fast as your legs will carry you."

Dorothy did not even consider this counsel. She was in a hurry to return to the ruins and there join battle with the enemy. She set off again at a run.

So the attack she had foreseen had indeed developed; but an hour earlier—that is to say before the signal was given—and the two men were forthwith posted on the path to the causeway with the mission to establish a barrage, then at the whistle to fall back on the scene of operations.

Only too well did Dorothy understand the motive of this kidnaping. In the battle they were fighting it was not only a matter of stealing the diamonds; there was another victory for which d'Estreicher was striving with quite as much intensity and ruthlessness. Now Montfaucon, in his hands, was the pledge of victory. Cost what it might, whatever happened, admitting even that the luck turned against him, Dorothy must surrender at discretion and bend the knee. To save Montfaucon from certain death it was beyond doubt that she would not recoil from any act, from any trial.

"Oh, the monster!" she murmured. "He is not mistaken. He holds me by what I hold dearest!"

Several times she noticed, across the path, groups of small pebbles arranged in circles, or cut-off twigs, which were to her so much information furnished by Saint-Quentin. From them she learnt that the children instead of keeping straight along the path to the gorge, had turned off to the left and gone round the marsh to the seashore so betaking themselves to the shelter of the rocks. But she paid no attention to this maneuver, for she could only think of the danger which threatened Montfaucon and had no other aim than to get to his kidnapers.

She took her way to the peninsula, mounted the gorge, where she met no one, and reached the plateau. As she did so she heard the sound of a second report. Someone had fired in the ruins. At whom? At Maître Delarue? At one of the three young men?

"Ah," she said to herself anxiously. "Perhaps I ought never to have left them, those three friends of mine. All four of us together, we could have defended ourselves. Instead of that, we are far from one another, helpless."

What astonished her when she had crossed the outer wall, was the infinite silence into which she seemed to herself to enter. The field of battle was not large—a couple of miles long, at the most, and a few hundred yards across; and yet in this restricted space, in which perhaps nine or ten men were pitted against her, not a sound. Not a mutter of human speech. Nothing but the twittering of birds or the rustling of leaves, which fell gently, cautiously, as if things themselves were conspiring not to break the silence.

"It's terrible," murmured Dorothy. "What is the meaning of it? Am I to believe that all is over? Or rather that nothing has begun, that the adversaries are watching one another before coming to blows—on the one side Errington, Webster, and Dario, on the other d'Estreicher and his confederates?"

She advanced quickly into the court of the clock. There she saw still, near the two tied-up horses, the donkey, eating the leaves of a shrub, his bridle dragging on the ground, his saddle quite straight on his back, his coat shining with sweat.

What has become of Maître Delarue? Had he been able to rejoin the group of the foreigners? Had his mount thrown him and delivered him into the power of the enemy?

Thus at every moment questions presented themselves which it was impossible to answer. The shadow was thickening.

Dorothy was not timid. During the war, in the ambulances in the first line, she had grown used more quickly than many men to the bursting of shells; and the hour of bombardment did not shake her nerves. But mistress of her nerves as she was, on the other hand, she was more susceptible than a man of less courage to the influence of everything unknown, of everything that is unseen and unheard. Her extreme sensitiveness gave her a keen sense of danger; and at that moment she had the deepest impression of danger.

She went on however. An invincible force drove her on till she should find her friends and Montfaucon should be freed. She hurried to the avenue of great trees, crossed the clearing of the old solitary oak, and mounted the rising ground on which rose Cocquesin tower.

More and more the solitude and the silence troubled her. The profound silence. A solitude so abnormal that Dorothy reached the point of believing herself to be no longer alone. Someone was watching. Men were following her as she went. It seemed to her that she was exposed to all menaces, that the barrels of guns were leveled at her, that she was about to fall into the trap which her enemy had laid.

The impression was so strong that Dorothy, who knew her nature and the correctness of her presentiments, reckoned it a certainty resting on irrefutable proofs. She even knew where the ambush was awaiting her. They had guessed that her instinct, her calculations, that all the circumstances of the drama, would bring her back to the tower; and there they were awaiting her.

She stopped at the entrance of the vault. On the opposite side, above the steps which descended into the immense nave of the donjon, her enemies must be posted. Let her make a few more steps and they would capture her.

She stood quite still. She no longer doubted that Maître Delarue had been taken, and that, yielding to threats, he had disclosed the fact that the second envelope was in her hands, that second envelope without which the diamonds of the Marquis de Beaugreval would never be discovered.

A minute or two passed. No single indication allowed her to believe in the actual presence of the enemies she imagined. But the mere logic of the events demanded that they should be there. She must then act as if they were there.

By one of those imperceptible movements which seemed to have no object, without letting anything in her attitude awake the suspicion in her invisible enemies that she was accomplishing a definite action, she managed to open her purse and extract the envelope. She crumpled it up and reduced it to a tiny ball.

Then, letting her arm hang down, she went some steps into the vault.

Behind her, violently, with a loud crash, something fell down. It was the old feudal portcullis, which fell from above, came grating down its grooves, and blocked the entrance with its heavy trellis-work of massive wood.

XVI

THE LAST QUARTER OF A MINUTE

Dorothy did not turn round. She was a prisoner.

"I made no mistake," she thought. "They are the masters of the field of battle. But what has become of the others?"

On her right opened the entrance to the staircase which ascended the tower. Perhaps she might have fled up it and availed herself once more of the rope-ladder? But what use would it be? Did not the kidnaping of Montfaucon oblige her to fight to the end, in spite of the hopelessness of the conflict? She must throw herself into the arena, among the ferocious beasts.

She went on. Though alone and without friends, she found herself quite cool. As she went, she let the little ball of paper roll down her skirt. It rolled along the floor and was lost among the pebbles and dust which covered it.

As she came to the end of the vault, two arms shot out and two men covered her with their revolvers.

"Don't move!"

She shrugged her shoulders.

One of them repeated harshly:

"Don't move, or I shoot."

She looked at them. They were two subordinates, poisonous-looking rogues, dressed as sailors. She thought she recognized in them the two individuals who had accompanied d'Estreicher to the Manor. She said to them:

"The child? What have you done with the child? It was you who carried him off, wasn't it?"

With a sudden movement they seized her arms; and while one kept her covered with his revolver, the other set about the task of searching her. But an imperious voice checked them:

"Stop that. I'll do it myself."

A third personage whom Dorothy had not perceived, stepped out from the wall where enormous roots of ivy had concealed him... D'Estreicher!

For all that he was still rigged out in his disguise of a Russian soldier, he was no longer the same man. Again she found him the d'Estreicher of Roborey and Hillocks Manor. He had resumed his arrogant air and his wicked expression, and did not try to conceal his slight limp. Now that his hair and beard were shaved off, she observed the flatness of the back of his head and the apelike development of his jaw.

He stood a long while without speaking. Was he tasting the joy of triumph? One would have said rather that he felt a certain discomfort in the presence of his victim, or at least that he was hesitating in his attack. He walked up and down, his hands behind his back, stopped, then walked up and down again.

He asked her:

"Have you any weapon?"

"None," she declared.

He told his two henchmen to go back to their comrades; then once more he began to walk up and down.

Dorothy studied him carefully, searching his face for something human of which she might take hold. But there was nothing but vulgarity, baseness, and cunning in it. She had only herself to rely on. In the lists formed by the ruins of the great tower, surrounded by a band of scoundrels, commanded by the most implacable of chiefs, watched, coveted, helpless, she had as her unique resource, her subtle intelligence. It was infinitely little, and it was much, since already once before, within the walls of Hillocks Manor, placed in the same situation, and facing the same enemy, she had conquered. It was much because this enemy distrusted himself and so lost some of his advantages.

For the moment he believed himself sure of success; and his attitude displayed all the insolence of one who believes he has nothing to fear.

Their eyes met. He began:

"How pretty she is, the little devil! A morsel fit for a king. It's a pity she detests me." And, drawing nearer, he added: "It really is detestation, Dorothy?"

She recoiled a step. He frowned.

"Yes: I know... your father... Bah! Your father was very ill... He would have died in any case. So it wasn't really I who killed him."

She said:

"And your confederate... a little while ago?... The false Marquis."

He sneered:

"Don't let's talk about that, I beg you. A measly fellow not worth a single regret... so cowardly and so ungrateful that, finding himself unmasked, he was ready to betray me—as you guessed. For nothing escapes you, Dorothy, and on my word it has been child's play to you to solve every problem. I who have been working with the narrative of the servant Geoffrey, whose descendant I believe myself to be, have spent years making out what you have unraveled in a few minutes. Not a moment's hesitation. Not a mistake. You have spotted my game just as if you held my cards in your hand. And what astonishes me most, Dorothy, is your coolness at this moment. For at last, my dear, you know where we stand."

"I know."

"And you're not on your knees!" he exclaimed. "Truly I was looking to hear your supplications... I saw you at my feet, dragging yourself along the ground. Instead of that, eyes which meet mine squarely, an attitude of provocation."

"I am not provoking you. I am listening."

"Then let us regulate our accounts. There are two. The account Dorothy." He smiled. "We won't talk about that yet. That comes last. And the account diamonds. At the present moment I should have been the possessor of them if you had not intercepted the indispensable document. Enough of obstacles! Maître Delarue has confessed, with a revolver at his temple, that he gave you back the second envelope. Give it to me."

"If I don't?"

"All the worse for Montfaucon."

Dorothy did not even tremble. Assuredly she saw clearly the situation in which she found herself and understood that the duel she was fighting was much more serious than the first, at the Manor. There she expected help. Here nothing. No matter! With such a personage, there must be no weakening. The victor would be the one who should preserve an unshakable coolness, and should end, at some moment or other, by dominating the adversary.

"To hold out to the end!" she thought stubbornly. "... To the end... And not till the last quarter of an hour... but till the last quarter of the last minute."

She stared at her enemy and said in a tone of command:

"There's a child here who is suffering. First of all I order you to hand him over to me."

"Oh, indeed," he said ironically. "Mademoiselle orders. And by what right?"

"By the right given me by the certainty that before long you will be forced to obey me."

"By whom, my liege lady?"

"By my three friends, Errington, Webster, and Dario."

"Of course... of course..." he said. "Those gentlemen are stout young fellows accustomed to field sports, and you have every right to count on those intrepid champions."

He beckoned to Dorothy to follow him and crossed the arena, covered with stones, which formed the interior of the donjon. To the right of a breach, which formed the opposite entrance, and behind a curtain of ivy stretched over the bushes, were small vaulted chambers, which must have been ancient prisons. One still saw rings affixed to the stones at their base.

In three of these cells, Errington, Webster, and Dario were stretched out, firmly gagged, bound with ropes, which reduced them to the condition of mummies and fastened them to the rings. Three men, armed with rifles, guarded them. In a fourth cell was the corpse of the false Marquis. The fifth contained Maître Delarue and Montfaucon. The child was rolled up in a rug. Above a strip of stuff, which hid the lower part of his face, his poor eyes, full of tears, smiled at Dorothy.

She crushed down the sob which rose to her throat. She uttered no word of protest or reproach. One would have said, indeed, that all these were secondary incidents which could not affect the issue of the conflict.

"Well?" chuckled d'Estreicher. "What do you think of your defenders? And what do you think of the forces at my disposal? Three comrades to guard the prisoners, two others posted as sentinels to watch the approaches. I can be easy in mind, what? But why, my beauty, did you leave them? You were the bond of union. Left to themselves, they let themselves be gathered in stupidly, one by one, at the exit from the donjon. It was no use any one of them struggling... it didn't work. Not one of my men got a shadow of a scratch. I had more trouble with M. Delarue. I had to oblige him with a bullet through his hat before he'd come down from a tree in which he had perched himself. As for Montfaucon, an angel of sweetness! Consequently, you see, your champions being out of it, you can only count on yourself; and that isn't much."

"It's enough," she said. "The secret of the diamonds depends on me and on me only. So you're going to untie the bonds of my friends and set the child free."

"In return for what?"

"In return for that I will give you the envelope of the Marquis de Beaugreval."

He looked at her.

"Hang it, it's an attractive offer. Then you'd give up the diamonds?"

"Yes."

"Yourself and in the name of your friends?"

"Yes."

"Give me the envelope."

"Cut the ropes."

An access of rage seized him:

"Give me the envelope. After all I'm master. Give it me!"

"No," she said.

"I will have it... I will have that envelope!"

"No," she said, yet more forcibly.

He snatched the purse pinned to her bodice, for the top of it showed above its edge.

"Ah!" he said in a tone of victory. "The notary told me that you had put it in this... as you did the gold medal. At last I am going to learn!"

But there was nothing in the purse. Disappointed, mad with rage, he shook his fist in Dorothy's face, shouting:

"That was the game, was it? Your friends set free, I was done. The envelope, at once!"

"I have torn it up," she declared.

"You lie! One doesn't tear up a thing like that! One doesn't destroy a secret like that!"

She repeated:

"I tore it up; but I read it first. Cut the bonds of my friends; and I reveal the secret to you."

He howled:

"You lie! You lie! The envelope at once... Ah, if you think that you can go on laughing at me for very long! I've had enough of it! For the last time, the envelope!"

"No," she said.

He rushed towards the cell in which the child was lying, tore the cloak off him, seized his hair with one hand and began to swing him like a bundle he was going to throw to a distance.

"The envelope! Or I smash his head against the wall!" he shouted at Dorothy.

He was a loathsome sight. His features were distorted by a horrible ferocity. His confederates gazed at him, laughing.

Dorothy raised her hand in token of acceptance.

He set the child on the ground and came back to her. He was covered with sweat.

"The envelope," he said once more.

She explained:

"In the entrance vault... in this end of it, opening into this place... a little ball on the ground, among the pebbles."

He called one of his confederates and repeated the information to him. The man went off, running.

"It was time!" muttered the ruffian, wiping the sweat from his brow. "Look you, you shouldn't provoke me. And then why that air of defiance?" he added, as if Dorothy's coolness shamed him. "Damn it all! Lower your eyes! Am I not master here? Master of your friends... master of you... yes, of you."

He repeated this word two or three times, almost to himself and with a look which made Dorothy uneasy. But, hearing his confederate, he turned and called to him sharply.

"Well?"

"Here it is."

"You're sure? You're sure? Ah, here we are. This is the real victory."

He unfolded the crumpled envelope and held it in his hands, turning it slowly over and over as if it were the most precious of possessions. It had not been opened; the seals were intact; no one then knew the great secret which he was going to learn.

He could not prevent himself from saying aloud:

"No one... no one but me..."

He unsealed the envelope. It contained a sheet of paper folded in two, on which only three or four lines were written.

He read those lines and seemed greatly astonished.

"Oh, it's devilish clever! And I understand why I found nothing, nor any of those who have searched. The old chap was right: the hiding-place is undiscoverable."

He began to walk up and down, in silence, like a man who is weighing alternative actions. Then, returning to the cells, he said to the three guards, his finger pointing to the prisoners:

"No means of their escaping, is there? The ropes are strong. Then march along to the boat and get ready to start."

His confederates hesitated.

"Well, what's the matter with you?" said their leader.

One of them risked saying:

"But... the treasure?"

Dorothy observed their hostile attitude. Doubtless they distrusted one another; and the idea of leaving before the division of the spoil, appeared to endanger their interests.

"The treasure?" he cried. "What about it? Do you suppose I'm going to swallow it. You'll get the share you've been promised. I've sworn it. And a big share too."

He bullied all three of them, impatient to be alone.

"Hurry up! Ah, I was forgetting... Call your two comrades on duty; and all five of you carry away the false Marquis. We'll throw him into the sea. In that way he'll neither be seen nor known. Get on."

His confederates discussed the matter for a moment. But their leader maintained his ascendancy over them, and grumbling, with lowering faces, they obeyed his orders.

"Six o'clock," he said. "At seven I'll be with you so that we can get off soon after dark. And have everything ready, mind you! Set the cabin in order... Perhaps there'll be an additional passenger."

Once more he looked at Dorothy and studied her face while his confederates moved off.

"A passenger, or rather a lady passenger. What, Dorothy?"

Always impassive, she did not answer. But her suffering became keener and keener. The terrible moment drew near.

He still held the envelope and the letter of the Marquis in his hand. From his pocket he drew a lighter and lit it to read the instructions once more.

"Admirable!" he murmured almost purring with satisfaction. "A first-class idea!... As well search at the bottom of hell. Ah, that Marquis! What a man!"

He twisted the paper into a long spill and put its end in the flame. The paper caught fire. At its flame he lit a cigarette with an affectation of nonchalance, and turning toward the prisoners, he waited, with hand outstretched, till there remained of the document only a little ash which was scattered by the breath of the breeze.

"Look Webster, look Errington and Dario. This is all you'll ever see of the secret of your ancestor... a little ash... It's gone. Confess that you haven't been very smart. You are three stout fellows and you haven't been able either to keep the treasure which was waiting for you, nor to defend the pretty cousin whom you admired, open-mouthed. Hang it! There were six of us in the little room in the tower; and it would have been enough for one of you to grip hold of my collar... I was damned uncomfortable. Instead of that, what a cropper you came. All the worse for you... and all the worse for her!"

He showed them his revolver.

"I shan't need to use this. What?" he said. "You must have noticed that at the slightest movement the cords grow tighter round your throats. If you insist... it's strangulation pure and simple. A word to the wise. Now, cousin Dorothy, I'm at your service. Follow me. We're going to perform the impossible in our attempt to come to an understanding."

All resistance was futile. She went with him to the other side of the tower across an accumulation of ruins, to a chamber of which there only remained the walls, pierced with loop-holes, which he said was the ancient guardroom.

"We shall be able to talk comfortably here. Your suitors will be able neither to see nor hear us. The solitude is absolute. Look here's a grassy bank. Please sit down."

She crossed her arms and remained standing, her head straight. He waited, murmured: "As you like"; then, taking the seat he had offered her, he said:

"This is our third interview, Dorothy. The first time, on the terrace of Roborey, you refused my offers, which was to be expected. You were ignorant of the exact value of my information; and all I could seem to you was a rather odd and disreputable person, against who you were burning to make war. A very noble sentiment which imposed on the Chagny cousins, but which did not deceive me, since I knew all about the theft of the earrings. In reality you had only one object: to get rid, in view of the great windfall you hoped for, of the most dangerous competitor. And the chief proof of that is that immediately after having denounced me you hurried off to Hillocks Manor, where you would probably find the solution of the riddle, and where I was again brought up short by your intrigues. To turn young Davernoie's head and sneak the medal, such was the task you undertook, and I admiringly confess carried it out from beginning to end. Only... only... d'Estreicher is not the kind of man to be disposed of so easily. Escape, that sham fire, the recovery of the medal, the capture of the codicil, in short complete redress. At the present moment the four diamonds belong to me. Whether I take possession of them tomorrow, or in a week, or in a year, is of no consequence. They are mine. Dozens of people, hundreds perhaps, have been vainly searching for them for two centuries; there is no reason why others should find them now. Behold me then exceedingly rich... millions and millions. Wealth like that permits one to become honest... which is my intention... if always Dorothy consents to be the passenger of whom I told my men. One word in answer. Is it yes? Is it no?"

She shrugged her shoulders.

"I knew what to expect," he said. "All the same I wished to make the test... before having recourse to extreme measures."

He awaited the effect of this threat. Dorothy did not stir.

"How calm you are!" he said in a tone in which there was a note of disquiet. "However you understand the situation exactly?"

"Exactly."

"We're alone. I have as pledges, as means of acting on you, the life of Montfaucon and the lives of these three bound men. Then how comes it that you are so calm?"

She said clearly and positively:

"I am calm because I know you are lost."

"Come, come," he said laughing.

"Irretrievably lost."

"And why?"

"Just now, at the inn, after having learnt about the kidnaping of Montfaucon, I sent my three other boys to the nearest farms to bring all the peasants they met."

He sneered:

"By the time they've got together a troop of peasants, I shall be a long way off."

"They are nearly here. I'm certain of it."

"Too late, my pretty dear. If I'd had the slightest doubt, I'd have had you carried off by my men."

"By your men? No..."

"What is there to prevent it?"

"You are afraid of them, in spite of your airs of wild-beast tamer. They're asking themselves whether you didn't stay here to take advantage of the secret you have stolen and get hold of the diamonds. They would find an ally in me. You would not dare to take the risk."

"And then?"

"Then that's why I am calm."

He shook his head and in a grating voice:

"A lie, little one. Play-acting. You are paler than the dead, for you know exactly where you stand. Whether I am tracked here in an hour, or whether my men end by betraying me, makes little difference. What does matter, to you, to me, is not what happens in an hour, but what is going to happen now. And you have no doubts about what is going to happen, have you?"

He rose and standing over her, studied her with a menacing bitterness:

"From the first minute I was caught like an imbecile! Rope-dancer, acrobat, princess, thief, mountebank, there is something in you which overwhelms me. I have always despised women... not one has troubled me in my life. You, you attract me while you frighten me. Love? No. Hate... Or rather a disease... A poison which burns me and of which I must rid myself, Dorothy."

He was very close to her, his eyes hard and full of fever. His hands hovered about the young girl's shoulders, ready to throw her down. To avoid their grasp she had to draw back towards the wall. He said in a very low, breathless voice:

"Stop laughing, Dorothy! I've had enough of your gypsy spells. The taste of your lips, that's the potion that's going to heal me. Afterwards I shall be able to fly and never see you again. But afterwards only. Do you understand?"

He set his two hands on her shoulders so roughly that she tottered. However, she continued to defy him with her attitude wholly contemptuous. Her will was strained to prevent him from getting once more the impression that she could tremble in the depths of her being and grow weak.

"Do you understand?... Do you understand?" the man stuttered, hammering her arms and neck. "Do you understand that nothing can stop it? Help is impossible. It's the penalty of defeat. Today I avenge myself... and at the same time I free myself from you... When we are separated, I shall be able to say to myself: 'Yes, she hurt me, but I do not regret it. The dénouement of the adventure effaces everything.'"

He leant more and more heavily on the young girl's shoulders, and said to her with sarcastic joy:

"Your eyes are troubled, Dorothy! What a pleasure to see that! There is fear in your eyes—fear... How beautiful they are, Dorothy! This is indeed the reward of victory—just a look like that, which is full of fear—fear of me. That is worth more than anything. Dorothy, Dorothy, I love you... Forget you? What folly! If I wish to kiss your lips, it is that I may love you even more... and that you may love me... that you may follow me like a slave and like the mistress of my heart."

She touched the wall. The man tried to draw her to him. She made an effort to free herself.

"Ah!" he cried in a sudden fury, mauling her. "No resistance, my dear. Give me your lips, at once, do you hear! If not, it's Montfaucon who'll pay. Do you want me to swing him round again as I did just now? Come, obey, or I'll certainly cut across to his cell; and so much the worse for the brat's head!"

Dorothy was at the end of her forces. Her legs were bending. All her being shuddered with horror at this contact with the ruffian; and at the same time she trembled to repulse him, so great was her fear lest he should at once fling himself on the child.

Her stiff arms began to bend. The man re-doubled his efforts to force her to her knees. It was all over. He was nearly at his goal. But at that moment the most unexpected sight caught her eye. Behind him, a few feet away, something was moving, something which passed through the opposite wall. It was the barrel of a rifle leveled at him through the loop-hole slit.

On the instant she remembered that Saint-Quentin had carried away from the inn an old and useless rifle without cartridges!

She did not make a sign which could draw d'Estreicher's attention to it. She understood Saint-Quentin's maneuver. The boy threatened, but he could only threaten. It was for her to contrive the method by which that menace should as soon as d'Estreicher saw it directed against him, have its full effect. It was certain that d'Estreicher would only need a moment to perceive, as Dorothy herself perceived, the rust and the deplorable condition of the weapon, as harmless as a child's gun.

Quite clearly Dorothy perceived what she had to: to pull herself together, to face the enemy boldly, and to confuse him, were it only for a few seconds, as she had already succeeded in upsetting him by her coolness and self-control. Her safety, the safety of Montfaucon depended on her firmness. *In robore fortuna*, she thought.

But that thought she unconsciously uttered in a low voice, as one utters a prayer for protection. And at once she felt her adversary's grip relax. The old motto, on which he had so often reflected, uttered so quietly, at such a moment, by this woman whom he believed to be at bay, disconcerted him. He looked at her closely and was astounded. Never had her beautiful face worn such a serene air. Over the white teeth the lips opened, and the eyes, a moment ago terrified and despairing, now regarded him with the quietest smile.

"What on earth is it?" he cried, beside himself, as he recalled her astounding laughter near the pool at Hillocks Manor. "Are you going to laugh again today?"

"I'm laughing for the same reason: you are lost."

He tried to take it as a joke:

"Hang it! How?"

"Yes," she declared. "I told you so from the first moment; and I was right."

"You're mad," he said, shrugging his shoulders.

She noticed that he had grown more respectful, and sure of a victory which rested in her extraordinary coolness and in the absolute similarity of the two scenes, she repeated:

"You are lost. The situation really is the same as at the Manor. There Raoul and the children had gone to seek for help; and of a sudden, when you were the master, the barrel of a gun was leveled at you. Here, it is the same. The three urchins have found men. They are there, as at the Manor with their guns... You remember? They are here. The barrels of the guns are leveled at you."

"You l-l-lie!" stammered the ruffian.

"They are there," she declared in a yet more impressive tone. "I've heard my boys' signal. They haven't wasted time coming round the tower. They are on the other side of that wall."

"You lie!" he cried. "What you say is impossible!"

She said, always with the coolness of a person no longer menaced by peril, and with an imperious contempt:

"Turn round!... You'll see *their* guns leveled at your breast. At a word from me they fire! Turn round then!"

He shrunk back. He did not wish to obey. But Dorothy's eyes, blazing, irresistible, stronger than he, compelled him; and yielding to their compulsion, he turned round.

It was the last quarter of the last minute.

With all the force of her being, with a strength of conviction which did not permit the ruffian to think, she commanded:

"Hands up, you blackguard! Or they'll shoot you like a dog! Hands up! Shoot there! Show no mercy! Shoot! Hands up!"

D'Estreicher saw the rifle. He raised his hands.

Dorothy sprang on him and in a second tore a revolver from his jacket pocket, and aiming at his head, without her heart quickening a beat and with a perfectly steady hand, she said slowly, her eyes gleaming maliciously:

"Idiot! I told you plainly you were lost."

XVII

THE SECRET PERISHES

The scene had not lasted a minute; and in less than a minute the readjustment had taken place. Defeat was changed to victory.

A precarious victory. Dorothy knew that a man like d'Estreicher would not long remain the dupe of the illusion with which, by a stroke of really incredible daring, she had filled his mind. Nevertheless she essayed the impossible to bring about the ruffian's capture, a capture which she could not effect alone, and which would only become definite if she kept him awed till the freeing of Webster, Errington, and Marco Dario.

As authoritative as if she were disposing of an army corps, she gave her orders to her rescuers:

"One of you stay there with the rifle leveled, ready to fire at the slightest movement, and let the remainder of the troop go to set the prisoners free! Hurry up, now. Go round the tower. They're to the left of the entrance—a little further on."

The remainder of the troop was Castor and Pollux, unless Saint-Quentin went with them, thinking it best simply to leave his rifle, model 1870, resting in the loop-hole and aimed directly at the ruffian.

"They are going... They are entering... They are searching," she said to herself, trying to follow the movements of the children.

But she saw d'Estreicher's tense face little by little relax. He had looked at the barrel of the rifle. He had heard the quiet steps of the children, so different from the row which a band of peasants would have made. Soon she no longer doubted that the ruffian would escape before the others came.

The last of his hesitation vanished; he let his arms fall, grinding his teeth.

"Sold!" he said. "It's those brats and the rifle is nothing but old iron! My God, you have a nerve!"

"Am I to shoot?"

"Come off it! A girl like you kills to defend herself, not for killing's sake. To hand me over to justice? Will that give you back the diamonds? I would rather have my tongue torn out and be roasted over a slow fire than divulge the secret. They're mine. I'll take them when I please."

"One step forward and I shoot."

"Right, you've won the party. I'm off."

He listened.

"The brats are gabbling over yonder. By the time they've untied them, I shall be a long way off. *Au revoir...* We shall meet again."

"No," she said.

"Yes. I shall have the last word. The diamonds first. The love affair afterwards. I did wrong to mix the two."

She shook her head.

"You will not have the diamonds. Would I let you go, if I weren't sure? But, and I've told you so: you are lost."

"Lost? And why?" he sneered.

"I feel it."

He was about to reply. But the sound of voices nearer came to their ears. He leapt out of the guardroom and ran for it, bending low, through the bushes.

Dorothy, who had darted after him, aimed at him, with a sudden determination to bring him down. But, after a moment's hesitation, she lowered her weapon, murmuring:

"No, no. I cannot... I cannot. And then what good would it be? Anyhow my father will be avenged..."

She went towards her friends. The boys had had great difficulty in freeing them, so tangled was the network of cords that bound them. Webster was the first to get to his feet and run to meet her.

"Where is he?"

"Gone," she said.

"What! You had a revolver and you let him get away?"

Errington came up, then Dario, both furious.

"He has got away? Is it possible? But which way did he go?"

Webster snatched Dorothy's weapon.

"You hadn't the heart to kill him? Was that it?"

"I had not," said Dorothy.

"A blackguard like that! A murderer! Ah well, that's not our way, I swear. Here we are, friends."

Dorothy barred their way.

"And his confederates? There are five or six of them besides d'Estreicher—all armed with rifles."

"All the better," said the American. "There are seven shots in the revolver."

"I beg you," she said, fearing the result of an unequal battle. "I beg you... Besides, it's too late... They must have got on board their boat."

"We'll see about that."

The three young men set out in pursuit. She would have liked to go with them, but Montfaucon clung to her skirt, sobbing, his legs still hampered by his bonds.

"Mummy... mummy... don't go away... I was so frightened!"

She no longer thought of anything but him, took him on her knees, and consoled him.

"You mustn't cry, Captain dear. It's all over. That nasty man won't come back any more. Have you thanked Saint-Quentin? And your comrades Castor and Pollux? Where would we have been without them, my darling?"

She kissed the three boys tenderly.

"Yes! Where would we have been? Ah, Saint-Quentin, the idea of the rifle... What a find! You are a splendid fellow, old chap! Come and be kissed again! And tell me how you managed to get to us? I didn't miss the little heaps of pebbles that you sowed along the path from the inn. But why did you go round the marsh? Did you hope to get to the ruins of the château by going along the beach at the foot of the cliffs?"

"Yes, mummy," replied Saint-Quentin, very proud at being so complimented by her, and deeply moved by her kisses.

"And wasn't it impossible?"

"Yes. But I found a better way... on the sand, a little boat, which we pushed into the sea."

"And you had the courage, the three of you, and the strength to row? It must have taken you an hour?"

"An hour and a half, mummy. There were heaps of sandbanks which blocked our way. At last we landed not far from here in sight of the tower. And when we got here I recognized the voice of d'Estreicher."

"Ah, my poor, dear darlings!"

Again there was a deluge of kisses, which she rained right and left on the cheeks of Saint-Quentin, Castor's forehead, and the Captain's head. And she laughed! And she sang! It was so good to be alive. So good to be no longer face to face with a brute who gripped your wrists and sullied you with his abominable leer! But she suddenly broke off in the middle of these transports.

"And Maître Delarue? I was forgetting him!"

He was lying at the back of his cell behind a rampart of tall grasses.

"Attend to him! Quick, Saint-Quentin, cut his ropes. Goodness! He has fainted. Look here, Maître Delarue, you come to your senses. If not, I leave you."

"Leave me!" cried the notary, suddenly waking up. "But you've no right! The enemy—"

"The enemy has run away, Maître Delarue."

"He may come back. These are terrible people. Look at the hole their chief made in my hat! The donkey finished by throwing me off, just at the entrance to the ruins. I took refuge in a tree and refused to come down. I didn't stay there long. The ruffian knocked my hat off with a bullet."

"Are you dead?"

"No. But I'm suffering from internal pains and bruises."

"That will soon pass off, Maître Delarue. Tomorrow there won't be anything left, I assure you. Saint-Quentin, I put Maître Delarue in your charge. And yours, too, Montfaucon. Rub him."

She hurried off with the intention of joining her three friends, whose badly conducted expedition worried her. Starting out at random, without any plan of attack, they ran the risk once more of letting themselves be taken one by one.

Happily for them, the young men did not know the place where d'Estreicher's boat was moored; and though the portion of the peninsula situated beyond the ruins was of no great extent, since they were at once hampered by masses of rock which formed veritable barriers, she found all three of them. Each of them had lost his way in the labyrinth of little paths, and each of them, without knowing it, was returning to the tower.

Dorothy, who had a finer sense of orientation, did not lose her way. She had a flair for the little paths which led nowhere, and instinctively chose those which led to her goal. Moreover she soon discovered footprints. It was the path followed regularly by the band in going to and fro between the ruins and the sea. It was no longer possible to go astray.

But at this point they heard cries which came from a point straight ahead of them. Then the path turned sharply and ran to the right. A pile of rocks had necessitated this change of direction, abrupt and rugged rocks. Nevertheless they scaled them to avoid making the apparently long detour.

Dario who was the most agile and leading, suddenly exclaimed:

"I see them! They're all on the boat... But what the devil are they doing?"

Webster joined him, revolver in hand:

"Yes, I see them too! Let's run down... We shall be nearer to them."

Before them was the extremity of the plateau, on which the rocks stood, on a promontory, a hundred and twenty feet high, which commanded the beach. Two very high granite needles formed as it were the pillars of an open door, through which they saw the blue expanse of the ocean.

"Look out! Down with you!" commanded Dorothy, dropping full length on the ground.

The others flattened themselves against the rocky walls.

A hundred and fifty yards in front of them, on the deck of a large motor fishing-boat, there was a group of five men; and among them a woman was gesticulating. On seeing Dorothy and her friends, one of the men turned sharply, brought his rifle to his shoulder, and fired. A splinter of granite flew from the wall near Errington.

"Halt there! Or I'll shoot again!" cried the man who had fired.

Dorothy checked her companions.

"What are you going to do? The cliff is perpendicular. You don't mean to jump into the empty air?"

"No, but we can get back to the road and go round," Dario proposed.

"I forbid you to stir. It would be madness."

Webster lost his temper:

"I've a revolver!"

"They have rifles, they have. Besides, you would get there too late. The drama would be over."

"What drama?"

"Look."

Dominated by her, they remained quiet, sheltered from the bullets. Below them developed, like a performance at which they were compelled to be present without taking part in it, what Dorothy had called the drama; and all at once they grasped its tragic horror.

The big boat was rocking beside a natural quay which formed the landing-place of a peaceful little creek. The woman and the five men were bending over an inert body which appeared to be bound with bands of red wool. The woman was apostrophizing this sixth individual, shaking her fists in his face, and heaping abuse on him, of which only a few words reached the ears of the young people.

"Thief!... Coward!... You refuse, do you?... You wait a minute!"

She gave some orders with regard to an operation, for which everything was ready, for the young people perceived, when the group of ruffians broke up, that the end of a long rope which ran over the mainyard, was round the prisoner's neck. Two men caught hold of the other end of it.

The inert body was set on its feet. It stood upright for a few seconds, like a doll one is about to make dance. Then, gently, without a jerk, they drew it up a yard from the deck.

"D'Estreicher!" murmured one of the young men recognizing the Russian soldier's cap.

Dorothy recalled with a shudder the prediction she had made to her enemy directly after their meeting at the Château de Roborey. She said in a low voice:

"Yes, d'Estreicher."

"What do they want from him?"

"They want to get the diamonds from him."

"But he hasn't got them."

"No. But they may believe he has them. I suspected that that was what they had in mind. I noticed the savage expression of their faces and the glances they exchanged as they left the ruins by d'Estreicher's orders. They obeyed him in order to prepare the trap into which he has fallen."

Below, the figure only remained suspended from the yard for an instant. They lowered the doll. Then they drew it up again twice; and the woman yelled:

"Will you speak?... The treasure you promised us?... What have you done with it?"

Beside Dorothy, Webster muttered:

"It isn't possible! We can't allow them to..."

"What?" said Dorothy. "You wanted to kill him a little while ago... Do you want to save him now?"

Webster and his friends did not quite know what they wanted. But they refused to remain inactive any longer in presence of this heartrending spectacle. The cliff was perpendicular, but there were fissures and runlets of sand in it. Webster, seeing that the man with the rifle was no longer paying any attention to them, risked the descent. Dario and Errington followed him.

The attempt was vain. The gang had no intention of fighting. The woman started the motor. When the three young men set foot on the sand of the beach, the boat was moving out to sea, with the engine going full speed. The American vainly fired the seven shots in his revolver.

He was furious; and he said to Dorothy who got down to him:

"All the same... all the same we should have acted differently... There goes a band of rogues, clearing off under our very eyes."

"What can we do?" said Dorothy. "Isn't the chief culprit punished? When they're out to sea, they'll search him again, and once certain that his pockets are really empty, that he knows the secret and will not reveal it, they'll throw their chief into the sea, along with the false Marquis, whose corpse is actually at the bottom of the hold."

"And that's enough for you? The punishment of d'Estreicher?"

"Yes."

"You hate him intensely then?"

"He murdered my father," she said.

The young men bowed gravely. Then Dario resumed:

"But the others?..."

"Let them go and get hanged somewhere else! It's much better for us. The band arrested and handed over to justice would have meant an inquiry, a trial, the whole adventure spread broadcast. Was that to our interest? The Marquis de Beaugreval advised us to settle our affairs among ourselves."

Errington sighed:

"Our affairs are all settled. The secret of the diamonds is lost."

Far away, northwards, towards Brittany, the boat was moving away.

That same evening, towards nine o'clock, after having intrusted Maître Delarue to the care of the widow Amoureux—all he thought of was getting a good night's rest and returning to his office as quickly as possible—and after having enjoined on the widow absolute silence about the assault of which she had been the victim, Errington and Dario harnessed their horses to the caravan. Saint-Quentin led One-eyed Magpie behind it. They returned by the stony path up the gorge to the ruins of Roche-Périac. Dorothy and the children resumed possession of their lodging. The three young men installed themselves in the cells of the tower.

Next morning, early, Archibald Webster mounted his motorcycle. He did not return till noon.

"I've come from Sarzeau," he said. "I have seen the monks of the abbey. I have bought from them the ruins of Roche-Périac."

"Heavens!" cried Dorothy. "Do you mean to end your days here?"

"No; but Errington, Dario, and I wish to search in peace; and for peace there is no place like home."

"Archibald Webster, you seem to be very rich; are you as firmly bent on finding the diamonds as all that?"

"I'm bent on this business of our ancestor Beaugreval ending as it ought to end, and that chance shouldn't, some day or other, give those diamonds to someone, without any right to them, who happens to come along. Will you help us, Dorothy?"

"Goodness, no."

"Hang it! Why not?"

"Because as far as I am concerned, the adventure came to an end with the punishment of the culprit."

They looked downcast.

"Nevertheless you're staying on?"

"Yes, I need rest and my four boys need it too. Twelve days here, leading the family life with you, will do us a world of good. On the twenty-fourth of July, in the morning, I'm off."

"The date is fixed?"

"Yes."

"For us, too?"

"Yes. I'm taking you with me."

"And to where do we travel?"

"An old Manor in Vendée where, at the end of July, other descendants of the lord of Beaugreval will find themselves gathered together. I'm eager to introduce you to our cousins Davernoie and Chagny-Roborey. After that you will be at liberty to return here... to bury yourselves with the diamonds of Golconda."

"Along with you, Dorothy?"

"Without me."

"In that case," said Webster, "I sell my ruins."

For the three young men those few days were a continuous enchantment. During the morning they searched, without any kind of method be it said, and with an ardor that lessened all the more quickly because Dorothy did not take part in their investigations. Really they were only waiting for the moment when they would be with her again. They lunched together, near the caravan, which Dorothy had established under the shade of the big oak which commanded the avenue of trees.

A delightful meal, followed by an afternoon no less delightful, and by an evening which they would have willingly prolonged till the coming of dawn. Not a cloud in the sky spoilt the beautiful weather. Not a traveler tried to make his way into their domain or pass beyond the notice they had nailed to a branch: "Private property. Man-traps."

They lived by themselves, with the four boys with whom they had become the warmest friends, and in whose games they took part, all seven of them in an ecstasy before her whom they called the wonderful Dorothy.

She charmed and dazzled them. Her presence of mind during the painful day of the 12th of July, her coolness in the chamber in the tower, her journey to the inn, her unyielding struggle against d'Estreicher, her courage, her gayety, were so many things that awoke in them an astounded admiration. She seemed to them the most natural and the most mysterious of creatures. For all that she lavished explanations on them and told them all about her childhood, her life as nurse, her life as showman, the events at the Château de Roborey and Hillocks Manor, they could not bring themselves to grasp the fact that she was at once the Princess of Argonne and circus-manager, that she was just that, manifestly as reserved as she was fanciful, manifestly the daughter of a grand seignior every whit as much as mountebank and rope-dancer. But her delicate tenderness towards the four children touched them profoundly, to such a degree did the maternal instinct reveal itself in her affectionate looks and patient care.

On the fourth day Marco Dario succeeded in drawing her aside and made his proposal:

"I have two sisters who would love you like a sister. I live in an old palace in which, if you would come to it, you would wear the air of a lady of the Renaissance."

On the fifth day the trembling Errington spoke to her of his mother, "who would be so happy to have a daughter like you." On the sixth day it was Webster's turn. On the seventh day they nearly came to blows. On the eighth day, they clamored to her to choose between them.

"Why between *you*?" said she laughingly. "You are not the only people in my life, besides my four boys. I have relations, cousins, other suitors perhaps."

"Choose."

On the ninth day, under severe pressure, she promised to choose.

"Well there," she said. "I'll set you all in a row and kiss the one who shall be my husband."

"When?"

"On the first day of the month of August."

"Swear it!"

"I swear it."

After that they stopped searching for the diamonds. As Errington observed—and Montfaucon had said it before him—the diamonds they desired were she, Dorothy. Their ancestor Beaugreval could not have foreseen for them a more magnificent treasure.

On the morning of the 24th Dorothy gave the signal for their departure. They quitted the ruins of Roche-Périac and said goodbye to the riches of the Marquis de Beaugreval.

"All the same," said Dario. "You ought to have searched, cousin Dorothy. You only are capable of discovering what no one has discovered for two centuries."

With a careless gesture she replied:

"Our excellent ancestor took care to tell us himself where the fortune was to be found—*In robore*... Let us accept his decision."

They traveled again the stages which she had traveled already, crossed the Vilaine, and took, the road to Nantes. In the villages—one must live; and the young girl accepted help from no one—Dorothy's Circus gave performances. Fresh cause for amazement on the part of the three foreigners. Dorothy conducting the parade, Dorothy on One-eyed Magpie, Dorothy addressing the public, what sparkling and picturesque scenes!

They slept two nights at Nantes, where Dorothy desired to see Maître Delarue. Quite recovered from his emotions, the notary welcomed her warmly, introduced her to his family, and kept her to lunch.

Finally on the last day of the month, starting early in the morning, they reached Hillocks Manor in the middle of the afternoon. Dorothy left the caravan in front of the gateway with the boys, and entered, accompanied by the three young men.

The courtyard was empty. The farm-servants must be at work in the fields. But through the open windows of the Manor they heard the noise of a violent discussion.

A man's voice, harsh and common—Dorothy recognized it as the voice of Voirin, the money-lender—was scolding furiously; reinforced by thumps on the table:

"You've got to pay, Monsieur Raoul. Here's the bill of sale, signed by your grandfather. At five o'clock on the 31st of July, 1921, three hundred thousand francs in bank-notes or Government securities. If not, the Manor is mine. It's four-fifty. Where's the money?"

Dorothy heard next the voice of Raoul, then the voice of Count Octave de Chagny offering to arrange to pay the sum.

"No arrangements," said the money-lender. "Bank-notes. It's four fifty-six."

Archibald Webster caught Dorothy by the sleeve and murmured:

"Raoul? It's one of our cousins?"

"Yes."

"And the other man?"

"A money-lender."

"Offer him a check."

"He won't take it."

"Why not?"

"He wants the Manor."

"What of it? We're not going to let a thing like that happen."

Dorothy said to him:

"You're a good fellow, Archibald, and I thank you. But do you think that it's by chance that we're here on the 31st of July at four minutes to five?"

She went towards the steps, mounted them, crossed the hall, and entered the room.

Two cries greeted her appearance on the scene. Raoul started up, very pale, the Countess de Chagny ran to her.

She stopped them with a gesture.

In front of the table, Voirin, supported by two friends whom he had brought as witnesses, his papers and deeds spread out before him, held his watch in his hand.

"Five o'clock!" he cried in a tone of victory.

She corrected him:

"Five o'clock by your watch, perhaps. But look at the clock. We have still three minutes."

"And what of it?" said the money-lender.

"Well, three minutes are more than we need to pay this little bill and clear you out of the house."

She opened the traveling cape she was wearing and from one of its inner pockets drew a huge yellow envelope which she tore open. Out of it came a bundle of thousand-franc notes and a packet of securities.

"Count, monsieur. No, not here. It would take rather a time; and we're eager to be by ourselves."

Gently, but with a continuous pressure, she pushed him towards the door, and his two witnesses with him.

"Excuse me, monsieur, but it's a family party... cousins who haven't seen one another for two hundred years... And we're eager to be by ourselves... You're not angry with me, are you? And, by the way, you will send the receipt to Monsieur Davernoie. Au revoir, gentlemen... There: there's five o'clock striking... Au revoir."

XVIII

IN ROBORE FORTUNA

When Dorothy had shut the door on the three men, she turned to find Raoul flushed and frowning; and he said:

"No, no. I can't allow it... You should have consulted me first."

"Don't get angry," she said gently. "I wished first of all to rid you of this fellow Voirin. That gives us time to think things out."

"I've thought them out!" he snapped. "I consider that settlement null and void!"

"I beg you, Raoul—a little patience. Postpone your decision till tomorrow. By tomorrow, perhaps, I shall have persuaded you."

She kissed the Countess de Chagny, then beckoning to the three strangers, she introduced them.

"I bring you guests, madame. Our cousin George Errington, of London. Our cousin Marco Dario, of Genoa. Our cousin Archibald Webster, of Philadelphia. Knowing that you were to come here, I was determined that the family should be complete."

Thereupon she introduced Raoul Davernoie, Count Octave and his wife. They exchanged vigorous handshakes.

"Excellent," she said. "We are united as I desired, and we have thousands and thousands of things to talk about. I've seen d'Estreicher again, Raoul; and as I predicted he has been hanged. Also I met your grandfather and Juliet Assire a long way from here. But perhaps we are getting along a bit too quickly. First of all there is a most urgent duty to fulfill with regard to our three cousins who are bitter enemies of the dry régime."

She opened the cupboard and found a bottle of port and some biscuits, and as she poured out the wine, she set about relating her expedition to Roche-Périac. She told the story quickly and a trifle incoherently, omitting details and getting them in the wrong order, but for the most part giving them a comic turn which greatly amused the Count and Countess de Chagny.

"Then," said the Countess when she came to the end of her story, "the diamonds are lost?"

"That," she replied, "is the business of my three cousins. Ask them."

During the young girl's explanations, they had all three stood rather apart, listening to Dorothy, pleasant to their hosts, but wearing an absent-minded air, as if they were absorbed in their own thoughts; and those thoughts the Countess must be thinking too, as well as the Count, for there was one matter which filled the minds of all of them and made them ill at ease, till it should be cleared up.

It was Errington who took the matter up, before the Countess had asked the question; and he said to the young girl:

"Cousin Dorothy, we don't understand... No, we're quite in the dark; and I think you won't think us indiscreet if we speak quite openly."

"Speak away, Errington."

"Ah, well, it's this—that three hundred thousand francs—"

"Where did they come from?" said Dorothy ending his sentence for him. "That's what you want to know, isn't it?"

"Well, yes."

She bent towards the Englishman's ear and whispered:

"All my savings... earned by the sweat of my brow."

"I beg you..."

"Doesn't that explanation satisfy you? Then I'll be frank."

She bent towards his other ear, and in a lower whisper still:

"I stole them."

"Oh, don't joke about it, cousin."

"But goodness, George Errington, if I did not steal them, what do you suppose I did do?"

He said slowly:

"My friends and I are asking ourselves if you didn't find them."

"Where?"

"In the ruins of Périac!"

She clapped her hands.

"Bravo! They've guessed it. You're right, George Errington, of London: I found them at the foot of a tree, under a heap of dead leaves and stones. That's where the Marquis de Beaugreval hid his bank-notes and six per cents."

The other two cousins stepped forward. Marco Dario, who looked very worried, said gravely: "Be serious, cousin Dorothy, we beg you, and don't laugh at us. Are we to consider the diamonds lost or found? It's a matter of great importance to some of us—I admit that it is to me. I had given up hopes of them. But now all at once you let us imagine an unexpected miracle. Is there one?"

She said:

"But why this supposition?"

"Firstly because of this unexpected money which we might attribute to the sale of one of the diamonds. And then... and then... I must say it, because it seems to us, taking it all round, quite impossible that you should have given up the search for that treasure. What? You, Dorothy, after months of conflicts and victories, at the moment you reach your goal, you suddenly decide to stand by with your arms folded! Not a single effort! Not one investigation! No, no, on your part it's incredible."

She looked from one to the other mischievously.

"So that according to you, cousins, I must have performed the double miracle of finding the diamonds without searching for them."

"There's nothing you couldn't do," said Webster gayly.

The Countess supported them:

"Nothing, Dorothy. And I see from your air that you've succeeded in this too."

She did not say no. She smiled quietly. They were all round her, curious or anxious. The Countess murmured:

"You have succeeded. Haven't you?"

"Yes," said Dorothy.

She had succeeded! The insoluble problem, with which so many minds had wrestled so many times and at such length, for ages—she had solved it!

"But when? At what moment?" cried George Errington. "You never left us!"

"Oh, it goes a long way further back than that. It goes back to my visit to the Château de Roborey."

"Eh, what? What's that you say?" cried the astounded Count de Chagny.

"From the first minute I knew at any rate the nature of the hiding-place in which the treasure was shut up."

"But how?"

"From the motto."

"From the motto?"

"But it's so plain! So plain that I've never understood the blindness of those who have searched for the treasure, and that I went so far as to declare the man who, when concealing a treasure, gave so much information about it, ingenuous in the extreme. But he was right, was the Marquis de Beaugreval. He could engrave it all over the place, on the clock of his château, on the wax of his seals, since to his descendants his motto meant nothing at all."

"If you knew, why didn't you act at once?" said the Countess.

"I knew the nature of the hiding-place, but not the spot on which it stood. This information was supplied by the gold medal. Three hours after my arrival at the ruins I knew all about it."

Marco Dario repeated several times.

"In robore fortuna... In robore fortuna..."

And the others also pronounced the three words, as if they were a cabalistic formula, the mere utterance of which is sufficient to produce marvelous results.

"Dario," she said, "you know Latin? And you, Errington? And you, Webster?"

"Well enough," said Dario, "to make out the sense of those three words—there's nothing tricky about them. *Fortuna* means the fortune..."

"In this case the diamonds," said she.

"That's right," said Dario; and he continued his translation: "The diamonds are... in *robore*..."

"In the firm heart," said Errington, laughing.

"In vigor, in force," added Webster.

"And for you three that's all that the word '*robore*,' the ablative of the Latin word 'robur' means?"

"Goodness, yes!" they answered. "*Robur* ... force... firmness... energy."

She shrugged her shoulders disdainfully:

"Ah, well, I, who know just about as much Latin as you do, but have the very great advantage over you of being a country girl—to me, when I walk in the country and see that variety of oak which is called the *rouvre*, it nearly always occurs that the old French word *rouvre* is derived from the Latin word 'robur,' which means force, and also means oak. And that's what led me, when on the 12th of July I passed, along with you, near the oak, which stands out so prominently in the middle of the clearing, at the beginning of the avenue of oaks—that's what led me to make the connection between that tree and the hiding-place, and so to translate the information which our ancestor untiringly repeated to us: 'I have hidden my fortune in the hollow of a rouvre oak.' There you are. As you perceive,—it's as simple as winking."

Having made her explanation with a charming gayety, she was silent. The three young men gazed at her in wonder and amazement. Her charming eyes were full of her simple satisfaction at having astonished her friends by this uncommon quality, this inexplicable faculty with which she was gifted.

"You *are* different," said Webster. "You belong to a race... a race—"

"A race of sound Frenchmen, who have plenty of good sense, like all the French."

"No, no," said he, incapable of formulating the thoughts which oppressed all three of them. "No, no. It's something else."

He bent down before her and brushed her hand with his lips. Errington and Dario also bent down in the same respectful act, while, to hide her emotion she mechanically translated:

"*Fortuna*, fortune... In *robore*, in the oak."

And she added:

"In the deepest depths of the oak, in the heart of the oak, one might say. There was about six feet from the ground one of those ring-shaped swellings, that scar which wounds in the trunks of trees leave. And I had an intuition that that was the place in which I must search, and that there the Marquis de Beaugreval had buried the diamonds he was keeping for his second existence. There was nothing else to do but make the test. That's what I did, during the first few nights while my three cousins were sleeping. Saint-Quentin and I got to work at our exploring with our gimlets and saws and center-bits. And one evening I suddenly came across something too hard to bore. I had not been mistaken. The opening was enlarged and one by one I drew out of it four balls of the size of a hazel-nut. All I had to do was to clear off a regular matrix of dirt to bring to light four diamonds. Here are three of them. The fourth is in pawn with Maître Delarue, who very kindly agreed, after a good deal of hesitation, and a minute expert examination by his jeweler, to lend me the necessary money till tomorrow."

She gave the three diamonds to her three friends, magnificent stones, of the same size, quite extraordinary size, and cut in the old-fashioned way with opposing facets. Errington, Webster, and Dario found it disturbing merely to look at them and handle them. Two centuries before, the Marquis de Beaugreval, that strange visionary, dead of his splendid dream of a resurrection, had intrusted them to the very tree under which doubtless he used to go and lie and read. For two hundred years Nature had continued her slow and uninterrupted work of building walls, ever and ever thicker walls, round the little prison chosen with such a subtle intelligence. For two hundred years generation after generation had passed near this fabulous treasure searching for it perhaps by reason of a confused legend, and now the great-great-great-great-granddaughter of the good man, having discovered the undiscoverable secret, and penetrated to the most mysterious and obscure of caskets, offered them the precious stones which their ancestor had brought back from the Indies.

"Keep them," she said. "Three families sprung from the three sons of the Marquis have lived outside France. The French descendants of the fourth son will share the fourth diamond."

"What do you mean?" asked Count Octave in a tone of surprise.

"I say that we are three French heirs, you, Raoul, and I, that each diamond, according to the jeweler's valuation is worth several millions, and that our rights, the rights of all three of us, are equal."

"My right is null," said Count Octave.

"Why?" she said. "We are partners. A compact, a promise to share the treasure made you a partner with my father and Raoul's father."

"A lapsed compact!" cried Raoul Davernoie in his turn. "For my part I accept nothing. The will leaves no room for discussion. Four medals, four diamonds. Your three cousins and you, Dorothy; you only have the right to inherit the riches of the Marquis!"

She protested warmly:

"And you too, Raoul! You too! We fought together! Your grandfather was a direct descendant of the Marquis! He possessed the token of the medal!"

"That medal was of no value."

"How do you know? You've never had it in your hands."

"I have."

"Impossible. There was nothing in the disc I fished up under your eyes. It was simply a bait to catch d'Estreicher. Then?"

"When my grandfather came back from his journey to Roche-Périac, where you met him with Juliet Assire, one day I found him weeping in the orchard. He was looking at a gold medal, which he let me take from him and look at. On it were all the indications you have described. But the two faces were canceled by a cross, which manifestly, as I told you, deprived it of all value."

Dorothy appeared greatly surprised by this revelation, and she replied in an absent-minded tone:

"Oh!... really?... You saw?..."

She went to one of the windows and stood there for some minutes, her forehead resting against a pane. The last veils which obscured the adventure were withdrawn. Really there had been two gold medals. One, which was invalid and belonged to Jean d'Argonne, had been stolen by d'Estreicher, recovered by Raoul's father, and sent to the old Baron. The other, the valid one was the one which belonged to the old Baron, who, out of prudence or greed, had never spoken of it to his son or grandson. In his madness, and dispossessed in his turn of the token, which he had hidden in his dog's collar, he had gone to win the treasure with the other medal, which he had intrusted to Juliet Assire, and which d'Estreicher had been unable to find.

All at once Dorothy saw all the consequences which followed this revelation. In taking from the dog's collar the medal which she believed to be hers, she had robbed Raoul of his inheritance. In returning to the Manor and offering alms to the son of the man who had been an accomplice in her father's murder, she had imagined that she was performing an act of generosity and forgiveness, whereas she was merely restoring a small portion of that of which she had robbed him.

She restrained herself and said nothing. She must act cautiously in order that Raoul might never suspect his father's crime. When she came from the window to the middle of the room, you would have said that her eyes were full of tears. Nevertheless she was smiling, and she said in a careless tone:

"Serious business tomorrow. Today let us rejoice at being reunited and celebrate that reunion. Will you invite me to dinner, Raoul? And my children too?"

She had recovered all her gayety. She ran to the big gateway of the orchard and called the boys, who came joyfully. The Captain threw himself into the arms of the Countess de Chagny. Saint-Quentin kissed her hand. They observed that Castor and Pollux had swollen noses, signs of a recent conflict.

The dinner was washed down with sparkling cider and champagne. All the evening Dorothy was light-hearted and affectionate to them all. They felt that she was happy to be alive.

Archibald Webster recalled her promise to her. It was the next day, the first of August, that she was to choose among her suitors.

"I stick to my promise," she said.

"You will choose among those who are here? For I suppose that cousin Raoul is not the last to come forward as a candidate."

"Among those who are here. And as there can be only one chosen, I insist on kissing you all tonight."

She kissed the four young men, then the Count and Countess, then the four boys.

The party did not break up till midnight.

Next morning Raoul, Octave de Chagny, his wife, and the three strangers were at breakfast in the dining-room when a farm servant brought a letter.

Raoul looked at the handwriting and murmured gloomily:

"Ah, a letter from her... Like the last time... She has gone."

He remembered, as did the Count and Countess, her departure from Roborey.

He tore open the letter and read aloud:

"Raoul, my friend,

"I earnestly beg you to believe blindly what I am going to tell you. It was revealed to me by certain facts which I learnt only yesterday.

"What I am writing is not a supposition, but an absolute certainty. I know it as surely as I know that light exists, and though I have very sound reasons for not divulging the proofs of it, I nevertheless wish you to act and think with the same conviction and serenity as I do myself.

"By my eternal salvation, this is the truth. Errington, Webster, Dario, and you, Raoul, are the veritable heirs of the Marquis de Beaugreval, specified in his will. Therefore the fourth diamond is yours. Webster will be delighted to go to Nantes tomorrow to give Maître Delarue a check for three hundred thousand francs and bring you back the diamond. I am sending to Maître Delarue at the same time as the receipt which he signed, the necessary instructions.

"I will confess, Raoul, that I felt a little disappointed yesterday when I discerned the truth—not much—just a few tears. Today I am quite contented. I had no great liking for that fortune—too many crimes and too many horrors went with it. Some things I should never have been able to forget. And then... and then money is a prison; and I could not bear to live locked up.

"Raoul, and you, my three new friends, you asked me,—rather by way of a joke, wasn't it?—to choose a sweetheart among those who found themselves at the Manor yesterday. May I answer you in rather the same manner, that my choice is made, that it is only possible for me to devote myself to the youngest of my four boys first, then to the others? Don't be angry with me, my friends. My heart, up to now, is only the heart of a mother; and it only thrills with tenderness, anxiety and love for them. What would they do if I were to leave them? What would become of my poor Montfaucon? They need me and the really healthy life we lead together. Like them I am a nomad, a vagabond. There is no dwelling-place as good as our caravan. Let me go back to the high road.

"And then, after a time we will meet again, shall we? Our cousins the de Chagny will welcome us at Roborey. Come, let us fix a date. Christmas and New Year's Day there—does that please you?

"Goodbye, my friend. My best love to you all, and a few tears... *In robore fortuna.* Fortune is in the firm heart.

"I kiss you all.

"DOROTHY."

A long silence followed the reading of this letter.

At the end of it Count Octave said:

"Strange creature! When one considers that she had the four diamonds in her pocket, that is to say ten or twelve million francs, and that it would have been so easy for her to say nothing and keep them."

But the young men did not take up this train of thought. For them Dorothy was the very spirit of happiness. And happiness was going away.

Raoul looked at his watch and beckoned to them to come with him. He led them to the highest point of the Hillocks.

On the horizon, on a white road which ran upwards among the meadows, the caravan was moving. Three boys walked beside One-eyed Magpie. Saint-Quentin was leading him.

Behind, all alone, Dorothy—Princess of Argonne and rope-dancer.

A fan of Sherlock Holmes?
Then meet Solar Pons

The original fan fiction from the great August Derleth—the Sherlock Holmes of Praed Street.

"the best substitutes for Sherlock Holmes known."
– Vincent Starrett

"an excellent series of adventures in detection in their own right." – *The Chicago Tribune*

For more details and a full list of titles:
visit https://www.hachetteindia.com/home/yellowbacks